The Gospel
According to Gracey

A NOVEL

Suzanne Kingsbury

SCRIBNER
New York   London   Toronto   Sydney   Singapore

SCRIBNER
1230 Avenue of the Americas
New York, NY 10020

SCRIBNER and design are trademarks of Macmillan Library Reference USA, Inc.,
used under license by Simon & Schuster, the publisher of this work.

For information about special discounts for bulk purchases,
please contact Simon & Schuster Special Sales:
1-800-456-6798 or business@simonandschuster.com

Text set in Bembo

Manufactured in the United States of America

1 3 5 7 9 10 8 6 4 2

Library of Congress Cataloging-in-Publication Data
Kingsbury, Suzanne.
The gospel according to Gracey : a novel / Suzanne Kingsbury.
p. cm.
1. Narcotic addicts—Fiction. 2. Heroin habit—Fiction.
3. Atlanta (Ga.)—Fiction. I. Title
PS3611.I63G67 2003
813'.6—dc21
2003045424

ISBN 0-7432-2305-5

For my family: Kasha Duffield,
Jennifer Katherine and Laurence Kingsbury

. . . for he maketh his sun to rise on the evil and the good, and sendeth rain upon the just and the unjust.

—Matthew 5:45

The Gospel
According to Gracey

Morning

———

1.

DAWN ON A SATURDAY in May. Officers Cole and Kelly are working out of a makeshift command post in an abandoned office building in Zone 1, Atlanta, a high-density drug area where twenty-five officers from the Red Dog squad dressed in black fatigues did a sweep of the Bluff at dawn. They are specially trained officers from the Narcotics State Academy, adept at undercover techniques, wiretapping, managing confidential informants, making buys, and targeting dealers. Investigators en masse form takedown groups and forty-eight uniformed officers from the field-operations division, usually working all over the city, come early this Saturday to the Bluff to help City Hall East slow the beating heart of Atlanta's drug-addicted neighborhoods.

The arrested are brought in just before daylight, hollering, spitting, biting, shaking their fists, falling asleep on benches, caught for possession, dealing, transporting, and smuggling. Their bodies are wired or they're just now coming down, losing their high and raging at the po-po for blindsiding them in the middle of their lives.

The woman they need to talk to is calm. Cole watches her, standing apart from the crowd in a casual way, doing what they tell her to. I'll get around to it, she says with her eyes, which are clear. Her body is clean. The blue dress looks just laundered.

Gracey Fill is her name. They picked her up in the Bluff, in Vine City, on Jett Street. She has old scabs on her cocoa-colored skin. Her slender form looks breakable. Cole finds her beautiful. He tries to talk to her gently, as one soothes a spooked horse. Hey, can you come with us? We need to get you set up here.

Officer Kelly stands next to him, with his red face, his high forehead, and his sandy-colored crew cut. Get moving! he says to the junkies around them. Get outta here. You think this is your living room? Move! While Kelly shouts, a woman wearing a diaper over her jeans and a bottomless handbag slung over her shoulder spits at him from behind. The mucus drips down his neck. He raises his fist in involuntary reflex and smashes his lips together in a white line. Hanging at his sides are two swollen-red omnipresent threats: his hands.

Cole watches Gracey pass through the door into the long hallway leading to a stairwell. At first, he does not know what he sees in her eyes. Then he recognizes fear, the locked, unblinking terror of a deer in the woods faced with a death-linked steel hole protruding from a hunter's eye.

Mug shot, searched, she's told to bend over and cough, flashlight up her anus, in her mouth, in her vagina. She's given an escort and sent to the questioning room, where Cole and Kelly are waiting.

Cole leans against the far wall. She sits at a table across from him, her wrists looped in handcuffs. The room smells of old coffee and dank, flat air. Boot treads and lopsided black spots mark the floor. To the left is a mirrored square. Someone outside can watch them. No one is.

I just wanna know you checkin on my mamma, Gracey Fill says. She lifts her shackled arms and rubs her nose with two fingers. I don't want her to lie like that for too long. That house don't have good memory in it. She needs to be prayed over and blessed on and visited, put in God's holy church where ain't no evil gonna enter. Eyeing them sideways, Gracey tosses back her hair. But I guess you the po-po, she says. If I tell you someone gone and passed on, you gotta investigate. She pauses. Don't you?

Kelly doesn't answer. Putting a boot on the ledge beneath the window, he shuffles through the papers in his hands, searching for something, not bothering to acknowledge the arrestee's dead mother. Cole looks around the dingy room. The walls seem to crack while they wait, long fissures of bleeding holes crying down the cement. Ms. Fill, Kelly finally says. Cole knows his partner is well aware of who the woman is, but he acts as though he has just found her name among the documents. You gonna talk? Kelly asks. Or are you gonna make us put you behind bars?

Gracey ignores him. She looks at Cole. Her eyes are chocolate brown. Her neck is thrice-corded and lovely, though muted old sores spot it. The collarbone, even, is scabbed. Cole tries to hold her stare. He finds he isn't able to. Somewhere a fly buzzes. A roped and jerry-rigged forty-watt bulb hangs above them. Cole looks up, expecting to see the insect there. It occurs to him it may be feasting on the woman's body.

We're listenin, says Kelly.

The woman continues to stare at Cole. You look familiar, she says. Do I know you? Cole thinks she is speaking only to him, then she moves her eyes to Kelly. I seen you in the West End or around Fourth Ward. Somewheres.

Kelly reddens and clears his throat. Cole reaches into his own memory. He has no idea if he has seen her before. Faces have blended together for him until now, when Kelly told him this was their out, Gracey Fill. She was married to The Rocket, the biggest drug runner in the city when it all began in the 1970s. Cole doubts the woman has anything for them. She appears done and tired.

Gracey crosses one leg over the other. The dress rides up her thighs. She tries to straighten it, but cannot with her hands bound. I wouldn't never have got to talk to you, though, she says. We be runnin and hidin when we see your blue ass. She pauses, pulls her arms around her, and says, It's cold in here.

No one speaks after this admission. The room is eighty degrees, set that way to make the suspects sleepy, worn out, and willing to talk. The other way they do it is to make the room freezing, and the suspects get edgy, their teeth chatter, they can't wait for the interrogation to be over. Addicts are always cold, their body temperature is lower from years on the drug.

Gracey shivers. You got a cigarette?

Kelly stares out the window. His face is pressed to the boarded slats. Cole, he says, go out and get the woman a cigarette.

Cole walks to the other end of the room. He wonders what Kelly sees out that window. He is probably only looking at the flat edge of another brick building. His partner's interest in the outside is a ploy to get the lady to want out. When Cole reaches the door, he puts his hand on the doorknob and looks back at her. She brings up the bound wrists and rests her chin on them. Her fingers are slender and long. The nails are unpainted and pearl-colored.

In the hallway, fluorescent lights bounce their glare off the linoleum floor. Radios blare dispatched messages and the sounds of sirens start outside. Ladies in heels rush by. Their bodies lack form. They shift paperwork in their hands. Cole weaves among them to a wooden box full of cigarettes, hands the intern from the local junior college's justice program four dollars, and fingers a pack of Pall Malls. Then starts back.

Officer Scott Cole, blond, blue-eyed, and six feet tall, on the job just three weeks, a virgin to the diseased streets of Atlanta, wanting in all his twenty-three years to be a cop, a man of justice and order, setting things straight, playing right. He grew up worrying his own father was a put-on, an actor, someone playing the part of a man. By day, his father managed the local grocery and sank the misery of his broken heart into philanthropy for the community, Little League coach and Boy Scout leader. He took it all too seriously, praised Cole when he received Cub Scout badges all the boys wore or when he made an easy home run.

Cole loves him. Is both ashamed of and grateful for him, and the confusion he feels about his father causes him to want to become what his father is not. He is going to be strong, tough, make a difference where it matters.

Where's Mom? he'd ask his dad's retreating shadow at night in the suburbs during a cricket-moaning summer, the daylight skulking beyond reach, leaving him with the knowledge that all was not safe, life could spiral out of control, blurring sensible form.

We don't know that, son.

At times he feels as if he is still that young boy in eastern Georgia, marred by the mother who left him. Now, women remain enigmas, out-of-reach soap bubbles, ruined to the touch. Without realizing it, he wants one he can save, make right, love her sorrow out of her until she is a weak-limbed, struck sparrow in his arms.

But he is in love with no one and so finds solace in his work. He reminds himself his purpose is bigger than quota and radio dispatch, the cosmology of crime in city streets, stop signs and coffee at late-night diners, after-hour ham sandwiches from the corner deli, HBO movies, and dates with hairdressers named Jennifer. He is proud of himself for enduring weeks of training when he learned to admonish fear and depend on quick reflexes while searching squatters' quarters, sweeping crack houses, cuffing dealers who sell to kids in abandoned basketball courts. He assures himself he is one of the good ones, adamantly saying no to temptations: smooth plastic bags of evidence wrapped in tape, free for cops to rob, use, and sell.

He enters the questioning room with the pack of cigarettes, a Styrofoam cup of coffee, and, slung over one arm, a tweed coat someone left behind. Walking over to the table, he sets the coffee and cigarettes in front of her and drapes the coat over her shoulders.

He can feel Kelly watching him when he goes back to lean against the wall. Out of the side of his vision, his partner's wide eyes mock him. He does not return the stare.

She manages to rip the plastic off the pack with her teeth and picks a cigarette out in the same manner. She sits holding it between her lips and then spits it out. Looking at Kelly, she says, You want me to light this with my asshole?

Officer Kelly does not move from his place in front of the window. You're lucky you got a cigarette at all, lady, he says. If you want it lit, you'll ask nicely.

Gracey stares at the floor in front of her, concentrating on one broken tile. Her jaw shakes. I want it lit, she says quietly.

Well, Prince Charming, says Kelly. Did you think of a lighter?

Cole goes back through the hallway. The intern is out of matches, and he asks everyone he can find for a light until Sandy, secretary for dispatch, gives him a book from the Stand Restaurant and tells him to bring it back to her as soon as he's through. When he opens it, there are ten left.

The interrogation room is sweltering. Kelly is a boxed dog, sniffing at the only air holes available. Cole lights Gracey's cigarette and leans against the wall across from her again. She smokes. Putting both cuffed hands to one side of her face, she squints at Cole and tries to find a nametag on his chest, in the wall's shadow. Can I name you? she asks. I'll name you Justice, she says. Justice, you young. You not more than twenty-three. My son's just about that. Yeah? She smiles. You surprised? I got me a son. I got a daughter, too. I'm a mother and a sister and a daughter, and I was a wife. Exhaling smoke, she says, But when you look at me, all's you see is prison bait and junkie, someone you gonna get for slingin powder, snortin, shootin, and skin poppin. You handcuffin these tattered wrists like I got a breath of energy left in me to fight it. She looks over at Kelly, smokes some more, and says, You doin it all in the name of *your* people. Ha! Ain't you just John Q. Citizen?

Kelly sighs. You gonna tell us about Sonny Fill? he asks. Or you gonna make us put you in the holdin bus to jail? 'Cause the mayor's on our ass. We got a drug quota from the city of Atlanta to fill and you might as well hurry up and let the cat out of that foul-smellin bag you been keepin it in.

She ashes her cigarette on the tabletop. Now you wanna know, she says. After you got your balls off watchin us. The pressure's on and the fun's over. You gettin tired of your lookout places, elbowin your brand-new partner, sayin, Check this out, Justice, she'll get her quick fix for ten minutes and then she'll be back on the street in fifteen puttin out for a two-dollar blow job to buy more. Yeah, you settin by smilin, watchin us lose our asses with our minds, satisfied we all goin to hell in a rowboat. Now the sugar's goin to shit, is that what you're tellin me? You need some names and numbers. Gracey Fill looks from one to the other. You gonna tell me it's about obeyin the law, doin the right thing. But no one's better than anyone else. You boys are workin for some pink-faced cracker politician sittin around chewin his steak bone, talkin about prayer in schools. She leans back in her chair and raises her chin. We lost prayer a long time ago, she says. Lost it with God himself. He run to high heaven from this mess we made. I just heard yesterday them big boys who pay your checks are levelin Herndon Homes. Where they gonna put all them people? Movin 'em off the street and into jail. They used to complain black men ain't ever home 'cause they got drug problems. Now the women ain't home either. Where you think the kids are at? And you gonna point your finger at me and say it's my fault.

Kelly gets up and goes to where she is sitting. He lifts a cigarette from the pack, taps it on the table, and strikes a match. It doesn't light. He pulls another one out, and while he is trying to get that lit, Gracey takes the pack from him. Bound-handed, she lights a match with her teeth. She hands it to him. He puts the cigarette to the flame reluctantly.

You gonna talk? he asks her after he exhales, 'cause we don't got time to stand here listenin to this bullshit. He lets that rest while the smoke withers and dissipates around them, giving them a cloud to abide in together. Or you could just go to jail right now, he says.

She crosses her arms over her chest and looks past Kelly. She smiles at Cole. I ain't never been to jail before, she tells him. Her voice goes soft. My grandma on my mamma's side, she used to tell me, Don't you never be common, doll face. Whatever you be, don't be common. I guess it's about come to that. Common. I always talk to her in my prayers at night. I got the whole list of sorries I gotta go through for my grandma. I tried to do right, I always tell her. But it's hard to come free.

She gets up and goes around Kelly, watching him while she does it. His body goes rigid. He doesn't look at her. She stands in front of the window; three strips of light mark the left side of her face, one eye goes golden, the other lies flat as a hole.

My IQ was a hundred forty-six, she tells them. They called Daddy that night after the testing to tell him. He said, Her brain might be smart, but she dumb everywhere else. She ain't never gonna be nothin. Gracey Fill sighs and hangs her head as though the neck just snapped. That's like the beast under my bed, she says. I went around proving it was true. She looks over at Cole. Really all I want is a chance, she says quietly.

He stops breathing.

Kelly stops smoking.

The room is still, waiting.

They have to strain to hear her. I want a chance to live right, start from scratch. I'm trying for that. If I can't have it, I just need it to be through. I know you want me to talk. You don't got nothin on me, but you could shove a pile of cocaine down my dress and tell them I came in with it. Ain't nobody gonna tell you not to. Let me say this, I got a story if you got time. There are some things I'd like to tell you. It might not do any goddamn good, but I'm gonna show you how long a road I been journeyin on. You need to know what it's like, 'cause you got it all wrong. You think somebody wakes up and says, Yeehaw, today's a gorgeous day. Thank you, Lord. Today I'm gonna get hooked on drugs.

Gracey faces each of them in turn. Raising her handcuffed hands, she rubs her eyes like a small child. That's your mistake, she says. It don't happen like that at all.

2.

THROUGH THE SLIT where the curtain meets the wall, a slice of
sun comes in the room, harsh and deliberate. Frazier Sky turns the
fabric back. He is twenty years old, naked and hungover. Behind
him, a girl sleeps in the hotel bed with her mouth slung open, in
the midst of a dream.

He can't see anything save a balcony with pale wicker furniture
and glass ashtrays. A waiter wearing black-and-white garb is serving orange juice in crystal carafes around a tear-shaped pool. Frazier is half-hard and needs to piss. He checks his watch. Nine. He
looks back at the girl.

She is seventeen years old and beautiful, auburn hair and
porcelain skin. She wears chips of emeralds in each ear, dug by
sweating, dark-skinned men in a country he wants to know about
and supposes he might someday if he can get it together, learn to
tell the truth, move forward.

He walks over and sits beside her on the bed. She doesn't
move. Each breast is splayed lazily, the nipples rose-colored and
soft. He thinks to reach out and caress one, suck her in sleep, but
he doesn't. On the right side of her neck is a scar they have never
talked about. He touches it now as he will when they make love.

11

His hand looks tan next to her opaque skin. He puts his arm across her stomach, interfering with the rise and fall of breath until she catches one inhale, holds it, and moans. Still, she does not wake up.

Audrey is his comfort, the constant in his life. There isn't a time he hasn't known her. The thought makes him need her desperately. He believes she might be the person who can mend everything with her memory of him as a boy.

Before he saw Audrey again, he used to come here, to the Ritz, with Lacy Stilts. She was two grades ahead of him in school. Her father also had an account at the front desk. Back when he'd first found out about his dad's affair, Frazier had wanted to know the secret experience of hotel sex as his father did. He remembers Lacy's tight vagina and the smell of her perfume, the shifting, shadowed light while they made love and the way she slept afterward like only men are supposed to. He'd found himself awake at three A.M., staring at the ceiling, plagued by vague, aching thoughts of suicide. He should have felt safe. Downstairs, quiet valets parked Rolls-Royces, guests walked under crystal chandeliers beside woven tapestries. But when Lacy awoke, they remained strangers. Despair riddled him.

Now he has Audrey. She is the unstranger in his life. He is contained in the pores of her skin. She knows him.

The faint sound of the air conditioner continues. At his feet, her overnight bag is open. It contains a pocketbook and her clothes, a mauve bra slung over jeans and blouse. He touches her things. Cloth slips loosely through his fingers. Under the clothes is a brown date book. Its cover says 2001 in gold letters across the leather. He leafs through the pages, where times and activities are listed in her fluid script. She has the handwriting of the rich and confident. He turns to today. May 19. PROM in capital letters across it.

Placing the book in the bag, he looks back at her. Her elbows frame her face, one knee is out, the blanket covers her to the belly button. He touches her cheek. Hey, he says.

She stirs, her hands flex, her head moves to the side. Her eyes stay closed.

He walks to the bathroom, takes a piss with the door open. Heavenly release.

You awake? she calls to him, her voice thick with grogginess.

No, I'm sleeping in the bathroom, he tells her.

The television comes on.

When he walks out, she turns it off. She is leaning back on her elbows, her hair messy and glowing red in the dim light, a pillow mark across her left cheek.

He loves to see her like this. When she looks as she does now, she is a Robert Frost poem that stirred him to erection in Mrs. Hetland's sixth-grade class. She becomes the feeling of a night when he was twelve and walked home well after dinner, surrounded by low-lying, misted fog, the houses like boats in a sea of vapor. Somewhere a person had opened a window and played a flute. He'd stood and listened. Wept without knowing why.

Her breasts are pale and full, and she lifts the blanket to hide them, smiling shyly. He sits at the desk, pulls a pack of cigarettes out of the denims slung across the back of the chair, and starts to smoke.

Patting the remote on the bed, she makes a drumstick out of it, and watches him. Last night she was cocaine drunk and dance weary, riding in the passenger seat of her own car, suddenly turning off the music and asking why he comes to her some days and otherwise goes away for long stretches of time.

I want to know where you go, she'd told him. I wish we could be . . . A cigarette lit and smoking in one hand, her eyes searching the dash for the word, her beautiful mouth wine colored in the passing gleam of streetlamps. Normal people, she'd said at last.

He'd chucked a beer bottle out onto Peachtree. Watching it roll away in the rearview, he'd laughed cruelly as the night hurried by in lusterless indigo. The scent of motor oil and spring air came at him through the window. What the fuck is normal? he'd asked her. You want me to be like your friends? My parents? Your parents? My father neck deep in your mother's pussy? Normal. That's good, Audrey. That's real good.

She'd cried on the way back, her face horrible in the flickering shadows, her cheeks plastic with tears.

In almost sleep, he'd held her, rolled over, and caught her waist. Felt her crying still.

He does not know how to talk to her, so he holds her like that, keeps her hand in his when they walk down the street, calls her late at night to hear her sleepy voice and know she is there. Hey, she says. Where are you? Are you okay? Frazier? After a few breaths he tells her he is sorry. It's late. Go on back to bed.

Piedmont Driving Club debutante, twice-crowned homecoming princess at the Lovett School. Her stepfather has bought her a horse for the riding stables on the property. He has built her an art studio behind the house and taken her to Florence so many times she says she is finally bored with the city. She has had lovers years older than her. She is old now, divinity sucked out of her at twelve when she was meant to perform her beauty, make it shine at her parents' dinner parties under Buckhead chandeliers after her father died, and her mother was free at last, liberated to pursue the glorious stages of the wealthy. Her mother had slipped out of upper-middle class and into the rung above like a snake wielding the last of its tired skin. She'd dragged her daughter into the world of the very rich as though returning to a mother tongue, welding her name with her new husband's, making a concentrated study of the manners and habits of generations of Atlantans who know their places in the ivy-laden, marble-topped world of Buckhead.

At seventeen, Audrey is just a remnant, a piece tossed around her mother's money-hungry hands. She wakes to the burden of her stepfather's visits, his shadowed form, sitting on a washed-silk easy chair, talking into the dark air about his troubles, molding her into confidante. His name means power except in late-night meetings with his stepdaughter, where he is allowed weakness, the worry of his loveless marriage. His contemporaries see prestige when they look at him, not the man but what his hand can offer them. In the muted light of her bedroom, her stepfather tells her he wishes he were still a boy summering at his grandfather's fishing cabin on the South Carolina shore. There he loved a dark-haired girl and lost her when the summer ended. Don't do that to yourself, he tells Audrey. Follow your heart when you are young; later there will be no way out. Her eyelids burn and grow heavy while she listens. He pats her hand, thanks her, tells her she is good, that she makes him feel peace again, being there in her room with him, asking for nothing. Closing the door, he leaves the lasting imprint of his secrets tattooed on her conscience. The whisper of forbidden words against her mother is merciless. By day money leaks like soiled power out of his guilty skin.

Somewhere within him Frazier Sky knows this. All of it. And he wants to search out her pain for the spirit it holds. He wants to reach inside her body and stroke it. Sometimes, though, he wonders if she is only a girl and no more. It makes him want to leave her.

You aren't happy, she says now, fiddling with the remote buttons.

He ashes his cigarette and raises an eyebrow at her. I am, he tells her.

She nods, bites her lip. Maybe just not with me, she says.

They are quiet. He sits picking at his thumbnail. Your prom is tonight, he says finally.

She shrugs.

Why didn't you tell me?

There wasn't anything to tell.

The cigarette is rough going down. Afterward all feels milky, easier. I would have gone, he tells her. If I'd known earlier.

They both understand this is a lie.

Outside the sun blooms, Saturday brings shoppers, golfers, the wide expanse of Frazier Sky's life, heading out before him like a Nebraska playing field without boundaries, seemingly eternal, the infinity of his own need for something to break the monotony.

She watches him. Fraz—

He looks up.

Aren't you ever gonna love me? She half-smiles.

He swallows, frightened by the question. Smoke works its way through the air.

Let's dip in, he tells her. Then I need to go to the Bluff, and if you want, you can come, too.

Okay, she tells him. Her seventeen-year-old resolve is a fraying thread. She lies back on the bed and closes her eyes.

3.

KELLY BRINGS COLE out to the hallway and leads him through the maze of men, navigating expertly, his hurried gait demanding acquiescence. Cole has to rush to keep up.

In the empty coffee-and-smoke room, Cole closes the door and turns to face Kelly. I don't have patience for that kind of shit, his partner tells him. His eyes are small marbles sunk furiously into his head. His lips are thin and violet. Cole has become a rebellious adolescent who needs to be disciplined for wet dreams and bad grades. Kelly rests his hands on his halter. The irregularity of his scalp shines through the crew cut. He eyes his wristwatch. Look, he says, she's gonna talk. Just follow my lead. None of this find-her-a-coat business. I got it under control. I'm waiting for her to spill it. She was The Rocket's wife, and that's all she's gotta be. The people who were running it then are running it now. The Rocket isn't dead, and no matter what she says, I'm gambling she knows he's alive. Kelly pries into his partner with his vermilion-rimmed pupils. The whites turn yellow while Cole watches. The eyes are devoid of emotion.

Back in the hallway, their boots make quick, somber lines on the linoleum. Kelly orders sandwiches, Coke, coffee with extra cream, two more packs of cigarettes, and a lighter from a neophyte intern, eager to please, his bangs slick with sweat, who says, Yes, sir, in a country-Georgia accent inherited from his father's father's father on some farm south of the capital.

They return to the room, each man dragging a folding chair, each holding a Styrofoam cup of police-station mud. Resting his forearms on the table, Kelly says, It's gonna be a long day, Miss Fill. You gonna talk?

Cole sips his coffee and watches her.

She shrugs. I ain't got nothin else to do, she tells them. Rapping her handcuffs on the edge of the table, she says, I want these off.

It is an order.

And I want to tell it *my* way, she says. She looks at Kelly. You honky boys want to blow bullshit up my asshole about gettin free, and you don't want it blown back at you, then I'm gonna tell you the whole truth and nothing but the truth, so help me God, and that's gonna mean starting at the beginning. The Bible starts at the beginning, and to understand anything you gotta hear it from there.

She thrusts her hands at Kelly. He leans over, reaches in his back pocket to produce a key, and unlocks the cuffs. Turning her hands this way and that, she stares at them as if they were marvels she just purchased. She rubs each wrist in turn. When she smiles, her straight white teeth shine in her beautiful mouth. The top lip curves up and Cole regards it with a curiosity akin to a student observing his brilliant mentor. She says, Now then, you boys comfortable?

Kelly rolls his eyes, presses Play on the small tape recorder slung to his belt, and places it on the table. You have the right to remain silent, he says. Anything you say can be held against you in a court of law.

Don't go Mirandaing me again, she tells him. I know that.

Kelly shrugs.

Gracey Fill starts to speak and the two men settle in their

seats to listen on this Saturday in May. Sun slips in like a sneaky malefactor, brandishing the truth of her face, scarred and scabbed, tired from treading the floodwaters of rotten experience. In all the world there seems to Cole to be only this room and one woman, her story reeling in lopsided circles like a drunk man. He wants to hear her words, but first he must examine her body, the curve of her neck. She isn't young anymore, and he can't help hunting for the traces of what she once was, innocent, lovely.

Gracey does not ignore her own wild beginnings. She was a race against time, pushed out on the heels of a hurricane, suffering her way through the threshold of her mother's fourteen-year-old cavity on October 1, 1960. The electricity had gone out at Grady birthing ward and bursts of staccato lightning illuminated the ghostly dark of the doctor's hands. He cut the umbilical cord by the light of a generator. In the aftermath of her mamma's screaming came tenderness. She had a star in her arms, a little girl to love. Hope resided in the newborn's flesh and tiny fingers.

Gracey talks without pause. The hollow cave of her mouth opens to spill veins of truth, which enter Cole like a transfusion. Her memories swallow him until he is out of his own mind and solely into hers.

Her mother was a love-struck teenager when she had her. You think I lost my memory with my habit? she asks Kelly and Cole, remembering for them her mother's face, her high cheekbones and full mouth, the glossy-black eyes, always just done with tears or about to start.

She recounts Jett Street before the eighties came to invade it with crack kids and squatting dope addicts. In Gracey's youth, children hopped barefoot through open fire hydrants, kids played kick the can in the street after supper while fathers mowed lawns and mammas made fresh lemonade in kitchens. There was penny candy in bins at Alfredo's store, where Gracey ran with two quarters rattling in her palm to get something cool from the freezer. A ceiling fan beat winged patterns on the store's wooden walls and gossiping men sat on porch swings chewing tobacco and telling stories. Afterward, she walked home with a Welch's grape soda, a Tootsie Pop, and four copper pennies to put in her piggy bank.

On the hottest Georgia afternoons she and her brother, Ray Junior, slipped under the house to drink warm Coke out of glass bottles, beneath the porch where the beating sunshine couldn't get them. They napped in that cool underground of safety.

She was a library kid, reading *Philip Hall Likes Me, I Reckon Maybe, The Cricket in Times Square, Anne of Green Gables.* Her mother sat beside her, arm to arm with Gracey, pinning fingers under each word to spell them out while her daughter looked on and helped her. Ray Junior, a grass stem in his mouth, dozed next to them. Until finally her mother was tired and laid back with him. Gracey read aloud, forming pictures in their minds with her deep, smart voice.

Long, lazy days of freedom until her father showed up at five, his six-foot-four frame sullying the door of the house. He was half Puerto Rican from his mother's side and kept his copper hair groomed and tinted. His body was fit. He was handsome. After heading the maintenance crew at the golf course all day, he drank a quart jar of vodka with Kool-Aid and ice and then started looking for someone to take his anger out on.

Her father's memories poisoned all his actions, always reeling him back to infancy, when he was the last child in a line of thirteen, stealing chicken bones off an East Georgia kitchen table, playing tug-of-war with slices of bread. He knew nothing about love getting him through the tough times. He believed it took only fight, pure will. He had come out of his worn-out mother with his tiny fists thrashing air. Always the baby, he was hit and beaten by his father and older brothers. His sisters were two ephemeral female shadows. They became, dying, martyred, almost-corpses for their brothers, who owned more strength and wanted to force their hate onto someone else's body.

The first time it happened to Gracey, she was swinging on an old board hanging by a rope off the oak in the backyard. Her father pulled her down by her legs, hitting her for leaving her bike out on the driveway, for being ugly and no good. Finally, for no reason at all. The blows fingerprinted her small body with sullen non-words. His veins stood out on his forehead. His eyes became like a rabid animal's.

In these spliced moments of disjointed time, Gracey watched her mother through the back kitchen window, rinsing pots and washing tiny rainbows out of the suds. Her yellow eyes, bruised to healing green from her husband's fists, were slits. I walked into the doorjamb yesterday, she'd tell their neighbors. I'm such a klutz.

Cole watches Gracey's lips shake when she tells them about the day she learned to drive, her twelve-year-old head craning to see over the dash, the steering wheel too big, her mother's blood staining the vinyl. She tried to manage that unwieldy animal, squealing around corners, braking at jolted intervals. Gracey did her best to imitate the adults she had seen driving.

She got them to the lights of Grady's emergency room, where she witnessed her mamma's almost death. Her mamma's head wept blood like car oil on the stretcher sheet. Drops of crimson fell on the white floor. The doctor in his green scrubs and plastic gloves acted as if he was going to catch a disease. He bandaged her head up. How'd you go and get yourself in a mess like this one, Miss Moore? he asked. And one nurse, pink and freckled, her hair in a bun, her green eyes kind, squatted down next to Gracey and asked her name. Why don't you tell me what happened to your mamma?

Daddy done it, Gracey said. Her body liquid fire inside, terri-fied of speaking that truth. The nurse nodded, put two dimpled arms around Gracey's body, and rocked her until her insides felt solid again.

They were sent back home. She did not see the nurse before they left. Riding back under a dome of stars, the night was horri-fying and exhausting with what it had brought them. Gracey's hands were tight on the wheel. She kept her eyes pinned forward, sometimes whiplashing her mother with her sudden stops. Her mamma's soft meowing moans filled the car.

At home, her father rocked catatonic on the kitchen stool, mumbling to nonwitnesses, blaming God and his broken angels who'd let it happen. *That woman deserves it, she be lucky if someone killed her.*

Gracey had no answer to her father's nightly scouring of her flesh in her childhood room. With survival instincts, she let her adolescent nails grow long and tried to carve up his handsome face. Tying her hands to the metal bed frame with a leather belt used to beat her bottom when she was small, he hit her with his bare fists. Your mamma shouldn't never have had you, he said between wrathful gasps. After what happened to her mother at the hospital, he always saved her face, beat her only below her neck.

She'd try to plug her ears when he entered Ray Junior's bedroom.

Sleep betrayed her and she stayed up the night through, waiting for him to return. The next day she suffered swollen flesh and bruises. Her eyes burned from fatigue. She woke to her mother's shame, a deep-rotting core beneath folds of denial. What you need a hospital for, child? You look fine to me. Couple of scratches is all.

She endured this her childhood through.

Cole watches while she stands by the window and looks out. Morning sun folds an awkward glare over half her body. The questioning room of the makeshift command post is quiet.

I was fourteen when I tried to kill him, she says. He'd brought me and Ray into the basement to show us his gun collection we weren't never supposed to touch unless he was home. I didn't want to touch them neither. I always hated guns. They're mean-spirited, and I don't trust 'em. Killin kids dead with one finger. I don't think them guns was loaded, but I always wondered if Daddy was testing us. Did we hate him enough to kill him? If we shot him and he didn't die, it'd be the best reason to beat us. If he did die, we'd have to live with that guilt all our lives.

I'd seen the rat-kill down there in its red box with the white skull and crossbones. And I couldn't get it off my mind. Every night he drank his quart of vodka with his Kool-Aid. One night, I said to Mamma, I'll make Daddy's Kool-Aid for him, you go lie down awhile.

Gracey is quiet. She turns to face them. I was just trying to survive. She looks at Kelly as if he had blamed her. Other girls with their lip gloss and movie dates, she says, and I was thinking, How could I kill my daddy? She lifts her chin to the air. Better him than me, she says. Better that filthy bastard than a young girl never did nobody a lick of harm.

She crosses her arms over her chest and stops talking, sets her jaw and waits, bravely withstanding silence before she is able to explain how her mother wanted to test the Kool-Aid at the dinner table before her father drank it. When she told her mamma no, her daddy saw murder in his daughter's eyes and she got up fast, tried to run, his fingers caught her belt loop and he pulled her back. What are you tryin to do to me, girl?

He dragged Gracey to the kitchen, aimed to beat her with a hot skillet low-frying on the stove. She fell and he scrambled after her. Gracey was up first, heading for the front door, breaking through a full screen and a pane of glass, taking off down a dark street in Vine City toward Boulevard. No jacket and only stocking feet on the coldest day in January.

4.

THE SEX-STUDDED WORLD of Deneeka Jones, four years into Atlanta, swimming behind the big guys, the Rockets, Jeromes, and Slip-Bones, and among the scarred, nicked, vein-jumping piles of men in hit houses and shooting galleries, wanting to get their freak on. The smoke-screened haze of their perversity licks Deneeka's pocketbook from the inside out. Under her skirt, leather straps hold up her snaked penis, unused, unwanted, tucked beneath her body like waste.

She stands now in line for works on Jones Street, above the magnolia tree on the corner of J.P. Brawley and Kennedy where they deal drugs by the bagful. The dealers switch their eyes like nervous horses' tails, watching for five-o-in-the-hole, the unmarked Ford Explorers, the GBI, and the Red Dogs, running their legal wheels slowly over the split and stained tarmac of the Bluff.

This part of Atlanta is obsessed with itself, has no sense of history. It contains the drug-struck multitudes who have welcomed Deneeka into their folds. They tolerate new meat, old scarred sisters they once loved, and death. Funerals are a weekly thing at Greater Springfield Baptist and the people accept them, are kind to the patterns of poverty, understand the dreams drugs offer. Everyone is trying to make a buck, survive, shuck reality for one earth-shattering moment of thrilling relief. When the addicts search out her now familiar form, something like compassion lives in their wild eyes. *Deneeka, baby, what you got for me?*

A needle on the street costs her clients two dollars. On Saturdays, she can stand here for nothing and wait for the Afroed lady in the baseball cap with slogan pins on it to give her brand-new syringes for free in exchange for old works.

She watches the wind take a beaten Pampers box sideways down the street. It hits a turned-over mail cart, holding damp leaves, Coke bottles, a sneaker, McDonald's wrappers, and thrown-out underwear slung there at five A.M. when Deneeka had her head between somebody's legs, screwing up her lips for the rehearsed power she knows is hers with the drug infested.

Late May sun seeps through the branches of Vine City in a latticework pattern of gold and orange. Deneeka turns her face away from it. She's wearing a black plaid mini and nude sparkling stockings she found at Value Thrift on Stewart. The elastic on her pink halter is loose and slips off to reveal shaved chest hair.

You got a cigarette on you? Fry Jones asks her. It takes him thirty seconds to get the words out. He stutters. He carries his limp left hand in the pocket of an old bathrobe, the other hand swings at his side in continuous motion. One blind eye's glued shut. He smells of destitution.

Deneeka's got a Newport in her mouth and talks with it in there. Nope, she says.

You got one between your lips, says Fry.

Lemon passes Fry a cigarette from behind his ear and sips his whiskey while he waits, his feet jigging from his heroin cold. His Brooklyn accent plasters against his vowels. That ain't the only thing he got 'tween his lips, he says.

Don't you wanna know it, Deneeka tells him. And I wish you wouldn't call me a man. It's a insult.

Fry breaks down laughing like that's the funniest thing he's heard.

A college girl sets up cardboard boxes of condoms and bleach kits and Band-Aids and ointment.

The lady running the program sits on the van step with her legs out the door. She's asking Charlene Dane the first three letters of her last name while shaking her plastic needle box like a tambourine. You got fifty in here, the lady says. Charlene's sweater is safety-pinned on the shoulder. Her tube socks are dirty. She's tried to squeeze her feet into Kmart flip-flops and the thongs on them are springing. Every few minutes, she bends down to tuck the rubber back in.

Kay Sum and Rollins and Healy come up in their Ford Escort with its spitting, sputtering motor that runs one minute and stops the next, a fading accessory to the impetuous trio. Most nights, they are screaming down Techwood Homes with dope to sell. The backseat holds young girls who give their pussy, sweat, and slack muscles for more freebasing. Deneeka's seen it. Those girls are pitiful, laying their beauty down in wait for tread marks from the uncaring. They don't know what they got.

Kay Sum does a U-turn in the street and drives up close to the sidewalk. His hair's in cornrows and he's wearing mirrored sunglasses. He says to the girl with the condoms, Give me some a those, baby.

This ain't a drive-through, says Deneeka.

Kay ignores her.

You want the green ones or the red ones? the girl asks him. The green ones are mint, for oral only.

Give me whatever you got, says Kay.

Deneeka sees the girl's shaking fingers handing over brand-new condoms from the state or wherever. Kay Sum grabs them, thanks her, and then screeches off down the hill.

Deneeka takes out her compact from her nylon bra top. She looks like straw, a stiff piece of colorless body. Bullet wounds of done dope are strung across her limbs and hold the memory of nights gone by in a host of cities: Hartford, New York, Baltimore, Richmond, Miami. One long time ago, Deneeka was a boy in Detroit with golden legs and blond hair. Her mamma let her keep it below her elbows and climbed in bed with Deneeka when she was a young boy, patting her head and saying, There, there, so beautiful, so sweet. The feel of her mother's hands and the smell of her perfume, she loved the lazy fingers on her back, the dream-like state of sleepiness touch brought. Her father had become a string of fathers, made-up fantasies her mother delivered in the hazy world of almost slumber. He was an airborne ranger, a sailor, a rich doctor, a war-torn Indian hero.

In waking hours, women came through their door and gave her mother pleasure until one fell in love with her. In a jealous rage she knifed her mother across the throat. Deneeka stood watching at the threshold, a silent child, listening in terror while her mother's broken cries sliced the air. Then she slumped in a closet and waited for three days for someone to find her.

You better not break that mirror, says Fry. That mirror ain't strong enough for you.

Deneeka puts a hand on her hip and rolls her eyes. Ain't you funny? she says to him. Yeah, you're just hysterical.

She goes back to her compact, fluffing up her strawlike hair, damaged from coloring and permanent waves, the stripping chemicals of home-done beauty products. Her painted eyebrows are falling down and she smudges them up with a finger.

You hear it? Lemon asks. The Red Dogs come 'round raidin this morning. They puttin people in jail for nothin. Yous didn't hear about it? He looks around. That's why this line's so empty. Everybody gettin their assholes checked by the po-po. Kyle warned us, but didn't none of us listen. They got Y for drunk and disorderly.

Drunk and disorderly ain't shit, says Fry. He smokes and ashes it in his shadow.

Deneeka's nylons are ripped and she tries to move them together with spit. They come around here and I'll whip their ass, she says.

The line grunts in humorous approval.

Yeah, you better watch yourself, Deneeka, Lemon tells her. Don't you want nobody tattletalin on what you doin.

Deneeka raises one fake eyebrow at him and shrugs. I ain't done nothin, she says. I ain't holdin.

A Jewish boy with big black hair and thick glasses comes from the back of the van to help the college girl with her condoms. How you all doin today? he asks them cheerfully.

Sunlight rises above the hem of trees and bathes their piece of sidewalk. Deneeka wants to run from it. It burns her eyeballs, rams straight into her head, and singes her mind.

Across the street, a woman in blue hair curlers appears out her back door, bends over, and attaches the chain on her German shepherd to the laundry line.

Fry stutters out, Hey, Irine! How you doin?

The woman shades her eyes with her hand and looks from Fry to the van and back again. The dog growls between her legs. All its free parts wiggle. Fry, don't you Hey, Irine me, the lady says. She shakes her head once and goes inside.

The dog can just make it to the chain-link fence. He jumps against it and barks. The metal shivers.

That there's the mamma of my first girl, says Fry. He's proud, picking his teeth with a dirty nail he found somewhere.

The dog or the lady? asks Deneeka.

Fry frowns. The lady, he says.

Deneeka goes back to her mirror. Her lipstick is fluorescent orange in the morning light. She picks a scab along her top lip. Why does it always get bloody without her noticing?

Backdropped against the sound of mutterings in their line is the woman sitting in the van, shaking the next box of needles.

Get me some of them condoms, Deneeka says to no one in particular. She frizzes her bangs by running two long fingernails through them. I'm a prostitute for a living, she tells them.

Semmes P. hears her while he saunters up in jeans and no shirt, a comb stuck in the back of his Afro. Ain't nobody's nothin touchin your white ass, Deneeka.

Hey, says Lemon, you leave him alone, he got some goodies tucked in there only a mother could love.

Maybe *your* mother, says Semmes. He smiles. His teeth are straight and white.

Those pearlies must be fake, Deneeka tells him. You probably slung powder for those.

Semmes fusses at himself in the blackened window of a parked El Camino. Wouldn't you like to know that, baby.

The girl holds the condoms out at arm's length for Deneeka. Deneeka lets her stand there while she finishes the last of her primping. She glances at the girl, who does not let her eyes go to the sores on Deneeka's legs, her broken nylons running in ripped streams down her thighs. You like my skirt, Semmes? she asks.

Hee-haw, he tells her.

I'm a fresh virgin schoolgirl, says Deneeka, taking the condoms. Thank you, honey, she tells her.

The girl smiles, ducks her head shyly.

Deneeka hates her smooth skin, the way she's got her hair tied back in a gold barrette, and the loose dangly earrings hanging around her neck. I could make a woman out of you, Deneeka says.

The girl looks up and swallows. Her eyes don't blink for some seconds.

Semmes laughs, Don't you listen to him, crazy, wore-out fool that he is.

Deneeka moves up in line and pouts at him. I ain't a crazy wore-out fool, she says. I got heart. I ever tell you I got a man at home, Semmes?

You never tol me no such thing, Semmes says.

And then the white kids come up, driving a new Jetta, the silver outline of their car glinting in the sun.

They park and the boy comes out the passenger's side. He has blond hair falling over one eye and a molasses-like jaunt, cool in its casual. His dark designer sunglasses hide his eyes. The girl steps out of the driver's side. She has auburn hair and fancy shoes, a no-fat body and a chiseled jaw. Golden Boy grabs her hand and they look both ways before crossing the street.

They might as well get hit by a car, says Semmes under his breath, they on their way to that end anyhow.

They take their place at the back of the line. The girl leans on a hip and the boy stands with his feet apart, still holding her fingers loosely in his. Between them they smoke a cigarette. He carries a Timberland shoebox full up with his needles.

You kids doin all right today? asks the boy with the frizzy hair. You want some condoms? Some Band-Aids?

The girl looks hit, visibly shrinks, but Golden Boy reaches out and takes a fistful of red condoms. He stares at the college girl while he does it. She smiles, blatantly fascinated. The boy looks down the line, at Deneeka.

Don't I know you? Deneeka asks him. She fluffs her hair. Her Newport's all smoked down and she toes it on the dirty cement, lets it roll into a gutter, plugged up and grime ridden with whiskey nips and excrement, four heinous vials of who knows what.

Golden Boy takes the cigarette from his girlfriend. I don't know if you do or not, he says.

He reminds Deneeka of the flying feeling of being young, wretched Miami men in convertibles taking her to clubs with gold-flecked bars, leather stools, starched white tablecloths. In back rooms, they'd feed her champagne and make her suck them, fuck her from behind until she screamed out in an ecstasy latent her whole childhood through. She primps her hair in a tangle of fingers and palm. I think you do, she says to the boy, know me.

And then the lady with the needles is saying, Next! Deneeka picks up the plastic box at her feet and walks toward the van.

I got about a hundred, she says, I'm sure it's about that. A hundred.

The lady is black and clean as a whistle. She's got a nonjudgmental look, the kind eyes of someone who knows the streets. Deneeka can see she is one of the few who understands where pain lies: in the childhood hearts of the lot of them. The lady shakes the box. You got about fifty, she says.

Deneeka huffs and puts her elbow out. I got at least ninety, she tells her. Or seventy-five, somethin like that.

The lady picks up her clipboard. You got fifty, she says, pulling out a box of new needles. Fifty will get you sixty. First three letters of your last name?

Deneeka gives her three letters, takes the box, and tells the woman thank you. Promenading back down the line, she sasses each person. When she gets to the boy, she stops, reaches over, and pulls his glasses down. She is looking into the green, down-to-earth eyes of a person who gets what he wants. The boy looks straight into her without fear, criticism, or interest. He holds on to the girl at his side as though she will blow away if a strong wind blew. There isn't even a breeze.

You want to know me better? Deneeka flirts at him. You just say my name in the streets. Deneeka. And I'll come runnin. She walks away flicking her hips from side to side. Don't you forget it, white boy, she calls back while she saunters.

Hey, the boy yells after her. You're white, too.

Deneeka turns and looks at him over her shoulder, a twisted, sultry pose she's memorized for years in front of an audience of mirrors. I ain't nothin you can put a label on, she says. And then she smiles, the sun a blinking torment in her eyes. Turning on her heel, she leaves them to go find sleep in that place it was when she last looked, days before.

5.

GRACEY'S VOICE IS DEEP, resonant, authoritative, the voice of cigarettes, risk, courage, and a hard life, lived on the brink of disaster. She leans against the wall, inspects her nails, and tells them how she couldn't ever go back to her house after trying to poison her daddy. She wound up running to her mamma's mamma's place on Angier. She looks at Cole. Y'all know where that's at? she asks.

Cole nods.

Kelly keeps his head down, moves the sludge in his coffee with a plastic stirrer.

Gracey studies Cole. Again he tries to hold her gaze.

Don't think Daddy didn't follow me, she says. My grandma put me behind her wide back and said, Ray Senior, get the hell out of my yard.

He aimed to shoot me dead, wavin a pistol in the air, screamin threats.

If you want to kill this child, my grandma told him, you'll shoot me first.

After that, Daddy slunk away like a beat snake.

I slept between Grandpa and Grandma every night. Grandpa

only had one leg, the other got torn off at the knee by a conveyor belt. I could feel its stub when I turned over in sleep, but it didn't bother me none. I knew he wouldn't ever touch me.

I grew up at my grandparents' house. My daddy's folks would uphold the wrong of their blood even if they knew it weren't right. I learned what love was from my mamma's people. I couldn't go back to Mamma, but I'd see her occasional and we'd hug and cry. Ray Junior left, too. I heard he hightailed it to Egan Homes to crib, and I couldn't never find him at school or anywheres else.

Gracey smokes and stares out the window until Cole is afraid she is done talking. Then her voice enters him again, filmed images slide across an invisible screen. She is fifteen, living on Angier and going to school at Charles Allen High School, hanging out with Rosy and C.C., Chris Byron, Fry Jones, and TBird. They'd go in back of Kmart with antique gold paint and paper bags, sniffing until their minds swirled, sounds echoed off the autumn blue skies, the cracked pavement and dandelion weeds. Someone was always puking over the curb from too much sniff.

Paint flecks on her nose, and a book bag on her back, Gracey could be seen running down the streets to her grandma's home cooking and backgammon games on the card table. Reading in bed until sleep came, she slept soundly, with only the vague memories of her father tingeing her dreams.

And then she got beautiful.

She looks down at her body. My curse and my savior, she tells it.

She saw the other beautiful girls with their twenty-one-year-old boyfriends, picking them up from school in Lincolns, fancy-dining them with cognacs and Dorals. She throws her chin in the air, pulls her curly hair back, and says she wanted to live high.

It was around this time Ray Junior came to see her at school, standing beneath the bleachers with his old reckless smile and a smoke in his mouth. They walked to Silver City Diner and ordered coffee, held hands over the place mats. Her fingers were small in his. She smiled so hard at seeing him again, her mouth ached. All the while, she was trying to make sense of his tight, gray skin, the black streaks coming from his eyes, how skinny he was.

Peggy, the waitress with Joan Crawford eyebrows and a bouffant hairdo, served them coffee refills.

The favor Ray wanted from Gracey was only one guy. Panic circled his voice. Just be a little nice to him, Ray told her. He's got money, and he's been watchin you. I owe him some cash. Ray's face was parallel with the table, lights bore down on him like a punishment. She noticed the white, foamy corners of his mouth. He was her family, and she would have done anything for him.

They left the diner and found themselves at the edge of darkness in an old baseball field on Ponce de Leon. From the windows of three parked Cadillacs came the Temptations singing Keep Holding On. The man Ray told her about arrived out of the shadows wearing a mustard-colored leather jacket, long sideburns, a beard, and a fat gold-chain necklace. Her grandma's words vaporized into air. *Don't you do what your mamma did, Gracey, the Lord loves you and these fast-talkin, hard-livin men don't.* He was Gracey's ticket to a fancy life.

Leroy lived on Northside Drive with white wall-to-wall carpeting, a tan leather couch, and a big-screen TV. He fed her reefer and got it on with her, buying her a Monte Carlo and consuming her sixteen-year-old body, new breasts, and unmarked face.

Gracey sits taller in her chair, pulls the hem of her dress down, and hardens her eyes. It wasn't anything close to tender, she says. But I knew men got money and women got pussy, and in order to get money, you give pussy. I did it with Leroy like I done it all my life.

Cole realizes his muscles are rigid. His hands clasp together on the tabletop and expose white knuckles. He watches the tape recorder, a single, turning eye between them, and wonders when a man first decides to hit a woman. He imagines it's a formula, time and trust over violence. Gracey Fill with four finger marks across her outer cheek. All I give her, Leroy said to his friends, holding court in his living room while Gracey went to get him a beer and then back to put ice on her cheek, and she's sassin me.

It was true, Gracey says. She looks wide-eyed at Cole. Anything I wanted, Leroy got me, so no one ever advised me to leave him off. She studies her nails and speaks softly about hoop earrings, silk scarves, manicures, going to school just to show off her fashion.

Standing up from the chair, she paces the room, finally finds a place on the wall, and leans her back against it with her head up. After that, he never hit me where you could see it. Just like Daddy. It was like it didn't happen. I thought I still had it good. I remember how nice spring was colored that year with bright flowers and green trees. The lawns were so pretty. I was comin on seventeen in three months, and Leroy was givin me all there was in return for rough sex and hittin me occasional to let loose his mad. I was missin something real bad, but I didn't know what it was. I didn't much want to think about it. Then one day I was walkin down the front steps of Charles Allen High with Rosy. A boy named Michael French come walkin up. He was the basketball center. I'd never looked twice at him until that day. He said, Hey, Gracey Moore, how you doin?

I said, Fine.

My friend Rosy said, Mm-hmm, under her breath.

Me and that boy stood there starin at each other. He got shy, looked at the ground, and then back at me. You doin anything after school some days? he asked me.

I could make myself free, I told him. I was fresh as they made 'em.

He said, My parents got a lake, and I wanted to give you a ride in a boat.

Rosy started laughin.

He just watched me.

I shrugged my shoulders. You tell me when, Michael French.

Gracey turns and looks at Cole and Kelly with pride in her eyes. A smile spreads across her face. Michael French's fish be fried in a skillet by a nice mamma when he got home. All winter he got basketball practice. He always did his homework. We set out toward Stone Mountain that very next afternoon in a little green foreign car that didn't rattle and sound like a gun goin off.

Gracey remembers how the beach didn't have one person on it. Sand on the bottom of her feet made her feel like the flesh there had been asleep forever. Down by the water, Michael turned over an orange boat and said for her to get in. She was all girl again, holding tight to both sides while they went gliding through the surface of mirrored glass that reflected trees on all sides. She listened to the dip of the oars and the rhythmic sound of wood against metal. Before her, the sun boiled down a sunset horizon.

I ain't never learned to swim, she told him.

He said, You ain't never had to. If you fall in, I'll save you.

There wasn't a lick of wind.

When they got to the middle of the lake, they lay with their backs to the boat floor, their legs up on the wood seat and their hands crisscrossed behind their heads. He asked her what she wanted to be when she grew up, something Gracey hadn't ever considered. He said he was going to get him a sailboat and go around the world. He listed countries, the names of which Gracey had never heard. He held her hand and kissed her fingers. The sky went a taffeta maid-of-honor royal-blue color. Stars pinpricked out like they were shy to do it and Michael French leaned over to kiss Gracey's cheek. He breathed there, then put his mouth on her ear and breathed there, too. He said her name so soft she didn't know if he really said it and then he kissed her lips. Gracey Moore, he told her, I like you. I really do.

Later, they lay hugging, faces half up to the sky, lips raw from kissing. Still fully clothed.

Make a wish, he said.

I ain't makin no wish, Gracey told him.

You don't have to say it out loud, Michael said. You just have to wish on the brightest star you can find. I'll do it, too.

She made a thousand wishes and hoped they counted as one.

His hand stayed in hers and the boat lulled in a quiet wave, bringing her to a place she'd never known before, where the world was kind, touch was tender. Mad voices in her mind stilled, were comforted.

All that spring, they went to the lake. Finally they made love. May 17 under a high full moon. Rowing out in placid water, Michael said, Gracey, I want to get me a present from you. I don't want to disrespect you none, but I want to be with you more than ever.

He knew about Leroy. He said he understood. Gracey had told him what she felt about him wasn't anything like what it was with Leroy. Michael touched her face and kissed her head and said, I know.

Their lovemaking was slow, so slow she thought she might die from wanting him. They went until they couldn't go anymore, the boat rocking them like a cradle, no distinguishable line between the two bodies. Gracey became the girl she never was. He held her, talked to her in a voice softer than air. The desire in her body came alive, and she screamed with delight. Her flesh laughed out its final pleasure.

Late that evening, he drove her back down the darkened roads to the city limits. The sun was long gone. Michael stopped the car by a curb in East Atlanta and kissed her on the mouth. Gracey Moore, I'm marryin you, girl. You gettin out of that man's hands and into mine. I love you.

At Charles Allen, her Monte Carlo was the only car in the school's parking lot. Gracey's heart deflated, the joy went out, knowing she had to go home to Leroy. Michael's voice was low and sorry in her ear, What do you want to do? I could take you somewhere else, anywhere. They didn't kiss before she got out. She drove all the way home with her heart in her feet, and there he was, Leroy, a dark form on the porch steps. Nobody else was around.

Not until he got to the driver's side did she realize he had a baseball bat.

Dragging her through broken glass onto a white carpet stained bright red from the blood of her smashed nose, her hit face, loosened back teeth, and broken jaw. An eyebrow hung from her forehead in a shapeless U. Leroy kicked her while the room spun, a carnival ride gone haywire. Vomit heaved tumult through her body. He flung words at her. *Whore, douche bag motherfuckin little dirty no-good gold digger.*

Down the stairs, tail over head, she lay on the moldy cement floor. Her arms and legs were bungee corded, and he climbed on. Blood leaked out of her wounds. Her right arm was broken, and her soft insides, loved tenderly just hours before, were torn up.

She doesn't know how long she lay there.

Her mouth works in jerky movements of lip-raising disgust at the memory. She turns and rests her forehead against the wall. Just like Mamma and me and Ray Junior got beat by Daddy, she says, I got beat by Leroy. She intakes a shaky breath. The police finally got him. He did fourteen years for statutory rape and kidnap and other things he'd had before me. He was thirty-six years old, always in the fresh underpants of some young girl wants a sugar daddy.

Gracey turns and looks at them. I'm forty-one, a old lady now, she says quietly. But if you asked me what Michael French's face looked like, I could draw you every inch of it. Don't think I couldn't.

6.

COQUETRY IS ABSENT in Tyler Sky's world, false. Except for her. On this Saturday in May, Rebecca Howe appears out of nowhere at his front door, elusive as holes in antique lace, a quick shimmer of sunlight reflected off diamonds. Her cerulean eyes are alert. She moves past him, into the room, where she walks among his things like visible breeze.

The last time they were alone together was in his ex-home, on West Paces Ferry Road. He never invites her, only hopes she will come at any hour, to be with him. He lies awake waiting, and when sleeping, dreams of it.

He hasn't bothered to dress this morning and stands before her now in an open Oxford shirt and the khakis he pulled on when the doorbell rang. Speechless, he watches her, as if studying a rare species of captured bird.

You are not welcoming, she tells him while she pours orange juice from the half-fridge by the liquor cabinet into a brandy snifter. Where's your wife?

I'm sober now. I've broken all my bad habits. Even marriage.

I know *that*. I mean, no one sees her. She and Dan have dropped out.

He shrugs, deliberate, careful. He doesn't know what will make her stay and he won't say anything to risk her going. You're still around, he says. And I think she's embarrassed because of that. They moved to Inman Park.

She walks the periphery of the room, touching the dictionary on its stand. Her hands were once familiar on his skin, drooling down his stomach, loving his hard cock with her palms. He wishes he could smell her, orchid and lilac. He wants to see her pale skin beneath those sheer, slip-lined dresses she wears. She is the sophisticated hippie of Buckhead with her 1920s scarves and heavy eyelids, her pert, small body. Atlanta women suck in breath and dare not think about the lust-filled pondering of their spouses when Rebecca passes by. Now she moves through his living room wearing white, at the nape of her neck is a single topaz and in her ears, two dangling sapphires.

Because he cannot bear the torment of his own thoughts, he loses all resolve and says aloud, I am still in love with you.

Her feet make short indents on the carpet. She looks back at him, her drink half-tilted. I want you to be, she says. But I've ruined you.

I'm not all ruined.

She moves her lip around so she can bite it softly. Everything she does makes him want to inhabit her body.

Swirling the drink, she looks into it. Her voice has a lilt of lullaby, as if she is still seven years old, asking to be picked up and carried. I think about the way you laid me down, she says. Sometimes when I slept, you sang.

But I thought you slept.

I slept best I could. I missed you when we slept, I wanted to be with you always.

She glances out the windows to the west, where the Olympic torch can be seen over the bridge. She said once it looked like a McDonald's fry bag and they'd laughed. He wonders if she remembers it. All of it, the soft promises, *I will love you forever, Tyler Sky. Forever.* Rebecca. Whenever he thinks he hears her name on the street, he turns to look, hoping she will be there. It was worst at the beginning. His body was a fresh wound without her. She'd gone to Paris to dry out from him, she said. Her husband went along with her, unruffled and impermeable. And Tyler had followed them, flew over with only the intent to see her, divorce imminent, his life a bottomless hole. There had been a shameful altercation with a doorman while Rebecca, in her husband's businesslike grasp, stood watching, wide-eyed and wild with confusion and want.

And now this one-bedroom apartment. He wishes it were less, a stone grotto beneath the Earth's surface, testament to how he loved and lost for her.

Fifty miles south at the southern end of the Appalachian mountain chain lies Piedmont Plateau, where he was born and generations of his family are buried. It has an elevation of 1,000 feet, its red soil forming gently rolling hills. Inside them, his ancestors quarried Georgia marble, 237-foot-high gold mines stood ready for his family's raping during the gold rush, when they made their final fortune. His money is juxtaposed against 2,500 years of Native American history. These forebears gave him his high cheekbones and olive skin, which bring women like Rebecca to him. Before the gold, he'd come from nothing, dirt and what it would yield. Often, after knowing her, he wants to return to that, but something in him keeps going. His pride perhaps, touted around the city in the architecture he designs.

Why today? he asks her. Why did you come to me today?

She takes a sip of her juice and turns to him. I came to tell you Audrey isn't doing well. I thought you might be able to help me think of something to do.

He thinks of when he saw Audrey last, a month ago. Frazier had come to borrow money. Audrey is even more stunning as she grows. She is kind, polite, but untouchable as any teenager. He has no hold on Frazier's love for her except that time will erase their bond. He believes it must, they were only kids together yesterday.

Where is Frazier? Rebecca asks. Audrey talks about him, but he never comes by. She's very secretive about him.

He's away from home now.

Really?

In Cabbage Town, actually. He wanted to try it on his own for a while, without Mom and Pop.

Cabbage Town? She frowns. How is he coming along there? Couldn't you have set him up somewhere else? I guess the schools wouldn't have him.

Not the ones Genevieve wanted to send him to. Cabbage Town is different now. Lots of young people are moving there. What's the interest in Frazier?

I want to know how he is. Like father, like son. She blinks luxuriously and half-smiles. Resting her hip on the back of the leather couch, she says, I think about it sometimes. The two of them together, you and I together. It's strange.

He watches her. That autumn afternoon comes back to him, lazy orange leaves falling onto the damp backyard while Genevieve was at work and Rebecca stood on the balcony in her slip. Wrapping his hands around her stomach, he'd kissed her neck until she stiffened, and he looked down to see his son emerge from a coverlet of maple leaves, bike in hand, sweat plastering his bangs to his forehead. Frazier had been fifteen years old, home on October break from school. He had kept his eyes on Tyler's, as if it was a challenge, while he moved the bike over the manicured lawn to the shed. Rebecca and Tyler hadn't moved.

He had never talked to Frazier about it. He had found it comforting when after the divorce Frazier started to go out with Audrey, someone his son could talk to, who shared his story. He makes the same stale promise to himself to stay available to Frazier, call more.

I worry about Audrey, Rebecca tells him.

Why?

She gets up from her place on the couch and stands by the window. He watches her from the doorway. Hair curtains her face. She's so beautiful. Men . . . She does not continue. In almost a whisper, she says, I need to tell you something.

He waits.

I think Audrey— She stops. Words stay frozen between them and then they rush from her. I don't know. She's getting very thin. And her grades are bad. Lovett sent home a note. I have a feeling it has to do with Howe. He hasn't made love to me. The other night I saw him go into her bedroom . . . She stops. He sees Rebecca swallow. She reaches one hand out and touches the windowsill as if to steady herself. When she lifts her head to look at him, her face is red. Hopelessness and despair wrestle in her eyes.

And he understands. Howe, he says softly.

The meaning is too much for him. Truth shakes his nerve center, makes him need a drink, a noose for his neck. Life is so brutal, he wants to tell her. Please, make it bearable.

He watches her touch her eye. He needs to bring her to him, to be inside her so she can feel tenderness again, know integrity, find reason. Rebecca. His Rebecca.

Outside the sun leaps from its city glare and finds metal car hoods and fenders and the flat surfaces of windows behind which he used to work. Before her, before drink, before he lost his way like a blind man running into things that made him stumble, hurt him, like these words before him now, asking the world to sleep, close its weary eyes and dream of other places.

7.

KELLY STANDS AND HOISTS his belt up with two thumbs. Let's try to get this on quicker, he says.

Gracey blinks slowly. You got a piss-poor attitude, she tells him.

He is about to reprimand her until he sees she's smiling, laughing at him. He resumes his place at the table, his brow creased. His top lip comes up slightly. I won't lie to you, lady. We want to know about Sonny. There's no use in us wasting time talkin unless you can tell us something about Sonny Fill.

Sonny is dead.

That may be true, but we still have to know about him.

She shrugs, shakes a cigarette out of the pack, and lights it. You boys are diggin for gold in a iron field.

Kelly watches her. We got all day and all night and we could stay here forever waitin, but if we don't start hearing somethin useful soon, you're in for a long vacation behind bars.

Gracey glances at him, wipes the back of her palm across her mouth, and says, You don't have to worry, Mr. Po-Po, there ain't nothin I like better than talkin about Sonny.

Kelly stares at her. I am an officer of the law and it would do you good to respect that title.

She holds his stare. I do apologize, she says.

You're going to be more than apologizing— Kelly starts to tell her, but Gracey interrupts. I met Sonny over in Summer Hill. After Leroy beat me like he did, I quit school and moved there to an apartment with three girls from Charles Allen. One girl was a Jamaican named Kaisem. She was a dancer at the Claremont. She had a little baby girl we used to play with all the time, just under a year old. Pierced ears and black eyes. She didn't never cry. Didn't smile neither. We had boys comin round with their Smokey Robinson tapes and Flag Brothers fashion, smokin Kools, and drivin them silver Sevilles.

Gracey ashes her cigarette on the windowsill and slides her back down the wall to sit on the floor. She tells them how Kaisem was dating Sonny. How high she was on him, all set up with her baby and her man. Back then they competed for men, wearing platform shoes and Diana Ross hairdos, lots of blue eye shadow. Gracey made her own money with her job at Crystal's and she had some boyfriends, not one running, lots of them, coming by the place trying for her to be their girl. She was shell-shocked after Leroy, promised herself she'd never be touched like that again. She was going to be real careful this time.

A lazy Saturday, Kaisem and Gracey, Randy, Sonny, Fry, and some others sitting around the velour couch. The boys had reefer and they'd smoked some. Fry had Kaisem's baby on his lap, making her dance with her hands in his.

Randy said, Hey, Grace, you know who asked about you the other day?

She said, Who's that?

He said, Michael French. You remember him? He went and got himself a basketball scholarship at Morehouse.

Gracey was quiet, trying not to think about how Michael was all she couldn't have. She didn't want to make herself miserable chewing on the fact she'd lost him, especially in front of all of her friends.

Oh yeah? she said.

Randy said, How you know that boy? He so square his head fit in a building block.

Kaisem laughed and said, Gracey used to go with him out on a rowboat every day.

No joke? Randy, hooked on Gracey, wanted to know all about it. He was standing behind the couch, tuning the radio. Keep Holding On was playing.

Yeah, Kaisem said, that lake must be pregnant from Michael French's spermies by now.

The lump in Gracey's stomach traveled to her throat. What lies you throwin around? she asked Kaisem.

Gracey, don't be caught dumb, girl, Kaisem told her. Michael French be takin all them other girls out there too, gettin 'em knocked up in that little rowboat of his.

Gracey got up from the couch slowly and walked to the other room.

Randy said, Hey, baby, where you off to?

Gracey closed her bedroom door behind her. She was real fragile, about to break apart after Leroy. In a way, Michael French had become her religion. She prayed to him at night, believing since he loved her once, maybe everything would be good another time. From the other side of the wall, she heard Sonny say, Kaisem, what in hell you say that for? That was her boyfriend in high school?

Kaisem said, He ain't no boyfriend. Anyways, I just spoke the truth. She'll be all right.

She ain't gonna be all right, said Sonny. She sad as a funeral.

Cole watches Gracey stub her cigarette out on the baseboard. She picks another one out of the pack and rolls it with two fingers across the floor.

When she speaks again, hot starts up Cole's cheeks at her spoken memory. She is nineteen years old and Sonny Fill is at her bedroom door, kicking it closed, walking over to help her unbutton the back of her work shirt, asking is she okay and telling her Michael French liked her better than the rest. His hand in hers is strong, a man's hand, his breath on her neck is gentle. His words are tender.

And then nothing could pull her from him.

Kaisem ran from the house at the pain of losing Sonny. Her baby was abandoned for long stretches of time while she wrapped her legs around a biker from Queens.

Son and Gracey were in love. Sonny had deep brown skin, eyes like almonds, black turtlenecks, and fat turquoise jewelry. And he was proud to have Gracey on his arm. She loved the confident way he touched her, how he brought her to pleasure with a skill that made her feel secreted, far from harm.

They lived together on Chandler Hill, in the Glenn Hollow apartments with matching '78 silver Eldorados, a canopy bed, fine linens, and glassware. He was twenty-nine and she was nineteen, a ripe plaything. He owned an import business and came home with roses, a finger to her lips. I don't want to talk about my day, baby, I just want to love you. She didn't work, watched the stories, did their laundry, talked on a gold phone to her girlfriends, and painted her toenails cherry-blossom pink.

On the other side of the door to Gracey's new house, drugs ran like undammed water down the streets of Atlanta. They were being hauled from the Golden Triangle, fields of ripe poppy plants on the Burmese border. In the fields of Colombia, coca crops bloomed promises of tax-free money. Single-engine Cessnas landed in vacant dirt fields under hot tropical skies. Sweating men brought boxes of cargo to hidden spaces and flew them to the United States. There they serviced the inner cities, college campuses, and black-tie dinners of America.

Meanwhile, Gracey had just turned twenty. She wore minidresses and high heels and sat in a high, twirling chair getting her hair done at Tucks on Auburn Avenue. Sonny came to pick her up decked fine in his gabardine and Stetson, and bringing her gifts of sable and mink.

On Saturday nights they could be seen on Cambleton Road, at Marcos and Siskos, drinking Rémy Martins, smoking Newports, and dancing to the music of Marvin Gaye, Smokey Robinson, and the Pointer Sisters.

Their wedding was six months later, a blur of tea roses and fine wine. Broad-shouldered men with car telephones and nervous eyes stood in the back of the outside chapel. Gracey, pregnant with her first baby, was vowed into marriage. Son was her true love and one desire, the person who could shield her from the unfair world.

Her daddy arrived uninvited in a shit-brown suit and graying temples, holding her mother by the waist. The wide bubble of the brandy snifter broke in Sonny's angry grip, a linen napkin had to be delivered and was stained scarlet. Get that bastard out of here, Sonny said. He hurt my wife. One spot of blood on Gracey's dress, four barking German shepherds at her father's heels, and Gracey's mother's face, pressed against the passenger window. Gracey waved her white-gloved hand at her. It's not you, Mamma. It didn't never have to do with you.

Two months later, she started to show. With a baby on the way, she became somebody, belonged somewhere. Grocery-store mothers touched her belly. *When's it due?*

At three A.M. the bed filled with her water breaking. Grinning widely, Sonny delivered happy chatter on their way to Grady Memorial. Just hang on, baby! he said. He took corners on a dime.

The girl baby came out slippery as chicken liver. Sonny held on to the bed's metal rail. I love you, Gracey, and I love our baby girl and ain't nothin gonna make me stop.

Later, six the next night, Gracey lay back happy and exhausted; Sonny brought her a velvet robe of rose yellow for house-wear when discharged. Her mamma came in afterward to hold her new granddaughter. A perfect child, she told Gracey. Just like you were. Leaning over her bedrail to place the grandbaby on her daughter's chest, she said, And you got you a good man. He the real thing.

Her daddy never did come.

Lakeisha Fill arrived into the world, and Sonny left. First just for three days, then seven, then longer periods of heartbreaking absence. He came home tired. Sorry, baby, I just got busy. Business is real crazy. Kissing her and then falling asleep while he did it.

The seventies. Heroin and cocaine were hitting the streets of Atlanta. Speed and crystal were old news. People wanted something different. Sonny was the welcome wagon, bulking up and running out, turning chippies into full-blown habits so the long-haired freaks with bugged-out eyeballs were waking Gracey and her baby in the middle of the night, begging for a hit of something.

Gracey leans back with her arms crossed in front of her. You want names? she asks. I'll give you names, but they ain't nothin you got a Social Security on. H, Y the Super K, Black Fly, T4, and all them juiced-up Betties they hired to carry their money through airports, exchange it for suitcases full of drugs, and back again. Son was one of the big guys. I remember waking up that first time to a fool addict on our front porch. I said, What's that guy want, Sonny? 2:11 by the digital and Sonny was in his pajama bottoms, pacin the room, his head twitchin. Go back to sleep, baby.

What he want?

Go on back to sleep, Son said. I ain't got time for you now. Then he walked out.

Cole sees the corners of Gracey's mouth twitch. My husband ain't never talked to me like that. She makes circles with a burnt match on the cement and does not look up when she continues.

The very next day piles of white powder were all around her living room. There were scales and rows of full Ziploc bags. Four guys were testing it on the black dinner plates she'd gotten as wedding presents. That your mamma? said one. He was cooking up and watching Gracey while he did it.

Sonny didn't look at Gracey. Yeah, he said. That's her.

Gracey went back to her bedroom. Sonny came in later to get his keys, and Gracey asked him where he was going.

Leave me alone, he told her. I got some business to take care of.

Not that kind of business, Son. We got a child. You ain't doin that shit with a child around. That's crazy. I'm fixin to be a wife on the outside.

He looked at her for a long time with his hard eyes and a rigid mouth. Real calm and level, he said, Who's payin for this house, Gracey?

She said, You are.

He said, That's right, and you ain't givin a red cent toward it so I don't want you hollerin about where the money comes from. You just keep your sweet mouth shut and let me take care of how we goin to pay the rent.

Then he left.

Gracey uncrosses her arms and fiddles with her hands on her lap. Not looking at Cole, she explains how she thought Sonny was only selling, that he wouldn't do anything as bad as shooting dope when he had a wife and a little girl.

But Sonny walked in five days later, his eyes gray and his nose running. He was pacing again. Two guys followed him, one big-shouldered and mustached, the other skinny and pockmarked. Sonny went with the big one into the bathroom and the little one sat with Gracey and Lakeisha. He had a squirrelly look in his eye, and his clothes hung on him wrong. She judged he was fifteen years old, and she shuddered at the sores on his face, bright red against his pasty skin.

You want to tell me what my husband is goin and doin with your friend in the bathroom? Gracey asked him.

The skinny one's eyes went wide. Don't you shoot dope? he asked.

Gracey never shot dope in her life and told him so.

He looked her in the eyes. Your old man do and you don't? he asked.

That day Gracey Fill's world did a 180-degree turnaround in the middle of a hell-bound highway.

Afternoon

―――

1.

Audrey drives them down Jones Street, swerving around a man leaning over his crutches, seemingly asleep in the middle of the road. She turns onto Marietta. I don't want to go home, she says.

They pass a store, hollow as an empty eye socket. That Korean's going out of business, Frazier tells her.

What Korean?

The one who sells syringes. Now that van lady gives us free ones, nobody's going to buy his two-dollar needles. Frazier rolls down the window and lets the air find him, plastic needle box on his lap. Going home!

The noonday sun bakes the car; inside it's warm. His skin is hot. They pass out of the Bluff by the electricity substation, the Good Samaritan Health Clinic, and the labor pool.

She lights a cigarette; one is smoking in the ashtray.

You lighting one for your imaginary friend? he asks her.

Shit, she says. You want this one?

Nope, he tells her. He knows she's coming down from the lines they did this morning, trying to keep her sad at bay. He tries to remember if he still has a Valium in his wallet for her crash. He is almost certain he does not. Maybe it will pass. He sticks his head out the window, opens his mouth to swallow wind. They pass over the tracks and take a right on Northside Drive.

She smokes furiously. Frazier, did you hear what I said? I don't want to go home.

Frazier feels the air in his hair, his face flat from wind. I heard you, he yells to the Georgia Dome. He has a nickel bag in his front coat pocket for him and JP, and then they can go cop somewhere JP knows about. He starts to sing the national anthem.

She slams on the brakes in the middle of Northside. A red Camaro honks and veers around them.

He ducks his head back in the car. Her beautiful green eyes are crying. She's sweating.

Aud, he says slowly, calm down. Let's get to the side of the road.

A whole family of cars goes by beeping, cutting into the other lane to avoid them. She is unruly now, dangerous. His voice is deliberate. We have works in here, he tells her. We have to be careful.

Her tears come fast. She brings the wheel over and they land on Northside's curb and then roll down again onto the side sand. She turns and looks out the window. Her hair folds into a canopy around her face and he hears her crying, watches her lift her finger to wipe her nose.

He gazes out at the hedge of skyscrapers that he hopes to enter to get back to Cabbage Town, JP, dipping in, new needles, a bliss-promised Saturday. Audrey's misery seems far off, the echo of something he doesn't try to make out, an irritating splinter in his finger. Before him the sky is a perfect blue, a great day for nodding, tripping out, feeling nothing. He's been mainlining for one month and nothing comes close to the anticipation of the high, cooking up, tying off.

While she cries, he goes through his connections, a name at a time. Who's gonna be there, how much money do they have left between them, him and JP? Absently, he puts a hand on the small of her back. So delicate. Audrey, take me home, sweetheart. I have to go home and get some rest, okay?

She turns, her face tear-streaked and tired, the eyes drawn and puffy. I want to go with you, she says.

Uh-uh.

How come?

Don't do this. Don't you have homework or something? Go shopping at the Lenox with your mom, you'll feel better.

Her eyes narrow.

He looks away, checks the side mirror for cops.

You shit! she says. She punches his thigh.

Ow.

You fucking asshole. I don't know why I do this. Wiping the tears away, she veers the car into traffic, driving fast. Smoke from the unused cigarette drifts up from the ashtray. I hate you, she tells him.

Don't say that.

I do.

He picks up the cigarette and starts to smoke it.

They drive in silence. She takes almost red lights with a vengeance, swings around corners like a NASCAR queen. Her face, even in its tired state, is so like a china doll's, the skin smooth, her neck long. He reaches out and touches her cheek, feels her soften, though visibly she is in the same fierce rage.

He doesn't know why he keeps her to him, mouthing words of lovesaying that will somersault them into marriage and kids. In his moments of bravado, he believes he stays with her because she wants it. He tells himself it is better than killing her with the pain of a broken heart. He pictures her waking up in her sun-soaked room, weeping and wondering to herself whether or not she is pretty since he doesn't want her.

In the deepest part of himself, where he rarely dares to look, he is scared Audrey will succumb to someone else. The thought makes him ache. He doesn't want someone paying her compliments, bearing gifts. Any guy would have taken her to that prom.

Some horny high school boy, high off her, hoping against hope for her round breasts in his mouth, her lovely legs wrapped around him, the way she has of leaning into her guy when she laughs. He chucks the cigarette out the window and tries to think what he can say to save himself from losing her.

She parks in front of his house. They don't look at each other. Go, she says.

Aud—

I *said,* Go.

He doesn't move, sits there thinking five more minutes of this and he can leave. He loves her, but he wants to be with JP, put the needle sideways in his mouth, roll up a shirtsleeve and fist a vein, feel that shame peeling from him like onionskin.

He turns to his lap. I'm sorry, he tells her from his neck-slack position.

She sniffs and looks out her window.

He reaches over and takes her hand, small and pale. Kissing the inside of her wrist, he watches her close her eyes, feels himself half-hard for her.

I am a shit, he tells her. He means it.

Why? she asks him, her voice pleading. Why do you act like that?

He shakes his head. I don't know, Aud. I'm scared of this. Losing you.

She moves in the seat and glances at him, touches his hair. He brings his face to hers. You won't lose me, she whispers. Just be good. A little nicer.

Her lips are raspberry, downy, the tip of her tongue moves on his own. He says her name into her mouth. She intakes a breath, long and shaky, and brings a hand to his cock. They lean, head to head like that. He puts his fingers up her shirt. She is braless. Her nipples are soft. Audrey Sullivan, I love you.

A tear rolls down her cheek. Do you?

But I'm not enough for you. You— You're in the pantheon, baby.

She lets out a teary giggle. Jesus, Fraz, you talk like a fucking gangster and then you're a prep-school boy all over again. What's a *pantheon*?

He touches her now coke-free jaw. The goddesses, Apollo and those guys.

She nods. Can I see you tonight?

I can't wait to see you tonight, he tells her. He suddenly cherishes her, knowing she is leaving him to his own day. I'll call you, he says.

When she smiles, her lips shake. I don't believe you, she tells him.

Touching her mouth, he says, I know you don't. But I will.

She checks both his eyes and nods. Okay, she says.

He feels in back of him for the passenger-door handle, then kisses her again, five times over. She closes her eyes and reaches for the side of his face, but he is slipping backward, out the door. He shuts it and puts his head in the window. She smiles at him through her tears.

Don't you go driving like that all the way back to Buckhead, he tells her.

She looks at his house and wipes her cheeks with her hand. I love you, she tells him. I never stop.

Standing on the curb watching her Jetta drive off, he feels the burden and relief of this. Her silver car flies through the tiny streets of Cabbage Town and disappears, leaving no remnant of the one person who still cares.

He starts up his cement porch, 350-dollar-a-month duplex in the Appalachian Bluff. The screen's pulled over and the aluminum siding, white once, is gray with age. Inside, JP lounges sideways on the couch, drinking coffee out of a juice glass and smoking a blunt. The walls peel olive-green paint, the couch is a worn tan-and-brown plaid, a sleeper with the mattress out so the cushions sag inward.

Hey, where you been? JP lifts his glass in salute.

Frazier inhales the sweet-herbed air.

I been waitin on you with my poor-man's speedball, JP tells him. He lets go of a gust of smoke through his nose.

On the TV, Barney's pearlike figure bounces to soft romper-room music. JP moves over so Frazier can sit down and points to the screen. That's somebody's *job,* man. Whoever's behind that getup's got serious problems. You holdin? He pulls up the hood on his maroon sweatshirt so it covers his skullcap.

Frazier takes out the nickel bag and shows it to JP, who sits up straight. No shit. Your girl get that for you? He hands Frazier the blunt and unrolls the bag.

JP is eighteen, quit school when he was ten to do street-corner dealing. At twelve he shared a crack pipe with a whore from Forest Park in a windowless seven-by-nine room on the third floor of a hit house. His easy charm and fine looks got him into the teenage upper-class cliques of the Masquerade's late nights, where he was paid in drugs for his knowledge of connects. There he met Frazier Sky, free of school and looking for a roommate, instant friend and cohort in adventure. No more crack for me, he tells Frazier when they smoke. I'm doin smack. H is the only way, man. You can't have a chippy with crack, that's the devil. You might as well hang your soul by a noose.

His pinkie finger's long, and he dips it in now, passes the bag to Frazier, who takes it and watches Barney bounce around his fake flowers. He nods his chin at the needle box. We got some clean works, he tells JP. Your turn next time. I saw that freak there with the yellow hair who knows Feather. She recognized me.

Deneeka? She sell you any?

I wasn't going to cop drugs while I was in line for needles. Frazier gets up and goes into the kitchen, stripped linoleum, rat shit, and no screen on a window that's held up by an old Bible left from someone before them. Greasy, gutsy stove grill is out on the counter from weeks ago. All they have in the refrigerator is powdered milk.

We should go to Feather's den, JP says. I think he picks up Tuesdays. I bet he's got a stash.

There's not even ice in the freezer, says Frazier. You got any money?

I don't got a stolen dollar.

I got that.

Your dick gets you that. How come you didn't ask her in? I like to look at her. She's something else. JP taps the blunt. There isn't anything left in it.

Don't talk about her like that.

Sorry, but you gotta know it. You hang with a beautiful woman, guys want to look at her. That's the price you pay, my man. Everything worth anything got a price. He stands up, pulls on his gloves with the fingers out.

You don't have to wear that shit on your hands, it's hot as hell out there.

I'm always cold. I get paid tomorrow. When I deliver the Sundays, they pay me at the office, so I'll get you then.

Yeah, says Frazier, you get your ass up at three A.M. so you can pay me back for the drugs you shoot. See if I care.

Hey, at least I'm workin for a livin. JP points a gloved finger at Frazier and winks. Anyway, I dig my paper route. Don't be dissin it. You might have to get yourself a job someday. You'll come beggin on me to help you do it.

There's nothing to lock in the house, but JP wants it locked anyway, puts the key on a string around his wrist and smokes a bent cigarette he found in his sweatshirt pocket. They walk past the Carroll Street Bakery. Check this shit out, says JP. Buckhead Realty sellin dumps in Cabbage Town for the price of a limb.

Gentrification, Frazier tells him. He lifts his T-shirt over his head and sticks it in his back pocket.

Gentri what? All's I know is my black ass is on the sidewalk if our rent gets any higher.

Our rent isn't getting any higher. We don't even got heat.

Easy to get heat.

They're walking by the Mattress Factory when they see the bicycle, lying on its side in the dirt. Blue with gold trim.

I'll be fucked runnin, says JP, glancing around like a pre-roadkill rabbit. Looky here. He passes his smoke to Frazier, who stands holding it between his thumb and forefinger. JP picks the bike up. He checks both brakes and then swings his leg over the seat. He cruises down Carroll, ringing the bell. The frame's bent and some spokes are out of the front wheel, but it goes.

It even has a goddamn ring-a-ling, JP says. Hop on, brother, here's your chariot.

They scream down the streets of Cabbage Town, Frazier with the smoke between his lips, leaning back on the seat, JP standing on the pedals, yodeling. Freedom is a bicycle, he tells the world. *I want to ride my bicycle I want to ride my bike. I want to be RICH, I want money, lots and lots of money, I want to ride in the sky.*

Those aren't the words, Frazier tells him.

But JP doesn't hear. He does riddles with the tires, makes snake signals in the street sand, and goes shrilling the bell by the Cotton Mill. A multicolored Ford pickup almost hits them. Fuckin idiots, the driver calls back.

Through the Krogg Street Tunnel they yell as loud as they can, howling like lonely dogs, hurling their voices. The acoustics are good. Sound bounces off the musty, mildewed walls while the dark cool swallows them. They come out into bursting sunshine. JP's ropy muscles work the handlebars, his denims are halfway around his waist, red-striped and fraying boxers stick out above them. His hood's off now and the skullcap covers only the top of his scalp. He pedals with a smile. Don't forget to wave to the women, he calls back to Frazier. But Frazier's looking at the turquoise sky, the trail of one airplane streaking exhaust through the blue.

Then they are downtown, past I-75, weaving in and out of the tourists in front of the Hard Rock Cafe, ignoring the DON'T WALK signs. JP stands up and leans forward. With one hand, he holds on to the side-rail of a truck. The truck's wind back-drafts through their clothes.

We lazy, he yells to Frazier, who grins, the luck of it hitting his gut in a tremendous surge of almost happiness. Behind them a cop car swirls its blues in the midst of noonday traffic. An officer says into his speaker, Hey, you, let go of the truck.

You don't have to tell me twice, JP says under his breath. I'm doin it.

They come up on the south side of the Four Seasons Hotel. Spanky Bank is standing on the sidewalk, sparechanging the tourists. JP is breathless and he slows down as they near the entranceway. Shit, will you look at Spanky? What's he gone and done to himself? His hair's got a nest in it.

Spanky's dreadlocks are wiry and long, his eyes like windmills. He pulls his palm over his head again and again, asking for a couple of dimes from the businessmen out on a Saturday to spend their money.

Frazier sees his mother. She's standing alone next to the curb on the far side of the hotel's entrance, looking expectantly down the street with four white shopping bags hanging off her wrists.

Spanky, yells JP.

Shut the hell up, Frazier tells him.

His mother's wearing a flowered sundress and her hair is blonder than Frazier remembers it.

You shut up, says JP. He pedals twice more.

Frazier throws his heel in the spokes, hurling JP forward and sideways. He catches himself with his foot on the pavement. What the fuck, Sky, you tryin to get us killed?

Just shut up.

His mother fluffs her hair once, presses her lips together, and looks at her watch.

Spanky is approaching her, circling like a vulture, finding a vein. Excuse me, ma'am?

Frazier watches her jaw tighten. Her eyes move anxiously down the street.

JP says, What? You owe Spanky somethin, man? Nobody owes Spanky nothin, it's bad luck.

Can you spare a little change? Spanky cows around Frazier's mother sheepishly. She becomes deaf, dumb. Frazier sees her swallow, the muscles in her throat go rigid. He realizes his mother is scared. Thinks to go up to her. Hey, Mom, how you doin? But she'd be worse then. Spanky's just a stranger. Nothing to her.

The white Jaguar comes around the corner. His stepfather is driving. Good old Danny boy. Dan slows the car and parks it. His mother hurries to it. Coming around her side, Dan helps her with her bags and throws his hand at Spanky as if he were a fly. Spanky, suited out in army garb with a blue bandanna around his ankle and two different sneakers on, says, Just a couple of dimes or somethin. He tries to help with the bags and Frazier's stepfather gets flustered. Young man, he says, please. His mother sits stiffly in the passenger seat. A dollar for Spanky comes out of Dan's billfold. Another flutters to the ground. Spanky reaches for it and so does Dan, they bump heads and then Dan is slamming the passenger door, and snarling at the beggar. His mother looks at the street man through the glass, bold now, irritated.

Spanky backs away, bows, and shows his rotted teeth as the Jaguar blends into traffic.

Frazier watches them go. A piece of his mother's flowered dress trails out the closed door.

Hey, Spanky, JP yells, mounting the bike again and pedaling slowly. What did you get?

Frazier wants to pay Spanky a dollar to watch the bike while they go up to Feather's, but JP says he'll take the bike with him. Hauling the bike over his shoulder, JP waits while Frazier puts his T-shirt back on. They enter through the tiny doorway of a narrow building to the left of the hotel. The tenement is in line for demolition, hazardous waste in that neighborhood. The stairs smell like urine and burnt fish. They mount them two at a time. By the first landing, JP is sweating, worn out. I'm leavin this shit here, he says, putting the bike down.

The fact of his mother is still on Frazier's mind, the powdered smell of her skin when she used to tuck him in at night, her face when she found out about his father's affair with Rebecca. Frazier was home from Chattanooga, freshly kicked out for smoking pot and leaving campus without a permit. She'd held him until he couldn't breathe. Ma, you're suffocating me.

Oh, Frazier, I'm sorry.

Always so dignified, she was ashamed, horrified, and kept apologizing.

It's all right, he'd said.

Later, his father's gaunt visage greeted Frazier when he went to the sparsely furnished one-bedroom he had rented. Witnessing his father's crying had been an awful scene, gruesome in its complexity. I'm in love with someone, his father had said. It isn't just what your mother thinks, sex.

I know, Dad. Look, I'm sorry. I gotta go.

The smell of his father's whiskey and sweat.

I have some people I have to see, Frazier had told him.

He'd watched while his father composed himself, wiping his eyes and blowing his nose. I hope you will think of this as your home, he'd said. Bring friends over if you like. You know Audrey is always welcome.

Okay, Dad. Yeah. Thanks.

No, son, thank *you*. For understanding.

JP stops at the fourth landing. That ain't piss, he says, holding his nose.

Something died.

Where's forensics when you need 'em?

They start up the fifth set of stairs. The smell's excruciating. It makes Frazier's stomach knot up and his head dizzy. He stops midway. I'm not going up there, he says.

Man, you labored up all those stairs to tell me that?

Frazier puts one foot in front of the other.

Feather's door has two street signs on it, a black rectangle ONE WAY and a red circular KEEP OUT.

JP knocks. Feather, he says. It's JP and Sky. He knocks fifteen times and then he kicks the door once. It creaks open. Shit, he says, open sesame the whole time.

When they walk in, the smell assaults them, sends them reeling backward as if a fire hose had hit them. Frazier stands outside, leaning over, waiting for the blood to come back to his head. Man, says JP, I didn't know I got a nose till I smelled some of that.

They look at each other. JP raises his eyebrows. After you, partner.

They walk inside.

Feather's sitting in front of a blue TV screen with the word *video* in digital white in the corner. His body is a large purple bruise, swollen to two times its normal size, a grotesque blow-up doll filled with canned jelly. His eyes are wide open, the sockets bursting a grid work of fluorescent red veins. On his neck, four gold necklaces are stretched to busting.

JP crosses himself. Jesus-son-mother-of-God.

Fine fuckin time to get religious, a voice says.

Turning to the kitchen, they find a woman standing there. On closer inspection, they understand she is a man, wearing a Goodwill housedress, smoking a GPI blue from a pack on the back of the couch. I'm used to the smell, she says, ashing her cigarette on the carpet. I wasn't going to take the needle out of his arm.

They look back at Feather. The needle's sticking out of his forearm like a miniature javelin. Next to him is a packet of brown powder with a picture of a red rocket stamped on it. I mean, are *you*? The lady-man smokes. What are you boys lookin for? Her hair is a brilliant orange. When she smiles, Frazier sees that all her back molars are missing. She's wearing purple heels and violet stockings and walks like Marilyn Monroe around the couch. As if to toast them, she raises the clear plastic cup containing a swallow of orange juice. It's all the poor darling had in his fridge, she tells them. And it's almost bad. She starts to come toward them. JP backs up. Frazier follows. Oh, she flops a hand at them, don't be afraid. You think I'd suck your little pinkies? I don't have any intention—

Mine ain't pink, JP tells her, his nose still plugged.

Touchy, touchy, the woman says. She throws her hand out, and he veers back. Snarling like a street cat, she goes around them to

Feather. Do you think he's dead? she asks. Then she laughs ten octaves too high. Immediately afterward she is sobbing, drawing her unwashed hand-me-down dress to her face and wiping her tears. Frazier sees a video case next to Feather, two women, a man, and someone dressed in a bear costume. The women's overblown breasts and pursed lips shout at the camera for attention. A pint of Zhenka vodka is sitting on the kitchen counter. He understands the man-woman is drunk.

We outta here, JP whispers.

Oh yes, the woman says, lifting her mascara-drowned face. You boys go. The meat wagon will be along any minute to take him to the morgue. I imagine it will be quite a scene down there, all those tourists standing around for a peekaboo while poor Feather gets his bones broke so they can straighten him out and carry him right. Sure, it's okay, leave me here. She is down on one knee, crying harder into her skirt.

JP pulls Frazier by the elbow. We need to get the hell away from here.

They head toward the door. Sorry, ma'am, says JP. We was just leavin. We got the wrong house is what.

You good-for-nothing dope heads, she yells after them. You aren't men, you're nothin, just—

JP slams the door and they take the stairs two at a time, hurdling the railings so they can get down sooner. JP vomits on one stair, not stopping long for it, letting it drip down the stainless-steel banister while he jumps the middle bars.

The cops are coming up from the front door when they round the second landing. Hey, one says. Slow down. Where you boys going? Were you up in number six?

There ain't no number six, says JP, looking the man in his beefy eyes.

The policeman narrows his eyes at JP.

Is there? JP asks. My aunt lives in four, we come all the way from Macon to pay her a visit, and she ain't there.

The cop raises his chin, deciding on the validity of JP. His radio sounds at his side. His partner keeps his foot on the stair, eyeing them.

Hey, says JP, what's that smell? I think some kid's hamster gone and died.

The cop on the bottom stair says, Frazier Sky?

Frazier's mouth goes dry; he looks at him without responding.

You were at that charity Christmas dinner with your mother and a red-haired girl at Lenox Plaza. He half-smiles and gestures shyly. I never forget a face or a name, he says.

The first cop relaxes, looks from Frazier to his partner and back again.

Oh yeah, says Frazier, putting on his best prep-school act, watching out for his consonants. That was me. My mother's always fund-raising all over the place. He laughs good-naturedly.

The cop is older, graying at the temples. They needed security, he says. I was filling in for someone who was sick.

Frazier nods.

There is a moment of silence while the smell curdles around them. More sirens sound outside. Frazier waits to see whether they will ask what he is doing with a black kid, down from Macon.

Well, you boys go on . . . says the first cop, we have an investigation to proceed with.

I'll see you later, says the second one.

Sure, says Frazier. See ya.

The two officers start up. Frazier and JP start down, one step at a time now. They stop to get the bicycle and listen to the cops talking to each other in low voices. They can't make out their words against the backdrop of shoes on metal and then they are out into the glaring sunlight.

Will you look at this cluster fuck, JP whispers.

People are gathered around the ambulance, asking questions, talking in voices thick with curiosity, looking up six stories to the worn-down tenement above. The ambulance's back doors are wide open, like a mouth, ready to ingest the food of the diseased and dying. The DOA.

2.

KELLY ANNOUNCES TO GRACEY they are taking a break. And he and Cole leave her sitting at the table, smoking. Kelly locks the questioning-room door behind them and brings Cole to the sarge's makeshift office, where the venetian blinds are drawn on the windows that look out over Vine City. A portable humidifier steams in the corner. Balled-up Kleenexes spot the area around a cardboard box used as a wastebasket. The sarge has a cold. He's red-nosed, pallid-faced, and in a bad mood. His uniform has a brown stain on the front and he's yelling into the telephone.

Cole and Kelly stand at attention like two privates new to the army.

The sergeant slams down the receiver. Sit down, he says angrily. Then he proceeds to explain about a suspected drug dealer dead in a sixth-floor tenement apartment in Atlanta's center. Sonny The Rocket Fill is his connect. We got a black book full of addresses, he tells them. And if you boys turn up names, I want them within the hour.

Kelly takes out a slip of penciled paper with the men Gracey named. The sergeant looks at them and frowns, throws the paper in the wastebasket filled with his cold tissues, and turns to Kelly.

Those guys are all dead, he says. We need 'em alive. What in hell is she giving you names from the 1970s for?

Kelly describes an air of helplessness with his palms up.

The sarge waves a hand at him. Just get me anything you can.

Walking back to the interrogation room, Kelly's chest is puffed out like a rooster's. We ain't listenin to any more of this life-story shit, he says. I'm sick of it.

Cole doesn't respond. He notices the rings around Kelly's eyes, how short of breath he gets, impatience flexing his jaw. Running his fingers over his uniform buttons, Cole says quietly, I think we made a deal.

Kelly stops walking. He stares straight ahead, not turning to look at Cole. Pulling his right hand into a fist, he says, Did you see me shake on it?

Cole takes a step toward him. I thought you said who's running it then is running it now.

I meant The Rocket, Kelly says. He starts to walk again.

Cole jogs to keep up. Listen, who knows what she could tell us about him if we let her talk? He catches a side glimpse of Kelly, whose eyes flit back and forth, thinking about this.

We're gonna be in that room till midnight, Kelly mutters.

I don't have anywhere to be, Cole tells him.

Yeah, well, I got a family.

I'd be glad to stay and listen if you want to leave.

I'll bet you would, says Kelly over his shoulder, his hand on the questioning-room door. I'll just bet you would.

She's standing by the window, the coat around her like a cape. Boys, she says when they come in.

Kelly sits down at the table across from her. How much longer we gonna be in here?

She looks at him. I don't own a watch, she says, but I'm judgin it's near two, and I just barely got married. She smiles at Cole, who smiles back. He sits in the chair closest to the window and turns it toward her.

Kelly looks from one to the other. Rolling his eyes, he punches the tape recorder. Go ahead, he says, bored, weary of it.

She balances herself on the windowsill, adjusts the heel of her shoe, and says, When my water broke with that second baby, I couldn't get Son out of bed. I near had to drag him out. He wanted to know if it could wait till mornin. Gracey shakes her head. They say with the second one, it comes out quicker, but Jackson's labor lasted twelve hours. I pushed and hollered. I sweated through a set of sheets. Finally, they gave me a epidural. Son had gone to get coffee somewheres. I was the first one to hold my baby boy. He smelled like a wet washcloth and was hard to keep still from day one.

Mamma, I said when she called, I just had you a grandbaby boy.

Mamma was crying so hard I could barely understand her. Your daddy's dead, she told me. He went down with a heart attack at three today and was dead when the ambulance came.

Gracey brings a hand up and rubs her forehead back and forth. A goddamn heart attack, she says. You'd think with those words the weight of the world would have been lifted. You would have thought the sky seemed brighter and all them daisies in the field be singin to high heaven. Truth is, I didn't feel nothin. That little boy in my arms didn't mean shit anymore. When Son come back, I told him to take Jackson to the nursery. I was tired.

Looking over at Kelly, she raises her chin. I stayed tired. Don't you never let no one tell you raisin kids is easy, it's hell on wheels and you gotta be the driver. Gracey leans against the window, her face limp. She grips the sill and tells them how Son would be gone for days at a time. When he walked in the door, he'd be wired up, doing circles around the living room, hyped on drugs. If she asked him where he'd been and why didn't he come home more, his face would change from happy to mad in seconds. Shut up, woman, he'd say to her. I'm here now, ain't I?

Son, she'd tell him, I need a stroller, the last one's broke. Where's all our money at?

What are you grumblin about? he'd ask. I'm the one makin it. Then Gracey would cry all night because that wasn't her Son. He'd put the pillow over his ears so he couldn't hear her. Jesus Christ, he'd say, shut up! He'd fall into comalike sleep while Gracey was trying to save their fall-down marriage.

Cole watches a breeze blow Gracey's dress collar up. Smoke dissipates in the air around her.

I tried to be a good mamma, she says. I was tired, like I told you. Especially after Jackson, but I wanted to do right by them kids. It was real hard on me. I was tryin to be everything, changin diapers and feedin them all hours of the night. I gave those kids all the attention and hugs I got left so they'd wind up right. It was hard. I never rested. They was nightmaring and crawling in my bed to sleep, Keisha kicking me in her dreams so I couldn't rest and askin me where Daddy's at. Every time they cried, I felt like I didn't know how to be a mamma and couldn't grow them up like I should. If I broke something or burnt the beans or spilled the gravy, Keisha be lookin up at me with her wise big eyes, and I felt stupid even though she was just a kid.

Jackson was real colicky, crying all the time, always had a cold or flu or somethin. He needed to be held constant. And I did. I'm burpin him one minute and feedin him the next, singin him lullabies and drivin him around for hours so he'd go to sleep. While Keisha's whinin she wants to be home. I didn't never nap when they did. I was vacuuming my heart out, cleanin them baseboards, bakin cookies and makin chicken dinners. I didn't want them to watch too much TV. I'd read aloud to those kids, took 'em to story-time at the library and all those little run-around neighborhood activities they be havin in the Bluff back then. On Sundays, I'm spit-shinin their hair, tyin ribbons on Keisha and little leathers on Jackson.

I had to put up with Keisha's terrible twos. She be on my last nerve, throwin tempers wherever we went, grocery store, park, library while I'm luggin around them sippy cups and Scholastic readers, so afraid they was gonna wake up in the gutter with gang tattoos on their behinds. I was doin it all on my own, and I was wore out tired. But still I stayed up past midnight readin books about potty trainin and how you gonna treat a child right and have patience. Son wasn't nowhere to be seen. When he did come home, he was more work than help. I thought we was gonna be doin all that together, raisin them up like we said. And I told him so.

Sometimes he was still good to me. I had them girlfriends whose boyfriends split soon as they got pregnant. Men who were makin it with someone else and weren't sending child support. These girls lived in Techwood and Fair Street Bottom. They couldn't even pay their electric. Son wasn't that. He was workin hard, tryin to maintain his high while bein a father and a husband. I guess for him it felt like the whole world was conspirin to stress him out.

About a year after Jackson was born, Son come home with a pile of bills in a suitcase and I sat down next to him on the bed while he counted it. I tried to talk reasonable. I was so tired of him not coming home, knowin he was doin drugs but not havin the words to talk about it. He was ignorin me and then lovin me and then short-fusin it with me. That day I pulled at his arm and told him I wanted him, tried to kiss him. I hadn't seen him in days and I was out of my mind. Hey, I love you, Sonny. Don't do this.

Real quiet he said to me, Grace, I'm sick of you naggin me, I want to love you, but I can't do it right when you always cryin.

I said, Son, please, you wouldn't do drugs if you loved us. You wouldn't be gone so much. We need you here. The kids, they want you around. I don't think we should raise 'em like this—

Son picked up my elbow, dragged me to the bathroom off our room. He said, Woman, you makin me do this, you makin me.

I'd put the kids in front of *Tom and Jerry*, so Son and I could talk and I could hear that stupid laugh track. Sonny closed the door. When he turned around, he hit me in the face. He hadn't never hit me before. The room buzzed. I slipped down the wall and snagged my backside on the toilet-paper holder. He hauled me over his shoulder and fixed me to the shower curtain with two rubber ties from his back pocket. He put a third one around my upper arm.

And then he stuck me. Shot me up with heroin and cocaine. Something happened to me. A tear come down my face and a orgasm went through my body, right into the hairs on my legs. The world went hazy, and I passed out. When I come up for air, Sonny was still starin me in the face. He stuck me another time. I threw up and passed out again.

When I woke up, it was so good. All that shit I'd been feelin about bein a perfect mamma and havin to try so hard, the hurt of how Son was doin me and my life turnin wrong, anything Daddy'd put in me and that ugly Leroy rubbed in my face and beat me with, losing Michael. Everything was just a bad old bird flyin out the window, and there I was, my head whipped up like a meringue and heat radiatin all over me.

Son shot me up till three in the mornin. Then he untied me, and I was slumped in the bathtub, noddin.

Gracey looks out the window and touches her hair briefly with her fingers. Cole is surprised when he glances at him to see an uneasy look in his partner's eye. Something like sorrow. Kelly shifts in his seat, brings a palm over his crew cut.

The next day after her first time, Gracey got up and did her routine, washed, cleaned, and changed the diapers. She didn't feel right, felt a flu coming on. She had a temperature, the shakes, body sweats.

Son came home at four, kissed her on the cheek, and started to help her fold the laundry. He watched her. The kids were sitting in front of *Sesame Street*. Gracey couldn't focus right on the bottom sheet she was trying to match up.

Son said, You all right, baby?

She told him she was sick.

You ain't sick, he said, you just jonesin. He dropped the sheet, held the small of her back, and kissed her neck. Then he took her to the bathroom and hit her again.

Gracey watches Cole. He tries to show no expression, though he can feel himself shaking.

I was cured, she tells him.

Later that night, they climbed in bed together. We didn't get it on, Gracey says. We just talked.

Sonny said, I'm sorry I did you like that last night, baby. But you had to stop botherin me. You was blowin my high.

She touched his face and kissed his mouth and forgave him everything that night.

It's how the drugs did me, Gracey tells them. I was feelin good. That was the beginnin of it all for a long, long time.

Gracey comes and stands between the two policemen, puts her thin arm in the middle of the table, and points to a spot below the inside elbow where a black scar is fixed in an O on her skin. This is where he hit me that first day, she says. This hole right here's where it all started, and I wasn't never the same again. Pulling the arm away, she moves the coat over her shoulders, walks around the table, and sits across from Cole.

Neither one of them looks at her.

You want to tell me somebody should have taken my kids away? she asks. That's bullshit. Those first years I functioned good, cared for my little ones. All that stuff I was tellin you I was tryin to be? Gracey snaps her fingers in the air. That was easy now. Sure, every chance I got, I was usin, but my kids didn't never have to know it. I kept it from them and it helped me be a better mother and a good wife. I was always cool and real mellow. You think it's all bad? She looks from Kelly to Cole and back again. You think junkies don't have nothin in life? They ain't worth shit? We're just stupid to start in on it and that's all? I'll tell you somethin, sometimes drugs can help people live. They can give people somethin to stay alive for. Gettin high taught me a lot of things concernin life. My eyes opened up. I found God while I was doin drugs those first years. I learned to love again and accept people. Before drugs, I was always half-thinkin how I could kill myself 'cause life was too hard for me. After Son showed me this new way, I started to look in the mirror and see I was a good person, worth havin. It was better than how I felt when I first got with Leroy or when Michael loved me or when I married Son.

She describes a heart on the table with her fingertip and says, That drug became my man.

3.

T YLER S KY IS AT HOME inside her body. He has been vacant for months. She is his spirit, gone for so long, inhabiting him. Through countries of desire, mapped across the length of her body, he is found again. She says his name, pulls her fingernails down his back. Her buttocks curve in his hands. He kisses her throat, her sweating brow, watches her in melted awe while she comes. During the ecstasy she asks, How can you do this to me? As though he has tortured her, she is beyond reason, a powerless hireling.

They have the energy of their first time between them still, that long-awaited, secret meeting at Polaris Lounge. Later they had undressed one another in a dimly lit hotel room by Piedmont Park. In the morning he had wanted to scream to the world that he had been faithful for as long as he could. His wife had been his best friend, a loyal partner, a good mother. But Rebecca had touched him in a way too erotic to ignore. When he held her, he felt drugged, and he could not leave her, made love to her again and again, desperately, as if his blood would stop its journey if he was not inside her. Without meaning to, he consigned his romantic soul to her.

Today they lie in his bed, satisfied and exhausted, smoking

rolled bidis he bought at an Indian smoke shop near his apartment. Rebecca has her head on his shoulder. His arm has fallen asleep beneath her. The smoke curls around them, lazily. Out the window across from his bedroom, skyscrapers of red granite, glass, and steel watch them, reflecting the warped sheen of passing cars below.

Who is she? Rebecca asks.

He ashes his cigarette in the coffee cup resting on his stomach and thinks how to answer this. She is Nancy, he says after a moment.

Passing the cup to the bedside table, Rebecca scoots down on the bed and rests her chin on his chest, looks at him with her flushed cheeks and bright eyes, her hair tousled, the cigarette up in one hand. Nancy, she says. She takes a drag of the cigarette. Living in a cluster house in Alfreda, I bet.

Don't be mean.

I'm jealous. I can't lose you, Tyler Sky. You're my everything. She says it looking down at her pointer finger, picking the cuticle with her thumb.

He tilts his head at her. Hey, he wants her to look at him, and she does, pouting, then turning her cheek on his belly.

I haven't seen you in a long time, he says softly. You don't want me.

She does not speak. He wants her to reassure him. He wishes she would tell him again that he is the only one she has ever really wanted since that first love when she was eighteen. She would recount for him again her life as a teenager. The time before she was someone's wife when she was just a poor girl in Northern Ireland, in love for the first time, climbing that rickety ladder to the upstairs fort, enduring mice and spiderwebs to kiss her boyfriend, lie naked with him under the tin roof listening to the rains. The boyfriend was three years older, fighting for The Cause, a young IRA rebel. He told her stories of bravery and courage. Rebecca said his virility made her feel delicate, feminine. When she talked about those sweet sweaty afternoons, Tyler

understood why her future had contained a lifetime of men finding strength from her fragile beauty. She had left that boy to
come to America. Home of the free. No one cares about politics
there, her first lover had told her when she said she was leaving.
She has described for Tyler the wind through the cracks of the
walls and the rain leaving mildewed green streaks on the wood
walls of the fort. Don't leave, the boy had told her, and then,
crushing his cigarette in the slat-board floor, he'd said, All the
smart ones are leaving. Shit, there's going to be no one left. You're
beautiful. That will get you anywhere. A gorgeous girl with an
accent is what all the American men want. You go get what you
deserve, a better life.

When Rebecca had gone to comfort him, the boy had shrugged
her off, taking his sleeve and brushing away the wide, shameful
male tears. Far below, youngsters yelled to one another through the
rough streets, boys ran in split leather boots and greasy hair next to
buildings butting up against the conflict-torn alleyways. Behind the
closed doors were hidden guns, kids with machetes, grown men
with terrifying secrets, women scared of drink and weapons and
the men who held them. Always fog and rain and news about the
killings and who was he? Just one man, he'd told Rebecca that day.
Stay, he'd finally said, marry me. I will love you right.

Tyler feels kinship with the boy whenever she speaks of him.
He sees him as a hero.

Rebecca rubs her cheek against his chest, and Tyler lifts her
chin. She looks into his eyes. I want to love you, Tyler Sky, she
says, but I don't want to marry you. There's that difference. Marriage is work. How we make money. Her voice vibrates against
him. You are not work.

He sighs, tries to hate her and yet can't. All Rebecca has ever
really done is touch the bottom block in the building of his world,
push it with her beautiful finger and then walk the other way when
it crumbled. How many times has he tried to ignore her, despise
her, and now here she is again, in this empty apartment, with her
problem.

And he loves her. Cannot find his way out of it. He wants to give her up. It is true, she ruined him. But when she comes to him like this, he is hypnotized, reason slips out the back door. Though he walks daily through his life, his spirit is always where she is. In the old days, when it was the clandestine drinking of her body in generic hotel rooms, he found he could not make love to his wife, went listless and irritable through his days. Alcohol helped it, abated it, but his great restlessness would never lie still until he could have more of Rebecca. He wished to see her in the mornings, putting milk in her coffee, her robe slipping from her when she dressed for the day. He wanted her bending over to get a newspaper from the porch, flipping the front page back, exclaiming about the weather. He needed to argue with her about inanities that held no circumstance for anyone but them.

He knows now she will never be fully his. She has been married twice before, to the grocer and the dentist, and now she has a third husband who is personal friends with Ted Turner, drinks with the mayor, owns houses in Seville and Patagonia. She loves Tyler, but she will not leave all that for love.

What about her? she asks. Will you marry again?

It isn't like that. He pauses. Nancy is uncomplicated, he finally tells her. Nice.

Rebecca frowns, her eyes open. How did you meet her?

AA.

You are still going to that? But, you have liquor in the house.

It wasn't just that I didn't want to drink anymore, it's that I wanted to find out why I did it.

Why not therapy?

He stubs the cigarette out in the ashtray, takes hers and does the same. I've been there, too.

She plays with the tiny hairs around his nipple. Remember when we first met?

The memory is like a blind man's name in Braille. Rebecca at Sea Island with the rest of them, how she looked in that plum dress and silver jewelry, her eyes painted, her hair long and wild about her. She'd passed him, smiling. Are you Tyler Sky? Twirling around once, she came back to him. I'm Rebecca Sullivan, just married to John Sullivan. Do you know him? She was proud, bold. Later she found him sitting alone by the swimming pool. She'd squatted down at his knee to feed him shrimp on a biscuit with hot sauce. Isn't that delicious? Her bright eyes were like a sixteen-year-old schoolgirl's.

I wanted you even when you were pregnant with Audrey, he says, remembering the day of the Fourth of July party at the Sullivans'; he'd watched her rubbing her sapphire-ringed fingers across her belly. She'd lifted the hair on the back of her neck and asked him to blow there because she was so hot. Pushing his hunger further, her attention was subtle. It could never be recognized as a true come-on.

She wraps her hand in his. He strokes her hair. They are quiet together, their bodies talking, as they will, in quiet comfort.

I would have married you a long time ago, Rebecca says. But you were so damn loyal. She takes her fingertip and traces his collarbone. Was Genevieve that good?

He pictures Genevieve's face, her high cheekbones and rosebud mouth, how she smoothed his hair in the morning, kissed him on the forehead. She made love to him with the lights off. He knew she came because the small of her back perspired and afterward her body relaxed as it never did otherwise. He says aloud, We talked well together. And we made some good love.

Don't mention about it.

You asked.

I know.

He had been standing at the doorway to their bedroom when he'd told his wife. She'd sat on the edge of the bed and he'd watched her face collapse in her hands. The sight of her weeping had been so foreign to him, he could not comfort her like he should have. She lifted her elegant hands to hide her mouth, muffling her own cries.

They had been college sweethearts, had built a steadfast, solid union where passion was a frivolity. Without realizing it, he had come to crave heated desire, the fire they had never had between them. Genevieve's deep love could have withstood anything but this. And then Rebecca fell center stage from the backdrop of their marriage and overshadowed it. Rebecca's own husband forgave her foolishness. Her spirit granted her immunity, her beauty left him no recourse but to stay with her. She was fragile, without family except for hoodlum brothers in Ireland who gave her an exotic air, dark and mysterious.

Sun streaks across her shoulderblade, curves around her side to her hip. He traces his hand over her. The way her bones move under her skin, how her voice weaves a promise of dreams realized, the movement of her hair falling against her back, make passion roar in him like fed fire.

Tell me what you want, Bec. What have you been doing?

I want advice on Audrey.

He nods. Silence hovers. He wants to know if she is dramatizing, as she will, for attention, or whether it is true. Howe. Audrey. Tell me about it, he says.

She shakes her head, and he can feel the cry beneath her surface. She puts her face against his chest. Are you really coming tonight? she asks.

He sighs. Yes. So nice of your husband to keep me on his invitation list.

He is trying to prove that he is sure of me, that no one can challenge him. Park Blaine will be there.

So I've heard; it's the only reason I'd want to be around those people.

She bites his nipple softly.

That was your doing, wasn't it? he asks her.

She nods. And that's the other reason I came, she says. I don't like to see you in public without knowing you in private first. She moves her hand around his thighs.

He holds her head. I love to see you in public, he tells her quietly. Only it tortures me.

He is forty-eight but feels Frazier's age, ready for her again so soon. She knows this and moves her body so her hand can grasp him. He moans, Rebecca.

She sucks him through the sheet, and then he is begging for her mouth, all of it. She does this expertly, her tongue a whispered answer, her lips so maddeningly familiar.

Later he gets up to make them coffee. At the picture window she stands wrapped in a chenille spread from his mother and watches the city take on golden-hued afternoon light. The planes pass back and forth, one with a runner says *Ladies Night at the Velvet Lounge*. The mirrored glaze of the circular towered Westin reflects it.

I know because when I saw him go in there it was two o'clock in the morning, she says into their shared silence. He stayed with her over an hour.

He freezes, refrigerator open, a container of cream in his hand. Bright light shafts over his profile. In one rush, images occupy his mind: Audrey's face when she was small, counting the cardinals at the feeder on a day when she was over to play with Frazier, her green dress blowing in the wind. Mr. Sky, can we have ice cream? 'Cause Frazier says the truck comes at three. Audrey, shy and sweet, the guileless, lone daughter always trailing behind her mother, never quite lost because of her auburn beauty.

But I'll kill him, Tyler says, without knowing he would.

Rebecca whips her head around.

He kicks the door closed without taking his eyes from hers. I swear to God; his voice is low. Audrey is mine as much as she is anybody's.

You can't say a thing to anyone, she tells him.

I can too, Rebecca. Don't be stupid.

Her lips go into a white line and she brings a finger out of the chenille blanket to point it at him. Don't you dare, Tyler Sky, I have come this far, I will handle it in my own way.

As kindly as he knows how, he says, You won't, Rebecca.

I will. Don't you go spreading this around before I've decided what I want to do.

But you have to tell someone, Bec. It isn't right. The child is going to rot inside. Something has to be done. Today.

I'll do it in my own time. She turns back to the window.

He stands gripping the counter. There isn't time with a thing like this, he tells her.

She won't look at him. I'll decide that, she says.

Don't be selfish, Becca. You pretend you don't give a shit about all of Howe's friends, but that's why you don't want to tell, you can't stand to look bad.

You should talk, Mr. I-Need-to-Meet-Park-Blaine.

That's different. Park Blaine isn't trying to sleep with my child.

The weeping is not hesitant. It pours down her face silently, a time bomb of frustrated grief. The plate-glass window reflects her. You don't know that, she says. She wipes her hand over her cheeks. You don't know anything.

He watches her without speaking. Once she had been the daughter of a miner. She'd met her American grocer in a rainstorm, taking refuge in a pub in Kingston. He had been her way to escape. She was nineteen and he was thirty-two and she knew how to love him until he was sick without it. She became the addiction he could not quit. Four years later, she would leave that grocer with their four-year-old son, walk out on them and the eastern Georgia heat, the drone of growing cotton, and the boredom of small-town life.

Her new lover had been an old friend of her husband. He had taken her away to the city of Atlanta, amphetamines in his brief-case, in a fine car. He'd made love to her in the murky drug-infested haze, bought her a house in Buckhead. His dying had been her chance to seduce Howe, a widower, the owner of a corporate buying firm, fifty-one years old and one of the wealthiest men in the United States.

Late at night after fitful, dreaming sleep, Tyler will wake to her story in his mind and tell himself the facts: she abandoned her own son. She leaves every lover she takes, slept with her first husband's best friend, and won't marry for love. Until this moment these things have mattered only when he was alone, able to abide that pragmatic place within him where he knows she is wrong. Now the reality of her hits him and curses the space between them. He understands there is something fatal about her, dead, valueless.

Still, he does not let her cry for long, brings her coffee, and then stands behind her, rubbing her back, being there for her.

I have to think of a plan, she says. Her accent is most noticeable when she is in pain. She turns to him, her head barely touching his chin. Will you help me think of a plan? she asks.

Sure, he says. Then he widens his eyes in mock surprise. Hey, I've thought of one. You can get her the hell out of there. Today.

She shakes her head. And go where?

He widens his arms to show expanse. Here, he tells her.

She turns back to the window. Be serious, Tyler. I need help. And I am offering it.

She looks at her wrist for a watch. Finding none, she brings her hand back to hold his waist. I have to go home and get ready, she says.

He watches her in the glass, her face still moist from tears. Bec, it could be nothing. You have to try to talk to Audrey.

But I'm always trying to talk to her, she says. I had a dream the other night, she was still a baby. I woke up crying. I wish she was. Her head smelled of talcum powder even when I hadn't used any, and I'd lie with her for hours, smelling it.

She looks up at Tyler. I used to put her feet in my mouth. And her fingers. I wanted to swallow her up. But when she grew a little, she didn't want to wear those Laura Ashley dresses and party shoes I got her. I thought I was going to be able to give her so much more than I had. But she always preferred her daddy. I'd sit by that picture window and watch her and John in the yard, making forts and things out of sticks and blankets. When he died, it was as if she went somewhere. Tyler, I can't get her back. I married Howe for her. I thought she should have someone besides me. She stops.

Tyler feels her breathing against his chest. When was the last time you really talked to her? he asks.

Rebecca bites her lip. She's quiet for some moments and then she says, Months ago. We went shopping at the Lenox. She looked so bored. She kept standing on her hip, how teenagers do. I was picking out things for her to wear. She didn't like any of them. And then she was angry because she asked me something and I didn't hear her. She told me I never listen to her.

Rebecca looks at Tyler in the window reflection. We didn't buy anything, she says. We just went home. I wanted to talk to her, but it's so hard. Everything I say is wrong.

He watches her swallow.

I feel like she hates me. I keep hoping when she grows up, then we'll be close. She turns to look at Tyler. Maybe you could talk to her. Audrey always loved you. Besides Frazier, she loved you best.

He puts his arms around her. She holds his wrists and leans her head against his chest. I'll talk to her, he says, resting his chin on her head. But you need to think about what I said. His voice is soft. It's not a small thing, Bec.

They stand in silence. He finds he is rocking her slowly back and forth. I wonder how Frazier would respond to this, he says.

Rebecca looks up at him. Frazier knows, she tells him. A lover always knows these things.

And there she is, Rebecca Howe: brilliant about the ways of lovers, a small child about all else, but a genius in the ways of desire.

4.

KELLY HAS GONE to get them a late lunch.

Gracey stands by the window, bending to pick up an unlit Pall Mall she dropped. Cole sees the backs of her legs are stained with scars. She watches him while she touches the match to the end of her cigarette. He concentrates on his hands, folded on the table. What do you think of me now? she asks through the clenched teeth holding her filter. Her voice is hard, but when he looks up, her eyes are pleading.

He swallows. I guess, he says, then pauses, considering. I guess I'm feeling weak, he finally tells her. Honesty is not hard for him, but he worries about his vulnerability. His mind does cartwheels thinking how he was a self-pitying fool before he heard her story. When he looks up again, no explanation is needed. She is nodding through her haze of smoke.

You don't do these? She points the cigarette at him.

He shakes his head no.

She nods again, this time slowly. What do you do for relief then, vaquero?

I just— He raps his knuckles on the tabletop. I don't know, he says finally. I'm not sure.

Kelly comes in. An intern follows with sandwiches and chips and bottled soda and paper cups and napkins and packets of mustard and mayonnaise. He puts it all on the table and then stands by the door as if looking for a tip.

Kelly gestures to Gracey, a rare find at a local zoo. Get outta here, he says to the boy. This is an interrogation room.

The intern is five-eleven with a crew cut of his own and a scar running from his ear to his chin. His eyes don't change expression when he looks at Kelly. You're welcome to say that nicely, he tells him. Then he turns the doorknob and is out the door.

Ha! Gracey says, nodding toward the exited intern in approval. Who that? He gonna make a fool outta the lot of you when he gets big enough.

Kelly says nothing. He sets up their plates and unwraps their sandwiches as if it is snack time at the nursery school.

Cole is surprised by how delicately she eats. One bite at a time, wiping her fingertips on the napkin and drinking with her pinkie finger out.

Kelly mashes his in his mouth and talks with a wad in his cheek. We don't got time for much of a lunch break, he says. Let's eat and start up again.

Cole watches her pull back her black, curly hair. He wonders on what secret parts of the body the needle found itself, pain accepted because of the barrel-rushing pleasure of the aftermath.

Thing is, she says, at the beginning it was so good.

Putting down her sandwich, she places both arms on the table, lengthwise, so the scarred underarms are faceup. She begins to pour out the memory of her first glorious years when the high worked. She was the kind of mother she'd always wanted to be, relaxed, easy, she cooked and cleaned, had the energy to play with her children and the peace inside not to lose her temper when they fussed.

And then they had to use more and more to get the high to work. Sometimes they mainlined five thousand dollars of dope a day. They were a new family, a young couple in love. She lists the things they could have done with the money, vacations in the Caribbean, a new house for Mamma, retirement and college funds, private schools for the kids, a house with four bedrooms and an in-ground swimming pool.

Instead they shot their profits in their veins, nodding off with needles in their arms, the bathroom a haven, Gracey almost ODing after returning from church with her kids one Sunday, the rush of cold water, Sonny beating her cheek with a flat palm and breathing into her. Her face blue, her lips white, she was a limp rag-doll over Son's shoulder and she collapsed unconscious for hours into evening on the canopy bed they'd always shared.

The kids stayed with her mamma for weeks at a time.

Eight kilos from L.A., cutting it, taking an eighth of a kilo out, putting a cut in. They got paid when they copped from the dealer, paid for delivering it, and then paid themselves with full needles. It wasn't ever enough.

You gonna to use up all the drugs? Son would ask Gracey. 'Cause I ain't got money for your habit.

You doin more than me, Gracey'd say back.

No I ain't.

Yes you are.

The kids had started school and Gracey was home, every hour on the hour, sitting with her legs spread on the toilet, the relief of the tourniquet, the throwing spurt of the needle, her head back against the wall. The house stayed a mess. When Keisha and Jackson came home from school, their beds were unmade, the sheets were dirty, dust covered tables, and the carpets weren't vacuumed. They were given cellophane-wrapped junk food and soda and told to sit in front of the television. Keisha would stand behind the bathroom door and call in to her mother, What you doin, Mamma? When you comin out of there? And Jackson sat with his eyes riveted to the television, his thumb in his mouth. His teachers called to say he was learning disabled, could not sit still. Wouldn't Gracey come in for an appointment to talk? Gracey made the appointment and then did not show up. When Sonny came home, they were cussing and fighting, never loving like they used to.

She found a job at a dry cleaners to make money for her habit. Pointing a finger at Kelly, she leans back in her seat and says, You ever been in the back of a dry cleaner? Smells like you workin inside a dead animal. Those fumes'll kill you. I'd stand there sortin clothes, thinkin how smart I was as a kid. An IQ of 146 and now I was goin through some fool's loungewear.

She explains the muted, half-good feeling of using too much. How the high betrays its lover, becomes less attentive, wanders off. The dose had to be thicker. The stuff had to be stronger. Pills fell out of the medicine cabinet when she opened it. Gracey could be found down on her knees, looking for blow on the living room carpet with the kids in back of her, silent as death, not wanting to understand the sickness that was their mother.

You know what almost did me in? she asks them.

Cole sees Kelly shake his head no. Kelly hasn't fidgeted in ten minutes; he watches her intently.

A goddamn Spic and Span commercial, Gracey says. That lady come on with her sparklin-clean kitchen, her kids runnin through makin a hell of a mess and she just wipin it off with a sponge and a smile. I thought, Shit, I was supposed to be that. What happened? I was crashin low and wantin out. I knew Son wouldn't stop sellin and the drugs'd keep comin. I couldn't never kick with him around. I'm faithful, but I ain't stupid. So who'd I call?

Gracey stands up and walks to the window. She puts her hand on the first wood slat and looks out. Mamma, she says. I told her I wanted to leave Son. You know what she said? You got you a fine man, Gracey, and if things are bad, you got to make good of it. Gracey puts the sign of a cross over her heart and says it's all her mamma knew.

In Gracey's words, Cole sees how she felt the uselessness of life. He understands why later that day she found herself stumbling through the SROs of Stewart Avenue. It is what she had become and she had to follow the line until it ended. She was a lonely wife, a bad mamma, and a loyal daughter, looking for something to put in her arm, obeying her fate.

At a filling station near Value Village, she found Randy G. He appeared clean, though she had heard he was a user, always had a stash. She got in his car with him when he said he wanted to show her something.

It was an autumn day, dry leaves were falling, and the windows were open to crisp air and a cobalt sky. Her blouse flapped in the breeze. Randy drove his Pacer past the dwellings of the drug-ruled. They saw scavengers hovering over trash bins. People Gracey had grown up with were holding out Styrofoam cups, looking for a handout.

Son wasn't home, mad with her for using all his drugs, and Lakeisha and Jackson let themselves in with a copied key, ate Oreos and drank soda, argued over the channel while in their small chests the ache of abandonment beat every half second. It had become what defined them, what they knew as normal.

Randy drove her through neighborhoods where Gracey saw the cowering, hollow faces of her peers. Her stomach was crampy. Her skin was tight. She needed a fix.

Finally, they arrived at the shooting gallery. An old house painted aquamarine, the roof caved in by an oak, victimized by storm and resting on its side. Rotted boards served as a porch. The door was a piece of plywood. Inside, a white girl leaned against the wall, wearing a leather jacket and no shirt, a bright orange curler in her bangs. Her bottom lip was split, and her desperate fingers tagged Randy. You got you some smack? Please, I'll suck you good.

Somebody in pain howled in the hole of an upstairs room.

People sat around the halls and rooms with scarred faces and wide, urgent eyes. *I got my magic in my pocket, ha ha. You gonna give me somethin for it?* Works, cookers, needles, and the drugs themselves, passing from hand to shaking hand.

In the back room, before a sheeted window, a guy sat in an old, found wheelchair, patched three times over by Bondo and held up by unmatching wheels. He was wearing a faded red bandanna on his head, and his torso was swimming in an oversize yellow windbreaker; his legs hung like two shriveled sticks from his body. When he looked up, his eyes didn't focus. Leaning next to him was a long, wooden stick, the end frayed from pounding cement. It was the seeing accomplice to his blind eyes.

Ray Junior.

Gracey dropped to her knees on the filthy floor and crawled to him. She put her hands on his face, her fingers in his laughing, drug-happy mouth.

Don't cry, Gracey, he said. He was crying himself, his mind a twirling wheel of nonsensical messages, memories buried together into one manageable lump.

Randy G. squatted next to Gracey, held the small of her back so she wouldn't fall and said, I'm doin you this favor. You want to turn out like that? Huh? I kicked and you can, too. Don't do this to your mamma. The both of yous.

Who that? Ray Junior was mad now, staring angrily into blank space. Who that? That Jokey? 'Cause I need my hit. Gracey, you got any money on you?

And Gracey repeated again and again, Who did him like that? Crying into the dusty floorboards where lice and rodents made their homes.

Gracey got the brains absent from Ray Junior, who'd always been smart as a dull nail and scared. Luck stopped short when it came to him. He'd shot the drugs in his ass and hit a nerve. He'd never walk again. He'd melted his drug with lemon juice, and made himself blind as a bat.

Gracey wanted to drop everything and be his eyes, love him back to something she remembered and knew: two young kids finding soda under the house, falling asleep in midday heat with their arms around each other's waists.

But Ray's Christ was not Gracey, it was a bald albino who came in now with his works and his drugs and a pile of hidden meat for Ray Junior's searching mouth.

I could smell you, Jokey, her brother said, his face eager, rigid, craving it. It's comin, he said, rubbing his hands together like a freezing person. He pushed Gracey's shoulder. Go on now, get where you goin. I got this thing to do with my man.

Ray Junior didn't want anyone else in on his cooker. He was slow-suiciding, heading for heaven in the shaft of a needle.

5.

DENEEKA LOITERS ON the streets of Vine City for the better part of the afternoon, socializing, setting up copping times, trying to make herself exhausted before sleep. She walks the entirety of the Bluff, part of the sun-dappled South that holds the haunts of the hard living. Someone's either a user, a lookout, a dealer, a distributor, or a supplier. Except for the grannies and grandpas, shaking their heads at the funerals, ducking from the drive-by shooting, asking God for a grandson's welfare to hold out one more day. Junkies are everywhere, copping drugs, fluttering like paper in air, shredded and holed, going with the wind, desperate not to hit ground, feel anything.

When she gets down the hill to Ashby and Simpson, Deneeka sees Slick X on the corner. That isn't his real name. Like Deneeka isn't hers. She was christened Mark. Imagine that. Mark. Since then she's been Olivia, Cascade, Angelika, Jezebel. Deneeka fit Atlanta. She'd picked it when she'd hopped off the rig and left the trucker with his orange tighty underwear and his paper bag full of crystal meth and dildos.

X is taking orders through a wireless phone. His sunglasses reflect the burnt-out skeleton of the church across the street, where cement crumbles from a fallen altar. Wiry teenagers hang around him, smarmy as alley cats, only a little more than a decade old and running guns, shirking the social worker's beige Honda that comes on Tuesdays and Fridays, their doors locked, driving in and out like priests coming for the dying. They arrive on the heels of the cocky high schoolers and frat boys, little rich kids with new sneakers and sullen faces, cruising slowly down the streets of Vine City, looking for a high, thinking they are better than their parents, they got something on them. Mr. and Mrs. Suburban Atlanta would be horrified to know Junior was steering their super-powered SUV through Egan Homes looking for girl, gutter water in his veins, swirling in a fancy suit down the mouth of a toilet.

Deneeka heads toward the sun, raising its white head above the bank building across the tracks and illuminating Atlanta's skyline, where the world freezes in a silhouette of buildings designed by John Portman. Urban development is the phoenix of the New South. The Georgia Dome has replaced *Gone With the Wind*. Shadows of those buildings curl around Deneeka, who supplies works for the city that will ram honey-gold magic through her clients' veins. The crack addicts save her life. She can walk in and be what they need, sucking one while the other watches. A spoon and heated powder act as food for their perversion, the candy the old man offers before he opens his raincoat.

She makes her way down Ashby, past the boarded-up graffitied houses, and steps over broken shards of bottle glass lying in fake diamond sprinkle across bloodied cement. Outside the east border of the Bluff, Deneeka passes the Georgia Dome. Ugly, she thinks. Fucking ugly. The colors don't match. It looks lumpy. A man in an old wheelchair with rags tied over his head and laceless boots rolls along in its shadow.

The day is starting to cloud some. Garbage blows over the street. On the other side of the road, Cecilia Cat pushes a shopping cart full of nothing. The woman is forty-two, but she is stooped like a senior citizen. She's done with drugs, tried suicide on the side of the I-75 overpass, wound up falling in a truck carrying a load of cotton from Alabama. After that, she went insane with religion. She talks God to the sidewalk. Her usual trade is to sleep in the day on the doorstep of the Salvation Army and then at night duck in and out of houses, eating food from kitchen cupboards whenever she turns up on the streets, out of jail, every few months.

Hey, C.C.! Deneeka calls, raising her palm.

C.C. stops pushing her cart, puts a hand up to shield her eyes, and looks at Deneeka. Then she keeps going, bent over and muttering to herself.

Crazy old fool, Deneeka says under her breath. She makes her way to the lot by the highway bridges. Underneath it, someone lies in a pile of blankets and moans like a hit dog. A few rattling cans fly down the blacktopped slope. It smells of the remnants of gone-by people who lit fires with damp newspapers, making smoke to warm themselves before claiming a corner for the night.

Deneeka feels for them. She knows how cold they get. Her gift is to offer a warm mouth. She understands how much a heart wants to quit pumping, and how it keeps asking for one small reason to go on.

It's been a warm day and now it has turned damp. The day's heat has drained into the pale, weather-weary paint of the stationary cars in the lot where Deneeka takes her afternoon naps. She arrives at this place where no one will find her, searches out her Ford Explorer parked seven cars deep on the north end. There she can stretch in the sun's leftover warmth and sleep. Ripped wire mesh surrounds the parking area. The cars' wheels are flat. Some have been replaced by cinder blocks. When night falls, she'll head to The Rocket's place on Stewart Ave. Afterward, she'll deal all evening long, until daybreak. She gives most of her money back to him. Hoping someday he will love her.

She's seen other people sleeping in that lot. Black boys with torn muscle T-shirts and bloodied lips from a hot crack pipe, white boys who have just sold their mamma's TV for drugs. Fifteen-year-old girls hiding from their pimps. The pimps themselves, knocking knuckles against every car door, looking for the girls, finally falling asleep in the littered sand until they wake, disoriented, pulling themselves up for one more day. One more dollar.

Deneeka has jerry-rigged a coat hanger to the door handle, and she tugs it now, pulls up once, undoes the bolt on the inside of the vaulted door, and climbs inside. She grabs a blanket from the front seat and sets it over the rear window, then feeds the plastic into the upper vinyl on both sides. She rolls down the back window partway. Slips of breeze come in and rest lazily on her scarred, exploited body.

She does not see her body like this. She is grateful to it, considers it and her mouth and her unique, genderless persona gifts from the Holy Ghost, offered to her on the day she was born. Long ago she'd wondered if the man upstairs had messed up. But as she grew, she began to think He sent her down as He sent His only son, to soothe those men who are different, outcasts, paupers, and grovelers.

Her life is like the little match girl's, fire up and have fantasies, then go cold again and fire up once more. It's been years since her adolescence when she knew the strange world of sobriety, ached for touch and love. What she understands about the world now is that you are colder if you don't cute up and sass around. In Detroit, she'd had to exist alone at foster homes in the lower-middle-class neighborhoods where people were clean and fun was simple. No one loved her. When you can't find the warmth you need, you deal farther into the streets. Human faces form where it once looked shut down. The cracked-out freak houses of the inner city welcomed her. She belonged.

In an almost sleep state, she thinks of the golden boy in line for works that morning. She remembers where she has seen him before, chasing the dragon with some brown from Feather, his face beautiful when he was nodding, like a small boy's. She had wanted to hold him, not masturbate him, but kiss his cheeks, take him somewhere unsullied. She could sing to him.

The thought is strange to her. She has to drag it back to the familiar, so she imagines the boy at her beck and call, her finger dragging down his bottom lip indulgently, her hips gyrating just slightly, his body hard against her.

She still has it in her to make those boys' dreams come true. She curls her knees to her chest, presses her cheek to the vinyl. She knows she does.

6.

KELLY RAPS HIS PENCIL on the tabletop, eraser side up.

Leaning over the table with her elbows on it, Gracey puts her face near his. You ever done drugs, cowboy?

The pencil tapping continues.

Hey, she says, chiding and singsongy. I asked you a question.

I'm thinkin.

Cole's eyebrows raise at this admission. His smart-ass partner's tone has changed, leveled.

Gracey leans back, shaking the empty cigarette pack. Tobacco pieces flutter onto the table. She pushes them around with her fingertip. Ain't nothin to think about, she says. Yes or no will cover it.

I thought we were the ones doing the questioning, Kelly tells her.

You don't want to talk, Gracey shrugs, that's your business. I was just lookin at you, wonderin how you got in this line of work. She juts her chin at Cole. Justice here does it 'cause he wants to love the world and make it better. But you, I'm afraid for why you do it.

Kelly lifts his head a fraction of an inch to look at her. She is gazing at the far wall. I'm askin you 'cause once you in neck deep, ain't no way out.

The recorder clicks. Kelly pulls the tape out. I'm serving my country, he says.

Gracey laughs. *Is that what you think?* You aren't doin a goddamn thing. It ain't up to you. I just learned the other day the U.S. makes up five percent of the world's population and consumes fifty percent of the world's cocaine. Go figure. Something's wrong with the United States of America. Haven't you found that out yet? I mean, they ain't all fucked up in Japan. They don't got meth clinics in Botswana, do they?

Cole looks at Kelly, who shrugs. Gracey waves her hand at him. You don't know, she says. You ain't traveled any more than I have. But I'll tell you one thing I know for sure. There's places where it's legal. The government taxes it. I heard about them countries where it's not a criminal act to get high if you need to. It don't cost you a paycheck and then some to get a little relief. Here, if you wanna be a junkie, you gotta pay your toenails and your scalp for it.

Kelly drums the tape on his palm and looks at her. That's 'cause it's against the law, he says.

Bein sick is against the law? Gracey asks him. You can't even buy a syringe so you don't get infected. Street syringe gonna run you two dollars. It cost twenty-five cents at the drugstore, but you can't get that shit without a prescription. Then you complain we causin AIDS? She laughs again, one quick bark. I'd guess y'all are puttin drugs on the street for us, chargin outlandish prices, then throwin us in jail so people can get jobs as prison guards and y'all can be rid of us.

Kelly turns the tape around to the other side. You gonna lecture us, he asks her, or you gonna go on with that story you keep sayin you want to tell us?

Gracey tilts her head at him. I'll tell you this, she says. I used to think it was easy to get cured. I thought Ray Junior was gonna save my life. I went right to Mamma's after I saw what it did to him. You see this dress I got on? She smiles. This was the same one Mamma was ironing in the kitchen when I come to sit down and be with her after I saw Ray Junior.

Mamma pretended not to see my cryin eyes. She clucked her tongue and told me, Don't you know what season it is? You need you a pair of slippers. Some of mine are by the bathroom, go put them on, girl.

I was too numb to feel cold. But I did what she said, 'cause I was tired.

She poured hot milk in a pan and made me a peanut butter sandwich. I know you don't want to eat nothin, she told me. But you just take care of what you can of this, make your mamma happy.

Gracey ate slowly, smelling the hot iron on cotton and listening to the slip-slip sound of its rhythm back and forth on the board. Her mamma hummed, the refrigerator made a small-town racket in the corner. Gracey's tears fell without her mother making mention of them.

They don't make dresses like this one anymore, her mamma was saying. I had this dress since you was a little girl. She knelt at Gracey's side, showing her all the places it had been darned. She pointed out the little hand-done stitches on the sleeves and stomach.

Her mamma's face was nearing old. She had a beaten look. The lips were pale. Wrinkles were growing around her eyes. Some gray was coming in on the temples.

She lived on Social Security. Her mamma and papa had been good people, and they'd died on consecutive days the previous January. Mrs. Moore could be seen kneeling on frost- or dew-ridden grass, pulling onion weeds and planting poinsettias in the cemetery behind the Baptist church.

While her mamma showed her the material, Gracey held the dress with chewed and bloodied fingernails, a result of the anxiety of her habit. Her hair was sticking out every which way. She needed a fix so bad, her mind was weary from want. Finally she put her head down on the table and let the hot tears warm her face. Her mamma stood, unplugged the iron from the wall, and came back to wrap her arms around her daughter. There, there, child, she told her. Ain't nothin in the world so bad you got to bend your head and cry about it.

The terry cloth on her mamma's toe slippers was worn down to raw rubber. Her heels were cracked and dry. Gracey came off the chair, knelt on the floor, and put her hands on her mother's ankles. She caressed and kissed the tired feet of her mamma, who had been loved in childhood, and then was startled into adulthood by the dark prison of a hellish marriage.

Baby, what you doin? Her mamma laughed nervously. Quit it. You ticklin me. Putting her hands around Gracey, she rocked her daughter back and forth. The rain was their witness. Gracey's question was bold in the quiet air. Why didn't you never leave him, Mamma? Why'd you wait for him to die like that?

Having tried never to break her mamma's heart by swearing, Gracey cursed that day, cursed a sorry man, dead in his grave, who drove Ray Junior to his crippled state and led her into a fantasy world of stuck needles and poisoned veins.

Her mamma explained how good her daddy had been when she first met him, the gifts he'd brought her, the way he'd held her and made her feel beautiful. He was a strong man who had a good job. The drinking changed him, came later and brought out a fierceness in him that could not be tamed.

Her mamma sat cross-legged next to Gracey on the scored linoleum. Underneath, swollen boards and rusty nails showed through. Her voice was crackly with cry. I ask God to forgive me every day for the mistakes I've made. I ask him to forgive you and your daddy in his grave and all them people out there tryin to make it in this world that's hell on earth. We will overcome.

The rain continued. Her blue dress hung on the board above them, pressed and mended. Gracey put her head in her mamma's lap. Her mother's hands held tight to her waist. They rocked and hugged for what seemed to Gracey like hours.

Cole watches Gracey turn her back to them. He sees her hand tremble when she brings it to her eyes.

It's like Mamma and me, we was really just kids, she says. Sometimes I think we never did grow up.

7.

AUDREY SPENDS THE AFTERNOON driving around the city, running the beltway with her CD player on Bob Dylan's best. She'd left home at three. She did not want to be around while the flower vans pulled into the driveway and the delivery boys came to the door with hothouse bouquets to be placed in strategic spots throughout the house for guests to admire. The busyness of caterers and cooks filled the huge kitchen and she could only sit in her room, trying to escape her mother, who'd come home after noon with fluttery, nervous hands and color high on her cheeks.

On Peachtree, she drives by the art store once, U-turns, and drives by it again. Finally she parks across the street from it and sits in the car trying to look in the windows.

She gets out of the Jetta and goes across to the entranceway. Three brass bells tied to a silk ribbon chime when she opens the door. She stands at the threshold, smelling the oil paint and turpentine. The store is empty of customers and she wanders listless through the aisles, touching canvases and easels, the black rectangular charcoal sticks and tubes of acrylics. The woman behind the counter is fifty-something with dyed black hair. Her nails are painted hot pink. Audrey does not remember her. She watches the woman lean over, draw a line down her sketchpad with a thick pencil. In the corner a phonograph from long ago statics out the *Sound of Music* album and the woman hums to it. Picking up her pencil, she eyes the drawing. Without looking at Audrey she calls, You need some help, honey?

Audrey stands in front of the racks of handmade papers. No, ma'am. Thank you.

A metal fan motors from the back wall, blowing in cool, musty air, the only sound in the cramped place. Beneath her feet the wood floor is old but clean.

She half-listens to the woman scraping her drawing.

Mrs. Yule arrives out of a side door. Her scarves trail behind her in a wave of color. The ankle-length skirt reveals bare feet and toe rings. Her slanted eyes are teal blue against her tan face. She is wearing a paint-spotted denim apron. My God, Audrey, where have you been hiding yourself, sweetheart? She looks Audrey up and down, puts a hand on her hip and a smile on her lips.

Mrs. Yule. Audrey touches her fingers to her nose to smell the cigarettes on them, then wipes them on her blue jeans. I thought you went to New York, she says.

I did, darlin, but I'm back here half the year. She points her ringed thumb in the direction of a wide wood door. I'm working today. You must be almost graduated.

Not till next year, Audrey tells her.

Mrs. Yule smiles and puts out both her arms. Audrey takes her hands, solid and substantial in hers.

You look like you need some sleep, Mrs. Yule says.

Audrey tries to smile. Exams, she says. That's all.

Mrs. Yule squeezes her hands and watches her. Well, Cynthia and Tatty are still coming to classes and we are always wondering where you are. Why don't you come on back and see some of the work?

Audrey hesitates, but Mrs. Yule pulls her hands and coaxes her forward.

I can't stay long, Audrey says. My parents are having a party.

Mrs. Yule looks back at her. You can call me Georgie now. Mr. Yule went back to California. It's only little old me by my lonesome, and it has been great for my art. I'm in love, but he's not taking my creativity with him like that other one did. She shakes her orange hair and laughs. We went our own ways and I'm a better lady for it.

In Audrey's post-cocaine nightmares, Mrs. Yule rises up to her and offers one outstretched hand full of colors, the fingers missing. She is just a palette. The vision comes to her clearly now and wavers before her eyes.

What on earth have you been doing with yourself? Georgie opens the door against the back wall with her hip. She looks down at her student. We were worried about you. Cynthia says she calls your house and you don't ever return her messages.

I've been so busy, Audrey says. School and all. Her voice trails off while she looks around the room. It is as if she never left. The hooks against the far wall hang the same aprons. Crude wooden-block tables are set up end to end. Tin cans with their labels peeled off expose the wooden ends of brushes, ready for their artists. Reams of rolled paper are cut and stuck to the tables with Scotch tape. The studio is a place she used to escape to. It held her for hours on the weekends, in the days before Frazier and what he offered, the late hours, lines of cocaine and lit cigarettes, whirling nights of dreamlike escape. The room is full of afternoon sunlight streaming through the six-foot windows. She can see the grocery lot where wind kicks up litter and people walk with carts to their cars.

Georgie straightens the place while Audrey stands watching, fiddling her shirt hem. We have twice as many classes now, her teacher says, smiling, proud.

Audrey nods, wordless.

Come see my new sculptures.

On wood pallets held up by two sawhorses are structures made of dried flowers and beach debris, faces etched in charcoal inside empty milk pods, broken pottery held with rope to weathered two-by-fours. One is a crucifix made of green wire, its head a mask of crystallized rose. Georgie watches as Audrey walks forward and looks at the things. A stirring rises in Audrey's throat and she wishes for what she used to know, time here when nothing mattered, making life out of a once lonely white space.

Georgie's structures have words scribbled on them. One reads *Fire is found within.* Georgie trails her fingertips over each piece, delicately, as you might the faces of sleeping children. This is what an unmarried lady can do with enough time, she says. I used to only have time to teach.

Audrey breathes. They're . . . beautiful.

Well, from a girl who's been to Florence, that's something. Where are you going to school next year?

Audrey eyes a rusty metal piece her teacher has turned into a wave beating against a sailboat made of a copper bucket and string. I don't know, she says. I haven't thought about it.

When Audrey looks up, Georgie is frowning. She reaches around and grasps the ends of her apron strings, and reties them. But you were such a good student, she says. I thought you'd go up to Chicago or to RISD.

Audrey looks at the floor. With her shoe toe, she fiddles a piece of dried gold paint.

Sissy Baker says you were the best potter in the tenth grade, Georgie tells her.

Helplessness turns the room in vertigo around her. She feels herself lift both shoulders.

Don't shrug it off, Georgie tells her. Most people wish for talent on their deathbed. She takes Audrey by the elbow again and leads her into a back room where stage lights line the molding next to the ceiling. Shelves and shelves contain neatly stored artwork by the students. Audrey sees her name there next to a stack of old sketches she never retrieved. Georgie points to an area above one of the shelves. It takes Audrey a full minute before she understands the pictures lining the wall are hers.

She walks toward the far side of the room and looks up at them. Staring back at her are the nameless faces she'd seen on street corners, the blind man on Ponce with his guitar and tin cup of change, a woman hunched over her woven bags, carrying a bird of carved wood. One is Audrey herself. Her gaze turned down, a strand of hair shadowing her eye. Another is a portrait of her grieving mother after her father died. Rebecca's teeth are on edge, her hair is wild in the whirlwind of survival. Pre-Howe, when, Audrey thinks, Rebecca did not have enough courage to live an independent life as Mrs. Yule has. Her mother's right eye is staring off in the distance, as if looking beyond reality into a hell she is afraid to enter should she die.

The sketches appear out of Audrey's past, wanting to betray her secrets to the world. She stands staring and then backs away. I'm late, she says. I have to go.

Georgie grabs a sketch from the shelf that has Audrey's name scribbled on it. As Audrey bumps into the paint-splattered gray desk, she hears her teacher behind her, the large paper flapping in the wind of her movement. Her voice has an urgent appeal. Here, she says. Take this, at least. You might start again someday.

I can't do it anymore, Audrey tells her. It just isn't in me like it used to be.

Georgie strides up beside her, nodding vigorously, understanding. Being a teenager always makes you feel like that, she says. She rolls the picture into a tube with her wide, capable hands, following Audrey through the aisles. It never leaves you though, sweetie.

Audrey stops by the cash register and lets Georgie give her the sketch. Her teacher is breathing hard, the jewelry at her neck panting with her. She smells of paint and flowers. You come back to me when you're ready, she says. A quick woman with a deep voice, Georgie shocks Audrey by running a gentle hand through her bangs. She puts a piece of stray hair behind her ear. Then, holding her wrist lightly, she says, If you ever need to talk, honey, you know where to find me. I'm always here for you.

Audrey looks down at the rolled paper, fingers the edge. Okay, she says. I will. She glances up again, into Georgie's searching eyes. Her teacher looks like she wants to say more than she has time for. She watches Audrey pull the door handle and open it to the windy day. The bells chime. It was nice to see you, Audrey says, her politeness ingrained, appropriate.

And then she is out into the street, the clouds rushing to cover the sun. While she walks across to her car, she turns once to see Georgie holding the door. Her teacher puts one hand up in a single wave.

Her car is safety, warm and silent. She sits shaking, not knowing why. She looks back at the store, thinks about what it would be like to go in and sit down with Georgie. Maybe her teacher would listen to her. Howe. Her mother. What Frazier has become. But she feels awkward, shy with how long it's been since she went to the school. She is not sure she belongs anymore.

Putting the tube on the steering wheel, she begins to unroll the paper. Revealed before her, inch by inch, is the face of her father. His eyes look to her as a man long seabound would look when he saw land. A daylily bows behind his ear.

The world goes dark around her as she stares at him. She does not remember having sketched it and is surprised by how clear he once was to her. She had been able to draw perfectly the length of his forehead, the cords of his neck, and the strength of his jaw. She believes for one solid minute that she can smell the leather and scent of his flesh. And then it is gone.

In those same cocaine nightmares where Georgie resides, her father comes out of the woodwork in the house where he raised her and scares her with his hollowed eyes and ashen face. Though she sleeps still, she dreams she is waking to her childhood home. She is a small girl again. In full dark, she pads down the hall and crawls to the side of his bed. He lifts her there between him and her mother. She tells him she has had a nightmare, picks up his hand to suck his fingers, as she used to when she needed to find sleep after nightmares. They taste of salt and home. Relief sweeps through her, calm comfort. Just as she is drifting back into her dream's sleep, she looks up to find her father a skeleton, decomposing beside her, one last inch of breath escaping his wooden mouth.

Evening

1.

KELLY, COLE, AND GRACEY sit in a dusk-filled room. Gracey's back is against the wall's baseboard. Her knees are up. Kelly has bitten his pencil down to a skinny middle of teeth marks. Cole sits across from him. Gracey opens and closes her palms as if they contain the story. Then she stops, rips a thread hanging from the armpit of her robe, sets it delicately beside her foot, and starts to talk. Her voice has turned raspy and tired.

It was fall, she says. I left Mamma's and went back home. I felt so sad. The flowers were dyin and a wind was blowin. I was tore up inside and couldn't get rid of the pasty feelin I had. Ray Junior was on my mind, livin right behind my eyeballs. I knew I needed to kick. I didn't know whether I was up or down. I couldn't remember what I'd taken last. I just knew I had to stop. I was on a roller-coaster ride minus the brakes.

That afternoon I had to get out of the house, get away from Son and the drugs he was bringin home. I took Lakeisha and Jackson to the park. My nose was runnin bad, and I was wipin it with my dress sleeve. Son had bought me that dress before the kids were born. It'd been in the window of Davison's, downtown. I said, I love that dress, that pink one. He said, I'm buyin it for you!

The store was open until eight o'clock that night, and it was five of. I was nineteen years old with stars in my eyes over Son. I wore that dress out of the store, left my blue jeans and my T-shirt on the bench in the fittin room.

Now here I was, thirty years old and geeked up on drugs. One button gone on the sleeve, the hem comin unraveled, coffee stains on the stomach.

Cole watches Gracey's eyes go downcast.

She says she sat on a park bench and cried for over an hour. She thought of ways she could end it. Too tolerant for pill use and too scared of guns for shooting, she really wanted to drown, put her head underwater and hear nothing, breathe liquid death. She needed it like a junkie needs a fix. Lakeisha and Jackson stood by with terrified faces. They had no way to remedy their mother. Shame built to a boiling infection within them. Mamma, what's the matter, Mamma? What are you doin? Why you cryin?

She knew she had to drown them with her so they could be dead and silent, away from all that misery.

She cried until she couldn't sit up straight, finally got to her knees down on the sidewalk and put her face in the gravel, sobbing, working to catch her breath. Saturday pedestrians walked by with their black Labs and neatly dressed children. They stared, watching her with condescending, scornful eyes.

Gracey goes quiet, leans her head against the wall, straightens her knees and wriggles the legs to stretch them. That's how bad off I was, she says. So when Merridew Lewis showed up, I didn't recognize her for the angel she was.

Cole watches her face turn languid. Her smile grows soft. She puts her head back, shuts her eyes, and tells them, I was rockin on that grubby sidewalk, curled up to myself, and Merridew come by wearin a purple windbreaker, a white slack suit, and a big hairdo that don't lie down for nobody. She had on gold hoop earrings and blue eye shadow. Pretty as daylight. Squattin her fresh body down near me, she said, Excuse me, miss, can I help you?

I said, Go away. I don't want none of what you got.

She didn't go away. She sat on the bench behind me, gathered Jackson in her arms, and held Lakeisha's hands. They quieted right off.

I wiped my wet face and said, Lady, what do you want?

I want to buy y'all lunch.

Keisha and Jackson looked down at the cement, too scared to hope for that.

The lady said, Afterward, we'll have ice cream.

My guts were all but wrenched outta my body and my eyes were swelled shut. I didn't have a bit of energy left to say no.

We started walkin the direction of Silver City.

Cole pictures it, the booths of the diner, the low din of lunch, Gracey with her red eyes and soiled dress sitting next to Merridew while the kids ate hamburgers and drew pictures on paper place mats.

When Gracey finally let herself eat the lunch in front of her, she bit her fingers she was so hungry. She choked on her sandwich and licked the plate.

Merridew ordered more: a large basket of fries, tall chocolate milk shake, banana cream pie. Smoking and smiling and shaking her head, she watched her new friend eat until Gracey was finally full, her body relieved of hunger. Relaxing her head on the table, Gracey welcomed the warmth of Merridew's hand massaging her neck. Tears collected on the Formica and formed a puddle before her.

Sometimes people get sad and we gotta let them, Merridew told the kids when they wanted to know why their mamma was cryin. Don't y'all get sad like your mamma's doing? she asked them.

They left Monroe Street in Merridew's white Ford Mustang flip-up convertible. The kids bounced in the back, pressing buttons that made the windows go up and down. She parked the car in a parking garage at Four Corners in Buckhead. Inside her apartment building, a man wearing a uniform pushed number eleven in the elevator and addressed the kids like miniature adults. How do you do? he asked them.

Merridew had ferns and flowers and spider plants on her balcony. While Lakeisha and Jackson went in to watch TV, Gracey touched a red, flowering geranium. She hadn't felt such softness in months, had not seen color as bright since she was a child.

Her kids ate the ice cream bars Merridew gave them. They made her rug sticky, put their dirty hands in her fish tank, and banged on the piano.

Merridew led Gracey into the bathroom, gave her four green pills and a glass of water from the basin. She knelt over the side of the tub to run her a bath. Gracey sat on the closed toilet seat looking at her naked limbs, wrecked with scars. She touched her uncombed hair and broken-out skin. She ran her tongue over her grubby teeth. When she lowered her thin, needle-pricked body into the bath, Merridew gave her a washcloth to suck on while she cleaned her. She scrubbed sudsy circles over Gracey's neck, belly, and arms, she sang, *We all live in a yellow submarine*. She poured cups of warm water over Gracey's hair. It turned slick and smelled of Prell.

Afterward, she wrapped Gracey in lime-green towels and took her to a corner room with window shades and lace curtains, a brass bed and a rose carpet. Gracey crawled in, putting her tired body between the cool, clean sheets.

At this memory, Gracey wraps her arms around herself and holds her elbows. Outside, rain falls. Cole can hear it washing the streets, slipping over the building's side. They listen to the sound of the storm while Gracey lets herself remember that first sleep at Merridew's house. When she woke up, it was night. Merridew was sitting on the side of the bed with more pills and water, and Gracey took them without knowing who this woman was. Merridew could have been anyone, but she was better than dying. She was a hell of a lot better than dying. She smoothed the hair along Gracey's ear and said, We need to get the kids somewhere till you feel better.

Gracey told her Mamma lived at 25 Jett Street.

Kissing her forehead, Merridew said she'd be right back.

I was on the brink, Gracey tells them. Goin to hell in a hand bucket. My body was about to give up, and my mind was already there. I was one sorry piece of blood, water, and bone with a little scarred flesh stretched over it. I didn't care who I gave my kids to, didn't want memory, couldn't think about life. Those pills pulled me into a lullaby state where the ceiling was interesting. And for some reason I trusted her. I ain't trusted no one in so long, I'd forgotten what it felt like.

2.

F RAZIER LEANS HIS HEAD against the back window of the MARTA. He watches the scenery go by in pink twilight.

They'd spent the better part of the day rummaging the city for it, running the bike through neighborhoods with boarded-up houses and broken windowpanes. Most knew JP, so they didn't give him a hard time. JP is known for being honest, making good, keeping a smile on his face, holding down a job. No one buys his drugs for him. There are never any pay-you-back-laters. Frazier's safe with him. All afternoon Frazier had tried to see the streets as he did his first time out, when they made him feel like a brave, tough sailor, far from home.

They'd passed through the Bluff into the neighborhoods of the get-off houses, where the whores with short skirts and penciled eyebrows stood on loose hips, sinking bottom lips at them. In raspy underground voices, they asked if they were holding.

They went up a flight of fire-escape stairs to a room JP had been to many times before, a haunt with broken floorboards and smashed sidewalls. Inside, men held tight, belted tourniquets, licked needles, pushed veins with their fingers, and then passed the needle on. In a side room, three guys and a girl were cooking baking soda and cocaine, shooting up, breaking a sweat. The girl pulled one breast out of her bra, as if about to nurse, and got off on a vein there. A man, splayed open-legged on the floor, pushed a needle in the back shaft of his arm, a quart jar of Pepsi and ice and a thing of alcohol for his works in front of him. On the Sheetrocked wall, someone had scrawled a cross and the RIP sign: *In Memory of SC Gonzales.* Frazier eyed the mud-colored stain of old blood the size of a head.

He and JP had told them no when they were offered the needle. They wanted their own stash, didn't want to share works. They'd not lost the brain that afforded them power over these brothers and sisters on twin mattresses nodding off with their inside elbows bruised and abscessed. So they left, walked down Ashbury, where a weather-beaten Chicano guy named Estevez stood looking at the bike. He offered them Tywal and Phenetol, pancake and syrup, for three bucks an ounce. JP raised his eyebrows. Ain't you a steerer? JP asked him, looking down at the pocket the guy had turned inside out to show the goods.

I'm done with that shit, the guy said. What the fuck you have against what I got? He'd played mad with them, glared and shrugged both shoulders.

Frazier and JP kept walking. We'll wait, JP said while he rolled the bike along by its handlebars. You can go down to the hotel tonight while I'm working and someone will come by like they always do to sell brown. We have all day tomorrow.

They exited the Bluff through an empty lot bordered by a brick wall with a Nazi sign inscribed on it. Empty of drugs, each one carried relief in a private place reserved for the terror linked to Feather's memory.

I need some mind candy after those shit-holes, JP had told Frazier.

Frazier nodded, opening the rotted-wood fence door with his backside. Dante's inferno, he said.

Straight and clean, they'd parked the bike in their front room and gone to catch the MARTA train going north.

Now Frazier watches the scenery turn from cityscape brown to green. Miles pass.

This landscape is well known to Frazier. It was a familiar friend when he would come back after prep school. He'd been twelve years old when they sent him away and he was expected to conform to life without his parents. The relief of coming home was shadowed by the knowledge that he'd be in the car again in a few days, heading back to school, cleats and a clean uniform in his packed bag.

He closes his eyes and feels the rhythm of the train in his body. He'd been too young to go away, ached for his mother's touch, his father's hand on his shoulder at night under a homework light. Loneliness would not let him sleep. He'd kept books and a flashlight under his blankets. They formed worlds. He entered an alternate reality where things happened and mattered. By day, he looked for the truth and passion of what he'd found in fiction to show up in real life. It was absent in the boys' school with sports and academics, bow ties and school assemblies. He stopped reading. The absence made him feel uncovered, exposed, left a cavern of want filled by the swift, sure feeling of a high.

It was the older boys who led the way. They played soccer and golf. They wore shined leather shoes and ironed collars. At night they congregated in the janitor's room down in the basement. The pipes clanged. Squatting on slop buckets next to work rags and damp mops, they cut lines of cocaine with razors across pieces of mirror. It was a relief to Frazier that the older boys liked him. He was a handsome, quiet kid, always picked for varsity sports teams without seeming to try, unthreatening, old money, their kin. His older cousin Thomas had been a quarterback, and as a freshman made the winning touchdown during a homecoming game against Pace.

These were places without adults where a teenager needed to learn to survive, within the walls of that utility closet, dorm rooms after dark, midnight circle jerks on Lawson's Field. The guys who were most admired brought home panties from the townie parties and rolled silver-barreled kegs out of Mercedes station wagons on Friday nights.

On Saturdays, the boys licked tiny rolls of paper with TV screens printed on them and went tripping through the woods surrounding the school's grounds, their limbs no longer straight, the trees coming to life as breathing, slate-colored monstrosities. The clouds were friendly beasts. Under their feet, the ground became a sponge. Faces melted and dripped, cigarettes got up and danced out of the pack.

Lying in bed that night, waiting for the trip to end, Frazier always believed he would die soon. There was no reason for him to live. Some hell or heaven would surely see this and afford him deliverance before daybreak. None did. Sleep finally came, his head welded to the pillow, his dreams dramatic. Five the next evening, he rose to eat. He did lines to bring him back to the living.

It was days like that. Drugs were friendly educators, lenient parents affording a world of repose and surety.

The money from his trust fund poured into the palms of Tatem Santangelo, from Manhattan, a big kid with a space between his teeth and ebony, cowlicked hair. Mafia coated his name with cryptic power. He tucked the drugs in a safe on the inside of a brick wall across from the dugouts. Only Tatem and Sis Owl knew the combination. The last week of school Sis was beaten black and blue. His pants and Jockeys were thrown over a telephone wire. One finger hung at a wrong angle. His wormy body slithered in May mud. Between moans of pain and pleading, Sis gave away the lock's combination to five senior boys. Commencement practice was to begin in half an hour. Frazier Sky turned the lock, distributed what would have been sold to the kids who were going home to dry towns for summer vacation. They were never found out. He sat in a folding chair with the others, holding his breath, wearing a navy-blue suit, and high on cocaine.

Without having to open his eyes from these memories, Frazier knows when he and JP get to their stop. They've reached the posh, aristocratic, blue-blooded, silk-stockinged world of Buckhead, bounded by the city limits and the Chattahoochee River. The suburb holds one of the largest shopping centers in the Southeast and sixty-seven thousand rich people, including a U.S. senator, the governor and lieutenant governor of Georgia, and three former mayors. Seconds later, they stand, single file, waiting for the doors to open. Then they climb the station's stairs, greeting the early evening light.

Five girls from Pace Academy are out in front of Phipps Plaza, on Peachtree. They grip Lord & Taylor shopping bags, waiting for their slick valet cars to come around the corner. Hey, Frazier Sky, one of them calls in her singsongy, sweetheart voice.

Hey, he says back.

JP tips an imaginary hat and tucks his shirt in, puts his hand in his pocket to keep down his hard-on.

They walk through Phipps Plaza. JP's good looks, his well-built frame, make him exempt from the kind of harassment black boys usually take. His ebony skin hides his scars. My father's a African, he used to say to Frazier until Frazier asked him in a cocaine burst of words where exactly his father was from. I don't know, but my mamma don't have skin like this.

They walk past jewelry.

Saks Fifth Avenue. Before he saw Audrey again after so long, Frazier had stood without his father's knowledge and watched him smelling perfumes here. An amused saleslady was holding out scented paper slips. Frazier had eyed him from behind sports apparel.

He'd known who his father was buying for because he'd walked in on them once, the sheets bunched at the end of the guest-room bed, one pair of lady's panties sprawled on the floor. Frazier had entered through the side bathroom and stood watching. Rebecca Howe was saying his father's name. Sunlight streaked in from the far window and shone on her heavy breasts and slender hips. He watched his father performing the act of a man. A true man. Frazier'd ducked out from that horrible secret. Leaving the door open a crack, he'd gone through the hallway, then tried to watch once more through the slit of door meeting wall, but he could see nothing, only moving shapes. The sound of his father's name turned into a groaning woman's wail of desire.

Though he didn't want it to, the memory aroused him again and again. Masturbation became a punishment. He envisioned her backside, the light shifting through her golden hair. The first time he was with Audrey, the image had entered him. He closed his eyes and prayed to God it would go away.

He and JP wander through the ladies-clothing section. Do a distraction, he tells JP. I need something for Aud.

JP's chin goes up, his shoulders square. Frazier watches him put a frown of worry between his eyes, pretending he's an out-of-place-honest-Negro type, leaning over the counter toward the coiffed saleslady with her ringed fingers and dyed yellow bouffant. I'm looking for something feminine, he hears JP say. I'm not ready for the big step. JP laughs nervously. But I want something kind of pre-big step.

Frazier fingers the scarves, burnt yellow and tangerine, a honeydew melon color. One is burgundy colored, the hue of spilled wine. Its ends are fringed with glass beads of rose and ivory. He takes three down and balls the burgundy one in a single-fisted wad, sticks his hand in his pocket for later when Audrey will kiss him with her full lips, slip it around her neck and tie it there.

He walks through gentlemen's attire to the double doors. Once outside, he leans against the mall's back wall to wait for JP and smoke a cigarette.

Stealing for her feels like jumping the NC bridge over Collard's Bay, years before he'd tried drugs. He was the brave one, the lone figure sailing through the air while the other kids watched. Audrey stood apart from the crowd, her hand to her mouth. When he looked up from the water, her hand was gone and she was smiling, proud, her head tilted. He'd watched her legs straddling the bridge's cement railing and then she was off, hands up, legs apart, floating through the air. The water swallowed her, and he searched for bubbles, his lip sweating, frantic she would not come up.

He'd wanted to call out her name but didn't want the others to hear. Hey, she'd said when she emerged, her hair slick and fine down her back, her eyelashes wet. Twelve years old and fresh from the death of a father no one ever mentioned.

Frazier had been fourteen, hard for her. You daredevil, he told her, ducked her once and held her body in his arms for too long. She didn't move from him, swam holding her hand on the small of his back until they reached the bank.

Lovebirds, shouted Sarah Pope.

Frazier'd shaken his head of the wet and they'd walked separately up to the bridge.

Toward the end of the summer, he'd gone to the window of her father's parents' summer place, climbed the roof with its bird shit and awakened her out of a deep sleep, told her to get her bathing suit and come on.

They didn't talk on the way to the bridge. Once there, she said she would jump if he held her hand. They flew through sable air under a slivered moon. There was a deafening sound when the two bodies hit water. He'd kept his eyes open to the salt so he could watch her murky form, her flailing legs, propelling her up and out of the water. Above the surface, the two of them gasped air, laughing. They'd laid with their backs to the cement pedestrian bridge, still hot from that day's sun, their eyes on the stars. And she'd talked about infinity; she'd learned about it in science class. She said it scared her.

Why are we whispering? he'd asked. And then he kissed her, touching her wet lips with his tongue. He remembers she reached for him, his waist in her hands, her fingers in his hair. A wind blew. The masts rocked and sang.

Later, they found a patch of blueberries on the far bank and fed them to each other.

He watches for JP through the plate-glass window on the far side of the entranceway. A wind kicks up and smells of cigarette ash.

What do you think of Audrey? he'd asked his cousin the next day. Thomas Keegan was first string in lacrosse and football, half

Italian on his mother's side. Girls liked his curly hair and blue eyes. Thomas had shrugged. I don't know. He shucked an old stick into the water and said, She's just a kid.

Meaning no tits. But she's brave, Frazier'd thought to say. She can jump. Years later she became one of the girls he'd masturbated to. She entered his dreams, making him shamed and wet in the morning with the embarrassing stain on his sheets. Her fragility was her deception. She was still brave, would love him without refusal, waiting for him to love her back with a patience that surprised him.

JP comes toward the doors. Fingering something in his pants pocket, he looks around the ceiling for cameras. He walks out the entranceway, stands and stretches his arms to the darkening sky. Winking at Frazier, he says, Stealing ain't gonna get you high. But it sure feels good.

3.

GRACEY STANDS AND WALKS to the window. She holds the sill and stretches her back, turning first to one side, then to the other. Mist rushes in and she tells Cole and Kelly how she slept soundly for days at a time, waking only when Merridew brought her drinks and food and pills. She got up to go to the bathroom and went back to bed. Once in a while, she'd go out for air, but she found herself staring down at the long space between balcony and street, trying to muster the energy to jump.

Often Merridew was standing at the kitchen counter with her coffee, reading a newspaper, smiling at Gracey when she came out of the bedroom. When Gracey got back in bed, bits of classical music drifted to her from a stereo in the living room and eased her back into slumber.

Over the telephone, Gracey's mamma asked, Who was that lady brought the kids over, Gracey? Where are you? You tell me where you're at. Sonny's sick. He's crazy for you. You call him. Get me your number so I can have him call you. He's cleaned up, and he wants you back real bad. You need to get home to him. He's the daddy of your babies. You can't do him this way. I'm happy to have the kids here with me till you two work it out. He's a good man.

Gracey held a dial-toned receiver in her hand and thought how talking to Son would just be putting a sledgehammer to a dam when the waters were high. She took more pills and they aided her withdrawal from him and from heroin. She didn't know the difference between sleeping and waking, could barely feel when she drifted off to dream and didn't remember the nightmares when she did.

It was close to a month later when she really saw the room. She woke to a mobile of seashells and rose walls. Next to the bed was a framed picture of two ballerinas leaping in the air. *What you dream, you become,* it said.

When she went back to sleep, she found herself in a driver's seat with no brakes, whaling around corners, the wheels slipping on ice. Merridew was there when she woke, touching Gracey gently and rocking her in her arms, listening as Gracey told her the stories of her nightmare and where it came from. The father who beat her, the way her sun was eclipsed. Life was always responding to her wishes in riddled, hateful answers. Merridew rubbed her ebony hair with her uncallused fingertips. She searched Gracey's deep brown eyes with her own, witnessing the pain tenderly.

I ain't had a pill in a long time, have I? Gracey asked her.

Merridew laid her fingers on her lids when Gracey closed her eyes. No. She kissed Gracey's face gently. They touched for hours.

It wasn't queer, Gracey tells Kelly and Cole. It was natural, better than natural. It's how it's supposed to be, woman with woman. She knew how to touch my body, didn't paw at it like men did, scrubbin it down like they wanna erase my most private parts. We played so good together like that, in bed, for days.

Gracey doesn't talk for some time. Her toe moves back and forth, barely touching the floor, giving her the appearance of dancing.

Somethin happened to me when I was with Merridew, she tells them. I was new again. I didn't worry about my next fix, money, the kids, Sonny. Merridew was my whole world, and I was safe. I'd never had that before. There was always something happenin or just about to happen. There was always the way my mind worked a problem till it was dead beat on the floor and stumblin to get up again. But with Merridew I was calm. Everything was okay. She was my new drug.

Gracey's voice gets low when she talks about Merridew leaving for a business trip. She hated Merridew's absence and searched the apartment for pills, tearing the place apart for something, anything that would soothe her. Finally, straddling the balcony's railing, she watched the Matchbox-size cars and people like small, busy ants rushing to their homes and jobs. The blazing concrete seemed to be waiting for her body. There was a Popsicle stick sideways on the balcony's floor. She pushed it down to see if she could watch it land. She couldn't.

Merridew's voice from the threshold of the sliding glass door scared her. Don't you do that, Gracey Fill. You do that and I'm after you.

All that afternoon, they lay together on the living room couch. Gracey cried and apologized. She told Merridew about the beautiful pain of being loved wholly when loneliness had always been there. Talk wound around the hours of that day. They told secrets so deep and dark the holder had forgotten them for years because there had been no one to say them to. Merridew's story spilled into Gracey. She told about her mother, home for Thanksgiving from the hospital where they were treating her for depression. On Friday morning, Merridew had woken to the horrible stillness of a sleeping house. At sixteen, she'd entered the room in early light to find drapery wrapped around her mamma's fragile neck.

Merridew's daddy had been a young black boy sent over to fight a war and defend a country that didn't even let him use a good public toilet or give him a bus seat. Her mamma'd been raped and beaten many times through by the North Koreans and her daddy fell in love with her, put himself on a rescue mission. In the end, he couldn't save her like he needed to.

My father's the best man who ever lived, Merridew told her.

People can be good, Gracey. You got to find the ones who aren't spirit hungry and soul weary.

She told Gracey of her own escape, Baltimore in the mid-seventies, using, months passing by like a minute.

She and her husband finally had to separate. We thought we were killin ourselves when we let go, Merridew said. But we had to leave each other off. Even though we'd both gone clean, we needed to find entire new lives so it didn't happen twice. She picked up Gracey's chin and looked into her eyes. Kicking makes you have to birth yourself all over again and that is hard. You're forced to be the mother and the baby and the doctor all at once. It's painful. I know how it is. I saw your face that first day in the park, and I understood you were good. You got treasure inside you. There's a flower down deep that got crushed by your daddy. You're usin to escape. But there's another reason, too. You want passion in your life, something to matter, a dream inside you to come alive. And there isn't anything wrong with that. Only drugs isn't the way to it.

Gracey found a mirror in those words, her savior, the only person who had ever understood her. Merridew.

She woke each day believing she'd be left. To her relief, Merridew was always there. They cooked and cleaned, cocooned each other into a life of comfort. Two rabbits in a safety den. Sometimes they stayed in bed all day long, loving each other.

Merridew showed Gracey the history they shared. Her voice drew pictures of the world they were both from and belonged to, Rosa Parks and M.L.K., Birmingham and Selma, Medgar Evers, the march against fear, how the kids filled up the jails so the parents could work. Grenada, Mississippi, 1966, black children beat to the ground by whites and the *Jim Crow Must Go!* signs. White government crippling black society by sending black men eight thousand miles away to fight for freedom in a Southeast Asian country when they didn't have any liberty here in southwest Georgia, Harlem, Chicago, anywhere.

Gracey let understanding seep through a history of denial.

She took sides for her own people. The two women spoke of what happened in Memphis, the Lorraine Motel on Mulberry Street in 1968 when the white guys in power didn't want to listen anymore. It was a drone that was getting too loud and the main voice in the civil rights movement was silenced forever.

Something's wrong with the psyche of America, Merridew told Gracey. Having to go to jail to promote equal rights, getting police dogs on young children while they're singing O Freedom. Ten thousand black Americans dead from the Civil War to the civil rights movement because of lynching, and killing Emmett Till for one comment.

Gracey came alive. She got angry. She loved. She was clean and well cared for. Everything was falling into place. Her smarts were finally exercised and working double time. Sitting at the dinner table over salmon bisque with her new lover, she threw ideas around, got energized, talked solutions, discussed how their history made the bad of today worse.

Sometimes people would call, and Merridew would say, I been busy fallin in love. I'll call y'all when I catch my breath.

Merridew read Brer Rabbit aloud to Gracey at night before long and unfitful sleep found her. She loved that book, only let Merridew read two pages at a time so they could make it last.

By day Merridew worked in her home office on designs for children's book jackets. Gracey flipped through magazines and cooked up breakfast, made sandwiches and cookies, called Mamma and had the same conversation all over again. She talked to the kids and listened to them cry. She cried herself. Her anguish was alive, but it was smaller than her knowledge of what would happen if she went back downtown, how she'd have to face the needle in her arm. She knew it was the only way she could handle that world.

Gracey comes to the table and circles it, watching the two officers. Neither Cole nor Kelly look at her or at each other. Kelly rolls his pencil across the tabletop with one finger. His mouth is small. His eyes are beaten.

Cole waits. Gracey says quietly, I know men better now. Once you find a woman who helps you live, it terrifies you to think of being without her. She runs her hand over the back of Cole's chair. He feels the breath of her fingertips, the sigh of her body. She says, I guess this other fear was lurkin, too. I was afraid that dark thing was still hoverin around, waitin on me. It wasn't never goin away. I was born with it and Merridew was keepin it gone for a while. It'd be back directly.

Gracey stays behind Cole, gripping the back of his chair.

I saw Son when I was out gettin a pack of cigarettes one day. He was on Roswell standin beside a cart that sold newspapers and magazines, shootin the shit with the guy behind the booth. I would have walked right past him, didn't recognize him until he touched my arm. Then I turned around, and there he was, my Son. His smile was so big and real, his eyes were clear, and his skin was smooth.

Gracey walks to the edge of the table, fingers the ledge, and tells them, We stared at each other like a couple of lovesick schoolkids. He didn't have a beard, but other than that, he was the same man as when I met him, white, straight teeth and those heavy-lidded eyes. Lookin into them made me feel like I was fallin.

Hey, girl, he said. How you been?

I was shaking from the inside out. I didn't know how I was gonna tell him about Merridew or what had happened to me. It felt like some other world I was livin that wasn't real at all.

I been okay, I told him. How you been?

He took me in with his eyes, up and down. He said, Baby, you look so good. You got thick. Your bright skin's back, girl. He tilted his head. You feelin better? he asked.

I said, Yeah, I'm feelin good.

He said, You sure look good.

I said, You, too.

I been cleaning up my act, he said. I'm layin wood floors for a livin, got some gigs up here in these fancy parts. I been lookin all over for you, about killed myself how bad I want you back. He was starin at the ground when he said it, then he lifted his eyes and smiled at me.

I was shocked silly he wasn't mad at me. And I was relieved. In the back of my mind, I had always loved Son. Merridew, she was what I needed at the time, but I was always half with Son in my mind.

I went to him. Right into his arms.

It was like coming home. His shoulderblades fit under my hands, and he smelled like that Mr. J cologne he always wore. When he kissed me, it was Son's thick lips with the little mustache growin in around them.

I ain't shakin 'cause of nothin, but I'm so happy to see you, he said.

I nodded. I had tears in my eyes and they was fallin down my cheeks.

Never again, Son said.

I shook my head. Nope. Never again.

He hugged me tight and rocked me back and forth and said, You and me, baby, we ain't never gonna let go.

Then I did to Merridew what I done to Son. I walked away from her in the middle of the day. I didn't never look back for one long while.

Gracey pulls the third chair out and sits across from Cole. She looks at his hands and then his chest, where his heart is.

We couldn't have lived like that, she says. It's what I told myself while Son was drivin me back downtown. You can't just off and live, two women alone. I wanted my children back and I missed my mamma and I never would have been able to explain to them about Merridew and what we was doin.

Cole watches pain flicker across Gracey's eyes. And then there was my Son. He was my man. Ain't no one never gonna be my man like Son, I told myself.

4.

DENEEKA OPENS HER EYES, stretches across the seat's blue velour, and feels her left leg cramp at the knee. Son of a bitch, she says, rubbing it. She pushes her fallen garter up, adjusts her .22, and grabs the ceiling's ripped vinyl to pull herself upright. It's almost as comfortable as her room on Cleveland Avenue, next to the Club Mexicana, where she used to be anonymous in the enclave of Latinos. Now when the Cubans, Mexicans, and Puerto Ricans want to get high, they know where to go for it.

She stumbles out the door, rights the heel of her shoe, and places the needle box on top of the car. Lifting her skirt, she uncoils her penis and pees on the edge of the car's tire. She looks around while she does it, at the dun sky, the slow, patient drizzle of rain. The sun has set for the day, and there is a cascade of blinking lights against evening's darkness. Night arrives and hides squalor, filth, the fact of this car lot with its bruised, crashed autos catering to the likes of Deneeka and other stray people who need homes and shelter.

Walking gingerly toward the east, she picks up various pieces of last week's newspaper while she goes and uses them as rain shelter for her hair and makeup. The ashen sky is a dull background to the silhouette of box-shaped buildings.

She hitches to Stewart Avenue from the east side of the I-85 bridge, walks backward with the new needles in her hand, her thumb out. Streams of headlights illuminate seven lines of criss-crossed highways. The streetlamps mouth an ever-present glow.

A Chinese man in a Domino's uniform picks her up. You need a ride, lady? I go as far as the Best Western on Airport Road. Then stop. His car smells of pepperoni.

Deneeka throws the newspaper to the wind and shifts from Norma Jean to Marilyn. She flips her hair at him and crosses her legs in the tiny front seat of his Chevy Nova. Sugar, can you just drop me off at the Alamo Hotel?

I don't know which one is Alamo. He has to raise his chin to see over the steering wheel. His chest is pressed forward.

I'll show you.

The heater is warm and Deneeka opens her window a crack to feel the breeze. So, what do you like on Stewart? she asks him. You like the Pink Pony, huh, baby? She reaches over and plucks him under the chin.

He smiles nervously and croaks out a laugh. Thumbing back to show her the pile of boxes in the rear seat, he asks her, You want some pizza?

She sidles over to him, puts her head on his shoulder and breathes in his ear, No.

Very well. He glances at her, then back at the road, then at her again. I married. New wife from Florida, very nice, very nice.

Deneeka plays with the hair around his ear. I'll bet, she tells him. Her voice is soft and welcoming.

They park next to Atlantic Trailer City, where old Gulf Stream trailers are hitched to the back of rusted-out Impalas. The inhabitants are in their cramped quarters getting ready for Saturday night while Deneeka opens the Chinese man's fly and rocks his hatchback. He steams up his own windows.

When they are on the road again, Deneeka wipes a hand over

her mouth and tells him in her man's voice, It isn't true what they say about you Asians. She punches his arm lightly. You horse, she says. You yellow slant-eyed stallion.

In his postcoital upset, the man understands Deneeka is not female. He pulls out in front of a semi. The driver honks for ten long seconds. Deneeka laughs, deep-throated, and thrilled at the man's surprise. Her voice is a brassy alto. Don't you worry, she says. The mouth is the dirtiest part of the animal. She laughs loudly and then abruptly stops to tell him, There's the Alamo, you big buffoon.

He screams in, and before she has gotten the door all the way closed, he screams out again.

Fuckin pussy, Deneeka yells after him. Standing in the rain, she takes the fifty-dollar bill from her pocket and kisses it. She raises her compact and arranges her hair. It's too dark and she can only hope she looks good.

Sonny Fill has ripped the dividers out of four rooms and made a house out of the old crumbling walls of the Alamo. A canopy bed with gauzy linen over it takes up the middle of the first room. A man stands guard, asking for ID and giving permission to see either The Rocket, the whore he owns and her companion, or both. Customers are charged fifty dollars payable in cash and drugs when they lay with the girl and the boy under the canopy.

One Saturday, when she came to pick up the score, Deneeka opened the gauze, lit a cigarette, and stood watching. The whore's expression was half-lidded, bored; she did not look up when Deneeka peered in. The customer's buttocks were round and muscled; his hands gripped the headboard while the girl lay idle. The young boy rested beside them, licking where he could, his hands groping the man's body gently.

Getting the freak on.

Later she watched the girl sit naked on the side of the bed, her eyes moistening and tearing, becoming soft and grateful when she pushed off.

Tonight the boy is asleep and the girl is crouched over her toenails, painting them an electric blue.

Deneeka walks through that room and one more. The gas lamps are low. Thick red velvet curtains with gold ties hang over the windows. A fish tank with purple and blue iridescent fish takes up a whole wall. The carpet is a deep maroon. Ace sits on a leather chair in the corner, a gun in one side of his holster and a Japanese Tanto knife in the other side. He's watching a rerun of *Three's Company*. The Rocket's waiting on your ass, he tells Deneeka without looking up.

At the threshold of the next room, she rings the doorbell on the jamb and waits. Saturday at Sonny's. All over the city tonight, drugs will be getting lowered by ropes, tossed out windows, hidden in drainpipes, tucked behind cement on the sides of buildings. They have been toted here hundreds of miles, from Asia and Colombia. Drug dealers in Miami and California, whose names Deneeka does not know, own plants in remote farming villages guarded by men holding semiautomatics, trained to kill for the fields of drugs. Or be killed.

Yeah? His voice is muffled, squeezed into the small intercom square.

She puts her mouth to the speaker and breathes into it. Rocket? she says, airy, fresh, ready.

What?

She licks her teeth and says, It's Dee.

Come on in, baby.

The buzzer sounds and she opens the door. It smells of the candied, sweet scent of The Rocket's drug. Hanging from four cameras in each direction of the room are the scenes of the other rooms: the front door; the sleeping male whore and his female counterpart, dipping her brush in the polish; Ace, laughing at the TV. In the back room Ralphy's eating from a bucket of KFC and Snort's leaning against the door next to him with a pistol at his knee.

Deneeka goes up to the plate-glass window. The Rocket is in a cradle of opium smoke, wallowing in a billow of unfiltered air. He is a haze of a man, the wizard of Oz, sitting in a wide black wing chair wearing a white salwar camise, a fat, gold pipe beside him. The smoking end of the tube is ivory and he mouths it amorously, his eyes half-mast, his smile permanent, unyielding to reality.

Deneeka, he says, baby.

She pokes her head closer to the space where the speaker is. Hey, Rocket, she says.

He heaves himself from the chair and goes to the safe. With a gold key attached to a chain around his middle, he opens it and takes out four metal boxes. He arranges the stash on the counter between them. A soundproof window separates her from him.

She bends forward to the speaker screen. How you been? she asks.

He does not look up. I'm fine, sweetheart. She watches his strong jaw, his hands pulling out baggies, sorting and piling. I got to deal with punks now, he tells her. I ain't dealin drugs with punks. They're no good for it. They cuttin it up with shit and smokin their lives up their noses along with my stash. But guns, I can't afford not to sell 'em pieces. I'm talkin armed youth, Deneeka.

I understand, says Deneeka. She fingers the speaker, puts her palm against it, imagines she can feel his breath.

He dips back and smokes one more time, then returns to the counter. Kids are runnin guns now. A few years ago kids only knew about .22s. Their heroes were Batman and the Incredible Hulk. Now it's the pusher with the Lexus and the weapons. They're askin me for .9mm automatics, old-fashioned .44 magnums, military guns, grenades, dynamite, shotguns, double pumps, .357s. The other night a kid come in here with a fully loaded Uzi, a .380 pistol tucked in his gangster pants.

What did you do, Rocket? Deneeka asks him.

Talk to Ace about what we did. I don't frisk 'em. They're not gettin at me if they wearin a weapon when they come here.

He puts the piles of white powder with red Rocket labels stamped on them into a large paper sack and packs it in a plastic carrier same as they use at banks for drive-up tellers. He sticks it in the metal basket and pulls the lever. It goes underground and shoots up on the other side where Deneeka can unfasten it.

Those kids are gettin rich, he says. They gold-cappin their teeth and they got twenty-five-year-old bitches givin 'em pussy anytime they want it. I'm gonna buy me white leather Reeboks and a sweatsuit and go girl hoppin, he says. These young punks, they have all the fun. He keeps an eye on Deneeka while she unpacks the goods. I'm givin you half a stash, he says. The other half got picked up Tuesday.

Deneeka knows that's Feather's half. Tonight he'll be selling to the college kids in the hotel by Morehouse. She smiles at The Rocket, but he isn't looking at her. He's filling his pipe. He backpedals to his seat, sits with the opium tube between two fingers, and nods at Deneeka. Go ahead, try you some, he says.

No, Rocket, I trust you.

He shakes his head slowly, puffs once, closes his eyes then opens them halfway. I knew you was gonna say that. You always sayin that. Don't trust me, baby. That's your problem, Dee, you trust everyone.

She presses her forehead to the window, leans in, and watches him. I trust you, Rocket, she breathes. I only trust you. And I ain't never told a secret.

Soon as you do, that dick you don't use gonna be blown off its base and shoved sideways in your mouth. He smiles warmly.

She runs her hand down the speaker. You know what it does to me when you talk dirty, she says. She is close to tears.

He shakes his head. It ain't happenin, Deneeka.

Rocket, she says, her knees buckle. Her insides go weak. Can I just see your bed? Please.

Go on now, he says gently. He rests his head back on the chair and closes his eyes. Pack yourself in there.

She puts the needle box in the tube and then passes it back in the metal basket to The Rocket, who has pressed a side button on the wall beside his chair.

You good to get me them clean works, he tells her. I don't want nobody sharin their works if I can help it, gettin the AIDS in their eyes and pointin the finger at me, sayin I done it. They want to get high, they can do it safe.

Deneeka nods furiously, watching the muscles in his arms, his heavy lips.

Ralphy'll take you into town soon as you're ready, he tells her.

While she is putting the bags of crack, meth, and heroin next to her falsies in her bra and down her underwear, Ralph appears at the side door. When he opens his mouth to smile, every tooth is gleaming silver. C'mon, baby, he says, hooking his elbow with hers. Where you goin tonight?

They drive down Stewart Avenue in silence. After seeing The Rocket, Deneeka has no room in her heart for sassing. It is all used up by her sorrow. The Rocket. When she closes her eyes, she sees his cocoa skin, the lazy way he moves. She opens her eyes. Stewart has just been renamed Metropolitan Avenue. City officials trying to clean up their municipalities with prohibitions, thwarting media attention. They ride past Haven Lingerie, not just for gawkers obsessed with nudity anymore, now open for your modeling pleasure. Niki's, the notorious strip club, has been renamed Niki's VIP Diner. Ralphy points to it. They're tryin to move the food at Niki's, he says. Good vittles with your titties. He laughs. Plenty of women still shakin their things in your face, he tells her.

But Deneeka doesn't want to hear about women and pussy. She wants the words voided. She aches for someone to show pleasure to.

The Oakland Cemetery goes by in a blur.

Ralphy gives the Mexican parking guy on Seventh and Peachtree a dollar and tells him he is just dropping his friend off. Deneeka pays downstairs and walks up, strutting her stuff, making herself forget The Rocket. Hey, baby, she says to the svelte, cool-looking patrons with their cigarettes and hard liquor. She ignores the gay boys with their shiny black ankle boots, collared polo shirts, V-neck sweaters, new blue jeans, and earrings.

On the drag stage, Nurse Holly is doing a comedy act, singing, *I got lots of friends in San Jose,* pretending she is blind. Large dark glasses owl her eyes. She has a Lucille Ball red wig on, a checked shirt, and a striped skirt. The words KICK ME are written across her back on a white sign with black Magic Marker. She's one of the opening shows before Charlie Brown comes on at midnight.

Strobe lights cover the room. People weave their way from the circular mirror at the back of the bar to the front. The meth is heavy beneath Deneeka's shirt. Her connect is Henry and she does not immediately see him. She takes a seat at a small fake-wood table next to Gloria, a six-foot drag queen in bright blue sequins and stiletto heels. Under the lights of the golden bulbs a painted picture of Cher is illuminated. The wall reads *BACKSTREET: Where the Men Are Men and the Beautiful Women Are Men.* How are you, Deneeka? Gloria asks in an Elizabeth Taylor accent.

Couldn't be better, says Deneeka.

Before Deneeka can ask, Gloria tells her, He isn't here yet.

When he enters, he makes eye contact with her and then heads to the rest rooms. She follows him. They stand in the doorless black-and-red bathroom, its shining red tiles like a bad trip, piss on the floor.

She gives him ice, ephedrine-based D-methamphetamine, glassine sheets of rock, all forms, to be smoked in a pipe, blunt, capsules, dissolved in water, finely ground, snorted like coke. The withered drag queens use it like water, oxygen.

Onstage they can hear the man speaking in a lavender-colored voice. The top hat's not near full, boys and girls, we're raising money for the AIDS fund tonight. I know we've all been affected, so let's share what's left in our pockets. And pay your bartender. Freddy's doing a marvelous job. Hey, let's give a hand to Freddy.

They sidle into the third stall for Deneeka's extra fifty. He pushes against her, puts his hands on either side of her waist and pushes her down so she's kneeling before him, Mary at the cross. She unbuttons his pants, slings off his leather belt, and ties it around her neck so he can pull and release her head when he wants to. We Are Family blares through the speakers and she knows Gigi String is onstage. The toilet has no cover.

Deneeka closes her eyes when she does it. If she plugs her nose, she will drown, so she tries to forget the smell and thinks of a field of poppies, The Rocket laying her down. Dollar bills falling around them like green rain.

Then it is over and Henry is dropping the money on the seatless U of the toilet. Go ahead there, Deneeka, eat it up. He zippers himself, licks his fingers, and palms their wetness over his scalp. Shame edges him out of the stall.

Hey there, he says to the mirror. Lookin good, lookin good.

Deneeka puts her wad of money from the sale in various places on her body, in a plastic bag up her asshole, down her shoe, across her breasts, under the panties. She ignores Henry when he yells good-bye. Even though he is a regular, she is careful of him. The meth makes him violent. It is said he raped and killed his girlfriend and her nine-year-old daughter in Nevada and told all he knew of the drug trade on a bargain from the feds to rearrange his face. The witness protection program sent him out of the state forever. Still he doesn't stop. Eventually he will kill himself with it and the world will breathe more easily.

Her next connect is Model T's, on Ponce. There she'll get rid of the last of her meth to Sid Hay, who can deal it all before the bars close. By the time she buses it to Ford Factory Square, it is half-past nine and there is a loose crowd. She missed Chicks and Dicks last night when the crowd would have been thick and ready for her. Tonight a barely clad man wearing makeup and a nylon skullcap is on deck for the strip stage. He's standing beside the nine-by-four platform in front of a window hidden by a filthy brown curtain, smoking Camel nonfilters and holding a rainbow lighter. An African-American drag queen named Lightning with a gold zigzag around her neck dances cobralike and lip-syncs, *I've been to Greece and the isle of Crete and drunk champagne on a yacht* with a feel-sorry-for-me look on her face.

Sid is in a blue leather coat by the GA lottery machine. Under the disco-ball lighting, the heart tattoo on his cheek looks like a hole in his flesh. He has an Ace bandage wrapped around his left hand.

Sid, what happened to you? Deneeka asks in her little-girl voice.

Rough sex, Sid says.

Before them the black drag queen collects her bills off the floor and steps from the stage. The little gay boy comes on in his rainbow G-string, his calf tattooed with a map of Florida. He's made a Mohawk out of his pubic hair.

Sid licks Deneeka's ear bottom to top, then pushes her face away with the heel of his hand. You got somethin for me? he asks.

She nods.

He glances around, pulls his coat back, and unsnaps the side of his pants to a nylon pocket covering the flank of his thigh. Come on, baby, do me in here. He smiles. His front teeth are crooked, and his eyebrow ring glitters in the twirling, diamond squares above.

She puts the meth in the holder, and he snaps up.

The leathered bartender glances back at them with his eyes narrowed. He shares looks with the older guy in front of the Pot o' Gold gambling machine and Deneeka sees it is Sandy Etch, the hired cop who has been paid off by the Bluff's hit houses to keep his mouth shut.

You hear about Miss Behave? Sid asks.

No, I didn't hear it. And I don't give a flying fuck since she's never nice to me.

Sid licks two fingers and runs them over Deneeka's lips. She's just jealous, he says. He turns back to the boy onstage, who is gyrating his hips. A long-haired drunk in green chaps and a western button-up puts a five-dollar bill in the back of his G-string. When the boy smiles, Deneeka sees he's missing a few teeth.

Well, what happened to her? she asks Sid.

She shot some of Feather's heroin stash, then smoked all day long. She said she wasn't feeling so good. Sasha helped her to the bathroom, gave her four 'ludes, and then she stopped breathing. Her eyes rolled back, *crash,* her head hit the sink, and she went dead as rock. They said it was the heroin. There's some bad shit going around. Feather got it, too. Word is, he's dead.

Deneeka feels nausea rise within her. Feather's toothy laugh echoes in her mind, the surprising powder-puff quality of his voice for such a large man. *Come on in, Dee, baby, sit down and have you some of this wine with your friend Feath.* He was gentle, generous, a junkie with a heart. *What you been up to? You lookin wore out. If I was your boss, I'd give you a vacation near the ocean,* leaning back, streaming lazy smoke into the room's stale air, *you and me both. How's that sound? Start saving our money, Deesee.*

Feather ain't dead, I saw his ass day before yesterday, she tells Sid.

Yeah, Sid says, taking out a pack of Lucky Strikes and sticking one between his teeth, but what about today? I sure as hell hope it wasn't you sold him that bad stash, Dee. 'Cause if it was, then you killin people with that shit. He smiles. His crooked teeth glitter.

Feather gets his straight from the source, Deneeka tells him. Her eyelashes bounce in rapid blinks and her skin breaks sweat. Anyway, you gotta die of something, right? she says.

He slips the money in her pocket and shrugs. I don't gotta die of nothin, he tells her. I'm gonna live forever.

With perspiring hands, she counts while she stands there, craning her neck between the juke and her hip to see the bills.

Meanwhile, Sid runs his hand up her back and whispers to her, I ain't got any of my own cash yet, but I could give you a verbal raincheck to pay you for your tongue around my nine-incher.

No money, no tongue, Deneeka tells him, as airily as she can manage. Anyway, I gotta be going to the hit house. You ain't my only customer. Can I bum a smoke?

He takes the pack of smokes and raises them above his head. No tongue for me, he says, then shit for you.

Give me the other hundred for the meth or I'll open your snaps and get it from you.

He sighs, takes the final bill out of his pocket, and slips it to

Deneeka, then raps four times on top of the jukebox. When he walks across the room to lean over the bar, all eyes, even the dancing boy's, are on him. They know what he's hiding, their trick, their crystal, the thing that helps them live. Deneeka goes unnoticed. She walks over to the door and pushes it open, crystal free and money rich.

Her mind turns circles, figuring who will know about Miss Behave and Feather. The Rocket hasn't ever had a bad connect and now he's gone and tombstoned two of them.

Walking out of the shopping center toward the rain-slicked sidewalk, Deneeka clicks into survival mode, how to make good of a bad situation. Feather would have been selling all his half tonight. Now he's dead and The Rocket must not know it yet. Or maybe he doesn't want to lose money on his stash. And he had offered it to her. *That's your problem, Dee, you trust everyone.* She cringes at the thought, rain slapping her face, her heels slipping on road sludge. Normally it would take her a week or more to sell what she's got of the heroin. But with Feather down, she can make all Feather's deals herself in only a few hours. She pulls her chin up, walks haughtily. She knows where to go.

This could be her last night in Atlanta, if the network gets wind of it, if the streets pick up breeze that she was the one. The Rocket's impermeable. He's indestructible, safe. She marks his fall-outs. It's her ass on the line.

Putting her thumb out, she heads west on Ponce. Guilt isn't a question. It's subsistence living. Where can she go next? What town won't hate her now? She walks backward, passing the Phoenix, the symbol of Atlanta and the town-hustler bar, male prostitutes buying and selling. She used to make her money there, but they won't let her in anymore, had another connect kick her out so he could be the sole dealer. Strolling by City Hall East, the police headquarters, she eyes the sex workers in front. She knows them all by name, and when they call hello to her, she raises a hand, saunters more.

Yeah. She'll go herself, sell the last of it to the college kids over near Morehouse. None of them will have heard about Feather yet. Even if they had, they wouldn't put two and two together. She can make enough money tonight to set herself up well in another place.

This thought hits her pleasantly, like the soft, cool rain on her neck. Louisiana, of course. She has always wanted to see New Orleans. It couldn't take more than eight hours to get there. Bourbon Street and jazz clubs, the nooks and crannies of cobblestone alleyways, a river and its constant pledge of goings and comings. She can make a connection down there.

Deneeka is feeling better, high. She has a plan. She likes Atlanta, sure, but life is long, she's got dreams of crayfish and Creoles. She could be good as gone. No one will find her, 'cause no one will look. She holds that one true American dream of being unattached. Free.

5.

LATER, WHAT WOULD BE said about her? Would she go down in history? A black woman, forty-one years old, the story of her life unraveled in Zone 1's makeshift command post on May 19 of the year 2001. Her words create a tapestry of the lost searchers in Atlanta's barest streets, cast-outs, misfits, the sick and tired, the once rich and loved, addicts and thieves, avoiding the ghosts of those who miss them, hovering about the forsaken city that holds Gracey Fill.

Drug users can no longer be jumbled into a mass grave of the almost dead and buried, for here she is in front of them, flesh-and-blood woman, a rotating planet containing rivers and jungles, salted tiding oceans and red-hot deserts. Savage beasts have stampeded in fellowship through the wild plains of her body. She has passion. Cole knows it by the way she speaks of her love: fierce, abiding, yielding to temptation without pause. He cannot get the sensual story of her recovery through another woman out of his mind.

Kelly has gone to get them dinner, file the tapes, talk to the sergeant, and run names. The room is spacious without him. Cole watches her at the window, stamping her foot out of her shoe and rubbing the Achilles tendon. The smoke from her cigarette drifts in a breeze coming between the slatted boards. She stands and looks out the window. Her voice is hoarse. Moon's coming up, she says.

Cole walks over and stands behind her to watch. The moon is a green and yellow paste rising through the belly of the sky. Turbid clouds move over it. He has these few short moments alone with her. His soul is naked from her talk. He wishes he knew how to tell her this.

She turns, leans her back against the wall, taps her toe in front of her, and smokes a cigarette from a new pack brought in by the second-shift intern. Her hair is curly and wild about her. You got a wife? she asks.

No.

She nods, ashes her cigarette on the floor. A girl?

He shakes his head.

She tilts hers. What about your mamma?

He looks at the ground, thinks of the moneyed envelopes, their blank space in the top left corner, remembers the glimpsed view of his mother through Buckhead windows when he sat crouched behind a hedge by a back-patio door, her ethereal form, floating through a grand house. He'd seen her again at his graduation from the police academy, a breezy day where she stood in slate blue under a pear tree in a cream-colored hat and heels. He'd wanted to go to her, but his oblivious father had come to hug him, and when he turned again, she was gone.

He'd called her once. Her hello had been cheery and confident until he said his name, and then her silence was a massive metal door, closing with finality. You don't want to know me, she had said. I am not good for you. She'd stumbled over words and then become composed. There are some things that cannot be forgiven, she told him. I know that.

Will you let me decide what's to be forgiven?

Please, there's nothing we can mend now. You live your life. I'll live mine. I was young, that's all I'll say. Reckless. Her accent was a troubled whisper.

I know I have a sister.

She's your half sister. Do you need money? I can send you money.

I don't want money.

She didn't ask him what he did want: for her to see him in his life, to smell her scent again. She used to sing James Taylor's Going to Carolina, rocking him to sleep in her Irish lullaby.

He starts to speak now, but cannot. When he looks up, Gracey returns his stare without fear, her eyes waiting. She dead?

No, he says. And then he tells her, Lost.

He thinks this an unacceptable answer until Gracey nods and sighs. A hushed look comes over her face, as though it were swathed in muted light and airbrushed. She says, You don't got a girl, a wife, or a mamma. You livin for the likes of me. My kind. If your mother is lost, then you gonna see her in every homeless crack lady bendin over for her next job so she can score a five-spot and spend it on relievin her wore-out self for fifteen more minutes. You know, you like God's son, savin all them sinners and gettin hung. You gonna go and get your heart broke all over this city. But you gonna save more lives than that chump over there who went to get us some supper. He's all boast and no bull. He ain't got heart. What we need is heart. Someone genuine to live for. She nods her head slowly. We need you, Justice, she tells him. We do.

He stands before this woman who has made sense of what he has decided to become and tries to think of something to say.

And then Kelly returns, surefooted, embracing the spring night smell of rain in the fabric of his uniform. His collar is drizzle-flecked. He's carrying three bags of takeout from Delaney's. Behind him, the intern brings a brown carrier full of three coffees and cream and sugar packets and brown plastic stirrers. Gracey watches while they lay the food on the table, opening the paper to reveal lettuce-heavy sandwiches leaking mayonnaise. Kelly licks his fingers and breaks open a cream. Come over here and eat, he tells her.

She stares out the window. How come you gotta talk to me like I'm a dog? she asks softly.

Cole's throat drops to his knees, knowing he has no power in this room.

Kelly fusses with the food. The silence that follows admonishes him. The intern throws away bags, cartons, and empty condiment packs.

Sonny and I done good for a while, she says to the window. Sonny and I done real good for eight long years. Maybe a little less, about that.

Kelly shakes a mustard packet and looks over at her. Don't talk now, he says. We're takin a dinner break here, the recorder isn't even on. You got a hot sandwich and a cola waitin on you. That's more than your sisters on Peachtree and Memorial are gettin.

But Gracey Fill's eyes are elsewhere. She is deaf to the sounds of the command post's questioning room. Again she pinpricks the nylon fabric of her past, revealing a punctured picture. She pulls her hair back with her fingers and tells them, When I first got home from Merridew's, I never wanted to be without my man again. I told myself women come and go, but you find you a good man and he'll be yours forever. I had my girlfriends with their four or five men who'd run on them or they were in prison or they were right then sittin on a La-Z-Boy, drinkin beer, without a dime. My Son was better than that. In the mornin we were lovin and in the evenin we were holdin each other tight. If he was in the neighborhood during lunch, we was in bed together, bitin and tearin and pullin our hair out, cryin for each other. Son'd watch my face and keep me on the brink. You could say it was a kind of abuse, like ticklin too hard, but I didn't never care. I knew it was 'cause he wanted to make sure he had a effect on me.

Cole sits with his sandwich untouched before him and watches Gracey's profile at the window, while Kelly unwraps the cellophane from another tape and sticks it in the recorder. He presses Play. Gracey throws her cigarette down and mashes it under her foot. She crosses one arm over the other and tells them, Merridew was so gentle. This was a whole different thing. It was more real to me with Son. I remembered Merridew like you remember a dream that maybe was true life and maybe it weren't.

Son was my family. He was a good husband too, takin out the garbage, comin with me to the grocery store. He took Lakeisha clothes shoppin, helped her with her homework. She was always in that room, studyin up a storm, keepin her light on all hours of the night. Her name was in the newspaper for the high honor roll. She was dead set for college same as, back in my day, I be set on findin me a man and livin high. She was thirteen. Son was so proud of her. I was too, only I was nervous it wouldn't last. I'd tell her, Don't you go wastin yourself on a man, Keisha. You better than that. She'd say, Mamma, can't you feel me? I ain't into all that. It was like she was older than me.

She was the real thing. Smart without the tart. I think she got a talent for takin the good and leavin the bad. Mamma had somethin to do with it. Her bein at Mamma's without Daddy beatin her black and blue like he did might have been how I'd have turned out if Mamma wasn't dealin with that beast for twenty long years.

Also, Keisha didn't have the looks. My baby girl be wearin big owl glasses and a short Afro and a flat body she didn't dress up for no one. She was plain lookin. That's the Lord's blessin on her. In those days, every chance I got I'm braggin on her, and I'd hear Son do the same. Most of our friends, their girls that age be already sleepin with their boyfriends and findin a way to smoke cigarettes and snort some cocaine. Not our Keisha. She didn't never want any part of that.

Jackson was a different story. He was hangin with the big boys, skippin school, loiterin on the stoops, stealin purses and car radios, smokin weed and drinkin liquor. He wasn't cookin it up or shootin it in, but he on his way.

One night he come home with a policeman on either arm. He'd been vandalizin the school with some other boys. They was gonna bring him down to Juvenile, then they saw our clean house and me and Son at home, especially Son. There ain't no daddies home no more. And they gave Jackson a second chance.

Soon as them blues hit the street, Son had him up against the wall with his neck in a elbow sling. He say, Jackson, you gonna let the streets raise you or you gonna do right by Mamma and me, 'cause you could join your brothers in a box behind Baptist or you could fly right. We love you, boy, and ain't nothin need to pull you down if you got love.

Jackson, he just soft as cake inside, bawlin and carryin on, knees on my carpet sayin, Word, Daddy. I'm gonna do right. I swear it.

We got him in a mentor program downtown where there was a smart older boy took him to ball games and home to his mamma's house, where they sung hymns and sat up straight. Son joined the gym with him and showed him how to get fit boxin on the bag, liftin weights, and eatin right. Jackson done good those years we was clean. He wouldn't bring no books home, but he weren't failin out neither. Son be scarin away all them gang members with his big muscles, standin on the porch with his arms folded over his chest, sayin, Y'all be gone. Go find you a new boy to play with, Jackson ain't followin your hides anymore.

We was good. I'm tryin to tell you, with a mamma and a daddy home and nobody usin, sometimes it can work. We went on family trips, down south to those farms you get to walk around on and feed the animals. We took rides to Stone Mountain and out to the coast. Day trips as a family. Keisha with her glasses on and her nose in a book, so serious. We'd get her to sing along to the radio. Once in a while, she'd let herself smile. And Jackson be bouncin around, puttin his head out the window, tellin Son to push the pedal to the floor. I'd be in the passenger's seat, sayin to myself, Here's my family. Here's what I been lackin.

I wasn't usin, I mean I drank some wine and whiskey, I took me some Valium and smoked some marijuana, stuff like that, but I wasn't injectin no drugs into me. I cared about my kids. They was doin okay.

When she got to be sixteen, Lakeisha found her a boyfriend named Tyrone. He ain't nothin like Leroy or anyone like that. He's a basketball player at GU now, and she's there with him. She got hooked into a good man early on. He lives down near Inman Park and his mamma's Justine Judge. Ms. Justine always walks like she got the world in her fanny and she gonna hold it up good. She knows how to protect her billfold. When she's carrying her pocketbook, she doin it with two hands clasped over it like a shield. She don't let nobody tell her how to run her life. She got a good man, tall and wiry, Tyrone Senior. He runs the soul-food place in Little Five Points. He and her, they compete for space to talk, but you know they love each other 'cause they hootin and hollerin at each other's jokes louder than anybody else. They're each other's best audience. They took Lakeisha in like their own. Ms. Justine was always sayin, Honey, we so happy to have your Lakeisha. She makes Tyrone Junior so happy.

Gracey shakes her head and smiles. Tyrone's bashful, but he don't let Keisha rule the roost all the time. Keisha thinks the sun rises and sets with her 'cause her daddy told her so and Tyrone most days goes easy with it, but sometimes he puts his size-eleven foot down and they go at it. They made for each other. Tyrone's played fine basketball since he could walk and Keisha's a good student. They study together so he can stay on his team.

His mamma's the one got me the job at that little beauty shop next to the Majestic. It was called Lovely Ladies then. Justine waddlin around the place, goin to burst, she so fat. I thought soon she wouldn't be gettin in and out of that itty-bitty door goin to the sink area. Everything smelled of hair tonic and blowers and polish, ladies with their perfume tellin each other, Girl, you so pretty, look at them cat's eyes. You made to be a movie star. In Lovely Ladies, all husbands and boyfriends were a problem you got to deal with. The stories about men kept that place goin. Those women talkin, sayin, Ah, my Gerald, he come home last night hollerin, wakin the babies at three A.M., pullin out that skillet, and tellin me to fry him up some gravy with his grits, wavin his shotgun like he goin to use it if he don't get his breakfast. I done tole him if he do that one more time, I'm skinnin his ass and settin him on the street.

And then another one pop in. Ooooweee, honey, that ain't nothin, my Henry, I set him out two weeks back, he come last night to set the house on fire, put a match to a old soggy bag of newspapers, every single one of 'em damp as a tongue. All he made was smoke. He can't even set my house on fire right.

Those girls be laughin. Holdin their new hairdos, slappin their knees, smokin Newports, puttin on lipstick and walkin out of there like they got the secret and the mens always knockin down the door tryin to find it out.

Gracey smiles. She kicks a cigarette butt away from her. The tweed coat is slung over the back of one chair and she looks at it. Throw me that, will you, Justice?

Kelly nods to the coat. You can come over and get it, he says.

Cole stands from his seat, picks up the coat, and takes it to her. Their hands touch. She blinks slowly. Thank you, she tells him. Very much.

Kelly shakes his head while Cole walks back to his seat.

Gracey gathers the coat sides around her to make a cape. She says, When Reagan got elected, all of Buckhead feasted on caviar and popped bubbly bottles. Meantime us black folks was losin our jobs. They had to hire a pile of blacks in the seventies 'cause of them laws for equal rights. Then a couple of years down the line, when they got the daffy old actor up there in the throne of power, the law hoopla died down and they fired all them black men so they could hire a bunch of crackers. What I'm tellin you is, Son come home from layin floors without a splinter on him. He don't got stain on his pants or nails in his back pockets. He drivin a sedan and lookin smart as a Confederate dollar in his khakis and button-downs and still I didn't want to have eyeballs for what Son was into. 'Cause he was clean, clear-eyed, and level. We was both clean, like I tole you. There wasn't any heroin anymore. Heroin was my thing and you couldn't get much of it for a while. Made it real easy to quit. Crack had hit the streets. It was called base back then and it wasn't cheap. I know you won't tell me, but I'm always wonderin if it ain't some conspiracy you got goin on, they pullin one drug off the street and for a while you can't get it and they puttin another one in its place. Looks like it's intentional to me. Somebody somewhere way high up got a master-plan strategy in mind 'cause when the pipe first started goin around, that's all there was. They was tryin to get us hooked. This shit was the worst.

I'm out on Ashby with Lakeisha when she was sixteen. We was goin to get something at Marc's for Mamma. Up come C.C., my girl from a long way back. She eighty pounds and dirty as a sewer.

Hey, C.C., I said, what you got goin on?

She say, Gracey, you got some money? I need some money.

I fished a five-dollar bill out of my pocket and said to her, What's wrong, C? You sick?

Lakeisha was standin a little ways from me with her arms crossed over her chest watchin C.C. like she the devil. I said to her, What's your problem, girl? You come over and tell your aunt C.C. hello, she an old friend of Mamma's.

Lakeisha come over and said hello, all sullen-like.

C.C. look at that five-dollar like it were a thousand gold pieces. Then she scurried off, bent over and gray-colored.

Lakeisha said, Mamma, don't you know what's happenin? She a crack head. Girls I used to think were beautiful are throwin everything away for that stuff. They're supposed to be goin to school, they just drop out. They got babies 'cause they're turnin tricks and they give the babies away.

I said, No shit, Keish, how do you know that?

She said, I know 'cause I'm around it.

I said, You not goin to visit Granny no more. The Bluff is bad. I'm scared for you, chile. I love you, baby, and I don't want to lose you.

Keisha laughed. She said, Mamma, you sure are naive, you think it's just in the Bluff? Boulevard is just as bad. All of Atlanta is that bad. I ain't doin it. And I never will. I ain't gonna turn out like you and Daddy did.

I never slapped Keisha before, but I turned around and hit her crossways over her mouth.

The sun was in my eyes so I couldn't see her face real good, but I could tell by her voice she was mad. Real quiet she said, Mamma, you ain't never hit me before and you ain't never gonna hit me again. Don't think I don't see the needle tracks on your arms. Daddy buyin me presents up and down and I love him like myself, but I know where he gettin the money—

I'm clean, and your daddy's a hardworkin man—

I know you clean now, and I'm not sayin he ain't hardworkin. I'm sayin he's gettin it from drugs and there are other ways to get it. Your head is stuck in a hole, Mamma, everybody knows, even Granny knows, Jackson knows. Uncle Ray's a half-dead heroin addict and you were one too and that's why you left us for so long. I'm goin to live with Tyrone if Daddy don't stop dealin. I told him so.

We walked down the street without another word between us. I kept lookin over at Keisha, sixteen years old, her head held high. Even though I didn't want to believe her and I was mad she would sass me like she did, I was proud of her.

My daughter had become what I never got the nerve to be.

6.

A MOTORCADE OF MERCEDESES, Jaguars, and BMWs turn right from West Paces Ferry Road onto a dead-end street leading to a security-laden house thrust deep into the forested properties of Buckhead.

Passing through an arched, eight-foot hedge, the guests enter the circular drive bordered by thickset, planted foliage of creeping ficus and Boston fern. The front lawn boasts dogwood and red salvia. Twisted bougainvillea vines curl around the center flagpole. Eleven feet up, America's stars and stripes and the Howe family crest snap in a damp evening wind. The lawn gazebo is filled with glass-covered candles. Carefully manicured shrubbery hems the four-story white columns, and two half-moon stained-glass windows frame the brass front door.

Inside the house, it smells of things polished: silver, crystal, wood, hand-blown glass stemware, and art fixtures hundreds of years old. Through the open parlor doors, butlers in waistcoats stand at attention while elderly men from old Atlanta families doze in antique easy chairs beside a low-flaming birchwood fire. Meanwhile, the young college valet from Georgia Tech escorts newly arriving couples to the door with umbrellas from the Howes' collection. He uses his best restraint parking forty-thousand-dollar cars in the unused stables out back.

Men come in holding the umbrellas over their jeweled spouses' hairdos, swiping rain off their own lapels good-naturedly. *Audrey, my God, you've grown. Last I knew, you were just a little girl. Rebecca, how often do you water her?*

The bowed heads of maids appear. They take coats, fetch drink orders, bring crystal ashtrays to side tables, and pass hors d'oeuvres smelling of crabmeat and caviar and shrimp and ginger.

Rumbling conversations curl around damask curtains, Turkish Orientals, Tiffany chandeliers, and gold door knockers. *Thomas is at Sewanee. Oh, he likes it fine. A little small for him. Pre-law, I believe, though he won't talk about it with dear old Dad.*

Audrey goes to the back window and looks out. The terrace bar is being taken down due to weather. Bow-tied waiters pack wine goblets into boxes and place tea roses in watered napkins. Blooming camellias and massed azaleas are forced inward, abiding the wind.

At least look happy for a minute, Rebecca tells her when she passes. She says it lightly, pecking her daughter's cheek and handing an empty martini glass to the maid. She keeps the toothpick stem of olives and plucks them off with her elegant teeth, ignoring Audrey's belated response, I *am*, Mom. Her mother seems to spend her time ignoring, breezing by, as if she lived life in a wind that carried her from one place to the next without recourse or punishment.

Audrey goes past her, to the back hall. The kitchen smells of roast and wine. Sixteen bottles of Taittinger champagne are lined up on the butcher-block counter. Weiss's bald chocolate-colored head shines in the overhead light. He stirs the tomato bisque. Hey, Red, he says to her, you want to taste you some of this?

Audrey smiles at him. No, thanks.

What? You ain't down with my cookin anymore? I cooked for you for five long years and I don't got it right yet? Sweetheart, you breakin my heart.

I'm just not hungry, she says, girlish, shy.

He shakes his head at her. Sure, yeah, that's what you always say. Whatever. I know when a lady's tryin to be polite.

She steals up the carpeted back stairs silently. The walls boast framed pictures from Tamara Kly's studio of her at each age. Running her hand along the banister, she comes to the landing and goes through the upstairs hall. Voices from the party float up from heating vents in the house's turn-of-the-century structure.

Her mother's room is hollow with emptiness. Audrey presses her palm against the rectangular switch. Light fixtures glow warmly from the walls, illuminating the gold rug and mahogany trim. Antiques, huge and regal, rear up on all sides, including two mirrored wardrobes, a tupelo vanity, her stepfather's oak dresser, and the cherry sleigh bed. A never-played harp sits with a Chinese silk tapestry draped over it. Money lies green and welcoming on the dresser next to photos of the three of them in Highlands, North Carolina.

She closes the door.

Here there are no party sounds, just the brief patter of rain on paned glass. She is alone.

The first drawer of her mother's bureau contains long white gloves with real pearl buttons, silver-and-ruby lipstick containers, fine jewelry wrapped in doubled satin from Italy. Audrey pulls out the last drawer in a set of them built against the back of the bureau, small, secret compartments, hidden and coital. She takes out the plastic-lined velvet bag and looks down at it, feels it with her fingers for bumps, and then opens it. Marveling at its white smoothness, she licks her pointer finger, sticks it in, and touches her tongue to it.

When she looks up, there she is in her mother's gold-gilded mirror. Audrey Sullivan, so pristine on the outside, walking the grounds of the Lovett School with its Olympic-size pools and riding stables, dating boys from Chattanooga when they are home on Christmas breaks. Politeness oozes out of their tweed coats. Inside they are acid heads, carrying nickel bags of pot, weaving their way down Echo Street to cop some cocaine. They turned into bleary-eyed college boys who loved her on their mothers' bedspreads after late-night parties. They kissed her lips, numb from drink, and she listened to the sound of their breath in her ear. All of it transported her from this house, this small, makeshift family where grief had no place and was pushed conveniently out of these expensive rooms. The boys with their nervous hands and cocky assuredness soothed her. Having spent many meaningless nights with them at the Masquerade, she'd watched some get caught in the web of rehab after being fooled out of their families' wealth by a candyland of drugs.

Boredom was beginning to catch up with her when she saw Frazier Sky last year for the first time in so long. He was sitting against the Masquerade's far wall, a cigarette in his hand, making fun of meth clinics and talking about getting his drugs from a guy who owned a Laundromat in Macon. He'd watched her walking toward him, his eyes taking on the appearance of someone seeing an apparition. They had not been in each other's company since his father's affair with her mother had been found out three years before. She'd sat beside him, smiling, wearing suede pants and a white silk button-up from France that fit snugly around her sixteen-year-old breasts. Audrey Sullivan, he'd said, sucking in his breath. But— He'd looked for words. Frazier, not a boy ever at a loss, was for a minute silenced by her. You're gorgeous, he said.

Later he took her to his mother's new house. No one was home. The next day she would wake to redwood floors and glass ceilings, satin draped curtains, ornamental balustrades, and nine-foot windows revealing rows of wicker lawn chairs around a black-granite circular pool. At three in the morning she could see only Frazier Sky, her childhood daydream. He'd laid her down on his mother's double-wide chaise longue and marveled at her body. His touch took her breath away, erased her hunger. That night he told her stories lazily. He'd been through five prep schools and had just been kicked out of Chattanooga. Get a clue, he'd said. I'm not the prep-school type. He smoked and watched the ceiling fan. While he spoke, she thought he didn't seem a teenager at all but an adult, wrapped in a nineteen-year-old body.

All through the following months turning into a year, she had not tired of him, making love to him, waiting for him to call, finding a gun in his glove compartment, and, lately, needle tracks on his arms. It was never dull, there was always something to learn, worry about, wait for. He was more than a distraction, he had become her ocean, and she a swimmer, never wanting the tide to go out or to feel the ground beneath her feet.

Tired, she says aloud. She looks away from herself and down at the bag. A part of her is sick of it, burned out. Her mother must know. How could she not know? It used to be every Saturday and now it is whenever she can be alone here. If it doesn't matter, she might as well snort the whole thing. What's stopping her?

In a ten-second period, Audrey's pre-cocaine voice fills her ears, a tiny violin serenading her from a place of knowing. It says, Just go back downstairs. Forget about it. You don't have to do this. She used to be able to take heed of that voice, answer it, stand around acting like Audrey, forget all about this room, the drawer and its bag. She would tell herself to wait until Frazier brought her some from the Bluff on Saturday nights.

These days, though, she cannot wait. She wakes up believing today she will be okay if she can only get to this bag. She is stuck in purgatory. The cocaine doesn't do what it is supposed to anymore, and yet she still comes here, expecting it to. She believes there is something wrong with her because she can't get high like she used to. The white powder and that short inhale no longer hold the promise of a princess feeling.

Since the cocaine has stopped its magic, the only thing left is Frazier. He is the one who makes her feel. She wants more than anything to be with him and feel the silky draw of their sex. She loves the frightening feeling that something might happen when he lets her stay at his low-rent duplex in Cabbage Town. There are cobwebs in the corners, Santana plays all night from a stereo on the floor, wax from his candles drips onto the crude shelves above his bed, and the sounds of JP fondling a one-night stand seep in from the room next door.

When she is not with Frazier, sensation stays hidden somewhere outside herself, weary of her, finished. She watches her face in the mirror, frowns, smooths her hair with one hand. She should be grateful for this secret high her stepfather's money has unwittingly bought her. A Colombian connection, pure from the plant, not cut up with lactose, speed, or detergent. She looks down at the bag, tries to muster up happiness at this prospect. Coming here has become a duty. Physical homework. She shakes the bag two times and sighs.

Rebecca's bathroom is done up in Moorish-style luxury. Gaslit candles surround the mirror. A small Moroccan rug of mauve and taupe lies across the Spanish-tiled floor. Audrey takes a hand mirror from below the sink and sits on the toilet, lining up the cocaine in five fat rows. Hallelujah, she says under her breath, working to elicit excitement. She remembers the feeling when Frazier first showed her how to sniff white lines off her powder compact in Buckhead's center late one Friday night, a year ago. Now, pouring a pile of cocaine out, she cuts it expertly with the Amex card from her mother's bureau, rolls a ten-dollar bill into a tiny cylinder, and puts her nose to it. Ignoring the smell of sweating money, she takes a sharp breath inward.

After five lines, she has had her share, but there is too much of it for her to regulate herself. She thinks of doing just a few more. Frazier hasn't called, and after the next couple of lines, she will be impatient enough to call him, track him down. She bends over and picks up the bag. When the outside door opens, five more lines are staring at her on the mirror, the rolled bill is in her right hand, and the credit card is clamped between her teeth. White powder spots her top lip. She sits frozen, listening to the sound of feet moving across carpet. Already her heart is beating fast and now it pounds out a rhythm foreign to her, a drumbeat of terror. The veins run icicles to her extremities. She takes the credit card from her mouth and calls out, Hello? Without meaning to.

He appears in the doorway, his hair not perfect like his contemporaries downstairs. He isn't wearing a tie and his camel coat reveals a sense of style she hasn't seen at her mother's parties. He's as handsome as Frazier.

She pulls her hair back so it doesn't get in the lines. Mr. Sky, she says. She swallows.

He looks down at the mirror.

She turns away. The faucet on the tub is gold and clean, revealing a contorted, oblong reflection of her face. She sniffs and puts her hand under her nose. I was just trying to get away from the party, she says.

Yes, well, I guess you came to the right place, he tells her.

She nods.

He looks down at the bag. Life is so bad without it? He gestures to her whole world by holding out his palms and flitting his eyes around the room. Then he seems to realize he is standing by a toilet, and he drops his arms.

Being in Tyler Sky's presence, she feels like a kid again. She lets her hair drop so her face is half hidden and tries to think of what to say. She notices the skin on her arms is almost translucent, she sees the veins. When she looks up, he is staring at her. How are you? he asks quietly. I haven't seen you in a while. You and Frazier been busy?

She shrugs. Pushes her hair back and looks at the mirror. We been kind of busy, she tells him.

You don't like these parties?

Biting her lip, she smiles, nodding her head at the doorway. They're all right, in their own way, she says. Her hand comes up in a jerky, swift motion and she rubs her nose.

He watches her. Did you come up here to use the bathroom? she asks him. Or were you following me?

He leans against the doorway. I won't bullshit you, he tells her. I've known you for a long time, Aud. He intakes a breath. I want to know you're safe. I want to know about Howe coming into your room at night.

She swallows. Silence echoes between them, creates great canyons of awkwardness.

He comes to her, squats by her knee, and picks her hair up, gathering it at the nape of her neck. She wants to move away, but the mirror is there and all that cocaine. Her body stiffens. His hand stops, he drops her hair and draws his body away from hers. I'm not trying to do anything, he says. You're a kid to me, Audrey. Nothing else. I feel like a father to you. He shakes his head. Look, he tells her. Let's start over.

Audrey turns away. He only talks to me, she says hurriedly. We don't do anything. The words stick in her throat. He's lonely. Mom—she lets out something between a cry and a laugh—loves you. Everybody knows she loves you.

Tyler Sky does not move from his squatted position next to her.

She stares at the floor. Can we talk about this somewhere else? she asks.

He nods.

We could go to Howe's study, she tells him.

All right. While he is standing up, he takes the mirror from her lap.

What are you doing? she asks. That's not even mine.

It panics her to watch him move to the double sink. The sound of the faucet washes over her like a heart attack.

Shaking water from the mirror, he bends down and picks up the bag at her feet. Your mother doesn't need it either, he says, putting it in his pocket.

He waits for her in the study off the second-floor lounge. The room is dimly lit and ornamented with gold-framed pictures of dead Howes who fought for America under George Washington. The mantel is black marble and there are Japanese floor-to-ceiling silk runners. The built-in shelves contain books on law and corporate business, a collection of Dickens novels, now and then a tragedy thrown in.

He fingers the bag of cocaine in his pocket and feels scorn for Rebecca. He had not been intending to talk to Audrey at this moment, had wanted instead to go to Rebecca's room and be with her things while she moved through the party downstairs. He'd wanted to feel her silks and lace, look at her jewelry, take in the scent of it all. He wished she would have found him there but knew she wouldn't. Rebecca rarely rewarded anticipation.

A fire is lit in the study to dehydrate any damp creeping in from outside. This means a bow-tied boy will come and put a log on it at some scheduled time Rebecca has decided upon or forgotten so the head maid has planned it. He considers this banality in order to escape the shock of seeing Audrey that way, taking refuge in her mother's drugs. It sickens him to nausea. He thinks again of her bedroom. Minutes before it was a magic, beguiling place and now the things in it are without intrigue, touched with evil.

Minutes pass while he watches the flames burn low in blue and gold. Audrey is so young, a mere child. The way to save a soul. He looks for this title among the many books lining Howe's study. Knowing it isn't there, he tries to elicit rage for Rebecca, but his hatred is not furious. It is limp, exhausted, an abortion of all other fascination he has felt for her thus far. This astonishes him, hits him hard and leaves him empty. If not for Rebecca in that place of emotion, then who? What?

He goes to Howe's personal stash in the antique dry sink and finds a good bottle of port, fills a snifter with it. He stands looking at the liquid, turning it around in the thin crystal glass. He stole liquor as a boy, drank it from a silver flask his father had bought him when he'd turned twelve. He smells the liquid, remembers the sick, pounding feeling of his first hangover. Walking over past the wall of windows, he feeds the port to a ficus tree next to the desk in the corner. While he does this, the benchmark of his passion bends with weight. At a quarter past nine by the antique clock in Howe's study, Tyler Sky's love for Rebecca cracks in half and leaves a space, a surprisingly wide expanse containing fields of light. Relief. Freedom.

He looks around. The colors in the Oriental are richer, wood gleams where once it appeared dull. He feels strong. After this he will go home and call Nancy, ask her to come for a latte at the cozy coffeehouse near his apartment. He wants to make love to her without guilt and the threat of complexity.

Just as he is about to go look for Audrey, she arrives. She has changed into a black silk dress that falls low on her pale, lovely neck and shows the beginnings of her breasts. But Tyler Sky does not see it like that. He sees only her unsmirched flesh and lineless face, how her teenage hands hang awkwardly and her large eyes flit nervously. Shaking the empty port glass, he watches leftover droplets spray on the rug and get lost in its thickness. He sets the glass on the desk, fishes the baggie from his pocket, and holds it up. Is Frazier doing this, too?

She brings her finger below her nose and nods.

He puts the bag back in his pocket. If you do this stuff too much, you could ruin everything. Your grades, your friendships, your shot at college. A high price, he says. I know about it.

She swallows hard and glances from him to the rug and back again. He begins to tell her one more thing, but she interrupts, talking quickly. Her pupils are huge, her mouth works at odd angles, words tumble out. You don't understand. It isn't like I'm bad off, Frazier's worse, Mr. Sky. He's so bad he doesn't come home for three days at a time. I don't know where he is. He's putting it in his arm. You know, injecting drugs you can't get anywhere except in the Bluff and out on Stewart Avenue. I can't find him sometimes for a week. My prom's tonight and I couldn't ask him to go. I mean, I do coke, lots of kids do, but we're not like him. He's crazy for drugs. It's all he does.

It takes Tyler Sky some moments before he understands she is speaking of his son.

When she begins again, the words reach him from far away. The sound of her voice is tinny and thin. How come you and Mrs. Sky— excuse me, Mrs. Layton, never go there? He lives in . . . nothing. It's worse than nothing with some black boy who used to run whores. Audrey wings her hands around while she speaks. The movements are jerky, unnatural on her slight, elegant frame. While she talks, the sharp edges of truth wreak havoc inside him. He is afraid he will throw up. He goes to the fireplace, his back to her, and places his hand on the mantel ledge to steady himself.

He does not think she is saying this to deflect their talk about Howe. He does not relive their scene in the bathroom. He thinks only of Frazier and how it could be his fault as a father. Images flash in his mind. He cannot keep up with them.

I'm sorry, Audrey says.

How long has it been? he asks the fire.

But she doesn't answer him. That's why he doesn't love me, she says.

He turns to see that she is crying. She looks like her mother, hours earlier.

She is desperate in her asking. Isn't it? Isn't that why?

He watches her. He nods. That's exactly why, he says.

I didn't know it until now, she tells him. Until just now when I said all that aloud, I didn't know why he couldn't love me. But that's why. Don't you think? Isn't that why?

He pulls his handkerchief from his breast pocket and brings it to her. Yes, he says. She takes it from him, and he watches her wipe her eyes and nose.

The phone rings.

Balling the handkerchief up in one fist, she runs to the desk. When she picks up the receiver, her voice changes to Southern politeness. Then it evens out again. Hey— No— How come you didn't call before? Don't hang up, wait— Where are you? Please. No, I won't. Well, can I meet you somewhere before that? Why not? I know it is, but if I'm with you, I'll be all right. She picks up a pencil and scribbles on a notepad next to the phone. Okay, she says. All right. And then she says his name, Frazier.

Tyler spins around on his heel and comes to stand at her elbow. I need to talk to him, he says. He can hear the dial tone as soon as he's spoken.

She hangs up slowly, replacing the receiver and looking down at it.

Audrey, I want you to tell me where he is.

No. He doesn't even want me to go. I'll take you to his house tomorrow.

I am going with you now.

But she backpedals. No, you can't. It isn't a place for you. I'll go get him, bring him back. Or I'll bring him to your apartment. She is cleaning up her tears, wiping her hand over her hair; she's lost, floating through the regret of what she has just revealed, trying to find her way back.

Her eyes dart around the room, her mouth works its tight, small muscles, the quickness of her breath makes her breasts rise and fall, which is noticeable in such a low-cut dress. She's seventeen years old. The same amount of years he was married. At seventeen, he was a baby, a hatchling to the world.

I need to get my coat, she says.

Her shoulder is brief beneath his hand and when he touches her she stops as if struck. She turns from him, he thinks to follow her, only he knows he will not win. She is not his daughter. He has no right to her. She goes out the door, through the leather-filled sitting room with its marble busts and topaz veneer. The room closes in on him. Anxiety runs through his veins, palpable energy he wants to save for Frazier, his only son, a child just yesterday.

He walks to the desk. Taking the pad of paper she wrote on, he shades the imprint with a pencil. She has written the words, *no cell phones,* in her hurried scribble and an address he doesn't know. He studies it as he goes down the back stairs, through the kitchen, ignoring the half-turned heads of the cooks wanting to appear incurious. In the front hall, he bumps into Rebecca, coming out of the bathroom, her hand fiddling with her hair. She smells of lilac.

Tyler Sky, what are you doing here? Her eyelashes flirt with her cheeks.

He digs the velvet pouch out of his sports coat and hands it to her. She raises her eyebrows, smiles slightly, and then glances around. Put that away, she says. Snooper.

He stuffs it down her dress, into the soft expanse of breast-filled bra. Great party, he tells her.

She blinks her eyes slowly, the lids perfected in gold.

You got some problems with the roof, though, he says.

She tilts her head, noticing for the first time his tone of voice.

You got leaks damn near everywhere, he tells her. There's a lonely husband and a near-starved girl who need your attention.

Essie Tree walks by. Why, Tyler Sky, she says, looking from him to Rebecca and back again. Rebecca smiles at Essie, but Tyler keeps his eyes pinned on Rebecca. He nods his chin at her. This house is too damn big for the lot of you, he says.

Out of the corner of his eye, he sees Essie Tree open her mouth, her ringed fingers come up and hold her chin. Well, she says.

Blood rushes to his temples. He raises his head and looks at the cathedral ceiling with its stained-glass skylight, picturing angels blowing trumpets and flying toward one another. The skylight's dark except for the staccato nonrhythm of lightning that comes to make heaven out of it. He glances down and watches Essie pick imaginary lint off her dress hem.

I don't know how they did the mushrooms, Rebecca, Essie says. They are outstanding.

Rebecca's voice trembles. Oh, Weiss does it all. He's wonderful. Tyler, maybe you'd like to come to the library a minute. Claire can get you a glass of water.

Tyler pulls his head down to look her in the eyes. I don't need a glass of water. He reaches in his pocket and holds up the paper. I need to find my son.

Rebecca raises her eyebrows. Yes, well. First, let me introduce you to Park Blaine. Excuse us, Essie.

Essie bows her head in permission, smiling, amused and comforted by the promise of gossip.

Rebecca's grip is hard on his elbow. He lets her steer him out to the main hallway. At the living room entrance, he pries her hand off. She puts it back. An edge of hysteria lines her voice. Park! Park, dear, would you be so kind? Tyler Sky is an old friend of ours and he would love to meet you.

The man is elderly, with blood-red skin around his eyeballs, a face spotted and gathered with age. He has an almost full head of white hair, is several inches taller than Tyler, and smokes a pipe. His voice is refined. How do you do? He puts his hand out for Tyler to shake, a leather hand representing all Tyler needs for new business, wealth, success, connections. The tried-and-true formula for getting him on his feet again. If Park Blaine recommends him, then the world will knock his door down with requests.

A pleasure, says Tyler.

Young man, Park says, investigating him with his eyes.

I'd love to stay, Tyler tells him. But I have a family emergency. I have to go see about my son.

The man appears concerned. Of course, he says. I hope everything is all right.

Rebecca laughs and grasps Tyler's elbow again. Mr. Sky worries too much about his son, she says.

Sophie Catchum, coming in with her drink and ivy-green pantsuit, says, Isn't Frazier at the prom with Audrey? Didn't they go tonight?

The prom? Rebecca asks. She looks into Tyler's face, begging him with her terrified blue eyes. Don't be silly, she says quickly, not looking at Sophie. Audrey wouldn't ever go to the prom. She's done with high school now. I mean, she has no use for it except for the academics.

Frazier's having a hard time, he hears himself say. He is aware he has spoken too loudly. The party swells with awkward curiosity. Feet shift, chests billow false pretenses. Fingers scratch imaginary itches behind ears. Men smoke. Tyler clears his throat. We all have our problems, he says. He has his shovel out and is digging deeper. A woman in blue silk turns to stare at him. Fred Reiner stops advising on capital gains. Half-smiling, Tyler runs one hand then the other through his hair. He can feel his right eyebrow begin to tic.

Rebecca's heels click on the front-hall tile. Peering into the coatroom, she says, Toots, will you see that Mr. Tyler gets his coat? Turning toward him, she pulls out her trump card, his reputation as a drunk in Buckhead. You must need a ride, she says. We don't want any accidents tonight because of overindulgence. We'll get you an escort.

Tyler stares at her, his hands dumbly at his sides. You know I'm sober, he says. I told you that at my place this afternoon.

Her face goes to nothing at all, a blank, inhuman mask.

She turns and walks back down the hall, toward the kitchen.

Toots appears with his coat. It occurs to Tyler in this moment of deafening social silence that Toots must have a photographic memory; he always knows whose coats are whose without being told.

Thanks, Tyler says, raising one hand toward the party.

He puts his arm around Toots while they walk to the front door. You should give this up, he tells an embarrassed butler. You're too bright for this.

Toots laughs uneasily. Yes, sir, he says.

When they get out into the slashing backlash of spring rain, Tyler says, Have you seen Audrey?

Yes, sir, Toots says, looking at his wrist as if there were a watch there. Miss Sullivan left about twelve minutes ago.

Tyler turns to his car in a blind panic. It is fast and reliable, but it cannot know all the inner streets of Atlanta. He hopes some latent wisdom can guide him there.

Night

———

1.

THEY ARE TIRED. Working double overtime after a twelve-hour shift, the umber half-moons beneath their eyes tattletale it. Their uniforms are wrinkled. Looking around, Cole realizes the room has become familiar, cracks in the walls are pages of Gracey's life he stared at while she spoke. The floor marks the geography of her body's endurance. That half-repaired window holds stories of her lost faith.

Kelly's top button is undone, he has his feet up on the chair seat. Cole is across from him. Gracey is squatting by the wall, to his left, smoking a cigarette, ashing it by the baseboard.

Maybe there weren't no works in our house, she tells them. No new needle tracks on Sonny's arms, no bags of white powder packed tight and users comin through, but there was Sonny gone a lot and sleepin late, and one day I was walkin with a full load of laundry and I tripped on a floorboard. Instead of putting the board down, I pulled it up. There was bags linin the house, warming it from the bottom up. While I'd been at Mamma's helpin her sew and at the beauty shop sweepin, while Lakeisha and Tyrone were drinkin sodas in the den, and Jackson was traipsin through with his muddy sneakers, those drugs had been sittin silent as dead people under our floorboards.

Gracey waits through the end of her cigarette before she tells them she was three months pregnant at the time. Lakeisha was already in college and Jackson was in the eleventh grade. We was almost free, she says. We was almost lookin at a life together, just me and Son. Our kids out of the henhouse and into the world. And now I was pregnant with another one and Son had gone wrong when I thought he was straight. I was so mad with him, my head was swellin and my heart was beatin and I couldn't swallow right.

She bare-fisted Sonny as he came in the door that afternoon. Skin under her fingernails, bite marks on his neck, tears and sweat down her face and the five o'clock winter day outside, silent and sad for Gracey's botched hope.

Kelly scribbles away while she says their names. Ralph Monroe, known as BC, from L.A., hooked into the Asian connection, and Lupe Rodriguez, known as 12, from Colombia, blackmailing Sonny for a gig gone bad before she met Merridew. Gracey'd never known about it, and he wouldn't tell her the details. Sitting on the bed, his head hanging and his hands between his knees, he would only say, I sold my soul, Gracey. I'm not kiddin you. These guys are the big time. When he looked up, his eyes were mad. I won't fall 'cause of you, he told her. They don't want their dealers hooked. They give 'em opium to keep 'em mellow, and that's it. You not gonna tell and you not gonna be tempted. My woman gotta be clean, too. After this debt's gone, I'm still not usin. I'm gonna make somethin of myself. Money's gonna flow. I'm owed.

Gracey couldn't have drugs under her floorboards. It was too close. How would she ever say no to it? Her body was a weak, unmuscled lover of it.

Son told her there was no other way. He wouldn't talk about it anymore. He walked out the front door, trading his presence with silence.

Dolor entered her. Demons she thought she had beaten

returned. A low-down, life-is-shit feeling came over her. It was so bad she wanted to jump a bridge, take some pills. End it.

Near ten o'clock she called her, could only whisper her name when she answered.

Merridew's voice was sweet, shaking with trepidation. Old emotion ripened again. Gracey? she said, as if it had been only yesterday.

Gracey pleaded.

On the other end was refusal. Girl, I want you, you know that. Only I'm scared to death you won't stay clean, and you won't keep away from Son. I got left and that hurt real bad and I can't do it again to myself unless you gone from him for good and gone from drugs for good and we can go at it like two grown women. I have to do it like that, Gracey. I been learning and growing, and that's the only way.

Gracey sat on the kitchen floor in an empty house, the telephone cord wrapped around her waist. She cried and tried to explain. Drugs in her floorboards, just a few feet away, eating the house from underneath. If only Merridew would come pick her up, save her.

Merridew's resolve was strong. You're tempting me, sweet girl, but I can't until you're done with your man and done with your drugs.

At quarter of eleven they hung up. No one was home. The clock ticked through the house in grim response to Gracey's loneliness.

Later Gracey could be seen walking down Northside Drive. Pretending she had no idea what she was looking for. TBird, a lawyer in gabardine and silks, came by in his black Camaro, duded-up lights, dice off the rearview, rug-wear seats. He rolled down his window and leaned toward her. He had a strong, chiseled face and a fit body, not a worry in the world and never would till he died. What's a pretty thing like you doin out on a night like this? he asked her.

I'm runnin away from home, Gracey told him.

The passenger door was a friendly open mouth.

Driving toward Macon, he said, I was always in love with you, girl. You out bad with Son?

TBird promised a good time. He said Son had got himself all uppity. No one knew who he was dealin with. He ain't usin, TBird told her, and he ain't sharin his stash. We all mad at him.

Out on the highway, she was treated to cool wind and the bright-coned light of passing streetlamps. At a lookout point south of Atlanta, TBird tied off, the needle lengthwise in his mouth. He turned to Gracey, inviting her. She was hypnotized. Memory went pungent through her body. She dove in. It swallowed her. The release was sweet and familiar, sex with your best ex-lover, relief again after eight long years.

Driving through the outskirts, they stopped at private clubs so smoky Gracey couldn't see her feet. Guys named Root and Forty-Five touched her back and called her beautiful. Liquor flowed and drugs were plentiful. Girls in nipple brags and crotch triangles lounged in back rooms on velvet couches beside pyramids of cocaine. Gracey was sick with the pleasure of the drugs, as if it were her first time. She knew she could die, doing it again after so long, but the worry disappeared with the high. Sitting back with her eyes closed, she listened to the sound of voices, the ring of ice against glasses, the bursts of tawdry laughter. She could hear the ladies making love to each other in the corners. Gracey, nodding off in a double-wide easy chair with ruby tassels, thought how it would be nice to die there.

Sometime later TBird was on top of her, his breath in her ear, his leather pants around his ankles, his strange mouth on Gracey's throat. I love you, I always loved you. Her legs and torso were numb, and her head spun like a child's top.

She fell in and out of sleep on a rust shag rug. When she was conscious, she prayed aloud to the woman who birthed her. I'm sorry, Mamma. I can't do good. I ain't right, Mamma.

All around her, long-limbed, half-naked girls were sleeping on stools. Their heads flopped over a crimson bar, their hands in some john's lap. People with cocaine jitters were still sucking powder up their noses. They watched her, mildly interested.

She woke with TBird asleep on top of her, his head on her collarbone, his penis cuddled inside her body. I want to go home now, she told him, pushing him off her.

He came to, sober and angry, rubbed his eyes, and zipped up his fly. What you kickin up all this fuss for, bitch? He rubbed a hand over his white lips and spit on the carpet.

He and some others drove her home. In the backseat, they did cocaine off vinyl records. The sky was a metallic gray. Run-D.M.C. pounded out the speakers, and Gracey's headache made it hard for her to think. She was jonesing, suffering the shakes and a fever.

When they got to her house, Gracey stumbled out of the car, mother of two grown kids, missing all her hairpins, her zipper jammed on the side of her dress so she had to hold it together, thirty-eight years old, a baby due in six short months.

Kelly interrupts, taps his pencil against the yellow pad. Where's TBird now? he asks.

Gracey's body is stiff from sitting, a starched and pressed camise left folded for too long. She stands tall and stretches her arms, shakes both her legs out. He's still there, in the Bluff. Maintenance user. Never goes down worse than he was the month before.

He's dealing to kids, Kelly says, watching her cross the floor.

Who ain't dealin to kids? Gracey asks. He's dealin to anyone who'll buy it. And he's runnin whores. Eighteen Simpson where he deals. Back of that house there's a garage, looks closed up. Saturday night at eleven o'clock.

Kelly's eyebrows rise while he scribbles.

That was the beginning of a whole 'nother time of druggin for me. Gracey follows the perimeter of the room, keeping one foot in front of the other, like a tightrope walker. Full-blown AIDS cases walkin around like skeletons in the Bluff. Kids who'd been hittin it with the syringe and the cooker were all fucked up from it. I always knew it when I saw someone with the AIDS in their eyes. Sonny and I used to say they got the black widow there. Them cases were dyin right and left and I knew if I let anyone in on my high, I could catch that shit in my blood. So my usin was lonelier than ever. All the drugs I wanted were in my floorboards, and after that night with TBird, I went solo. I'd go to the Korean over there on Ashby, get two-dollar syringes. I always used clean Johnsons. Never let anybody in on my cooker. My usin was a secret from Son, my way to get back at him. Also, it was how I escaped from that feelin that my life ain't never gonna come to good anyhow. He'd leave for the day and I'd pick up the floor to see what I could find. He got all kinds of shit under there, crack, cocaine, heroin. Guns.

Kelly moves his feet so Gracey can sit down. She brushes the chair with her palm and puts the coat across her lap, smooths it with her long fingers and tells them she was high when she went to the doctor for her prenatal appointment. He was a skinny, square-headed cracker with a cold stethoscope. She sat on a stiff paper runner on the examining table while he lectured.

You have to clean up your act, he said. Your age, your history, it doesn't bode well for this baby. You've got to stop everything— cigarettes, alcohol, cocaine, heroin, pills. Everything.

That doctor was so smart, Gracey says. White and educated, the world at his fingertips. You try quittin everything, Gracey thought to say to him. You be me for a day.

No one wants this baby anyhow, Gracey told him as she got off the table.

Their house had a chute on the side of it. Drugs were sent down it on wheeled runners in the middle of the night. There were days when she picked up the boards and nothing was there. She'd sit waiting, biting her nails until they bled. She learned the schedule—drop off Friday and Tuesday, pick up Saturday and Wednesday.

Gracey was on the toilet at ten o'clock one Thursday morning when Son came in, his clothes reeking of the sweet smell of smoked poppy. Gracey, you shootin our money, he said. I know what you been doin. This ain't no small-time shit. I got to distribute to six different dealers, and they got hundreds of clients. There's a runner for guns and a runner for drugs. And that's the least of it. I got bankers, politicians, business owners. All of 'em want their drugs. I can't handle you smokin the profits. I'm savin up, Gracey, workin off my debt to them jackasses, and I'm gonna make it big when it's all said and done. But I won't be married to no junkie.

Gracey's nose bled while he talked. She had no energy to wipe it off. She just lifted her chin and let it run sideways down her face. You ain't divorcin me, she told him. You got to be dead if you want me gone, 'cause I got a load of your business and I can turn you in like that. She tried to snap her fingers, but they were rubber. You deal, I use, she told him. That's the rules. I'm a junkie and I love it.

My ass is on the line for you, Gracey, Son said. You walkin on thin ice. You got three days to get cleaned up or I'm leavin your ass. I'm sick of this.

She knew he meant it. But she was high, laughed in his face, and spit blood at him.

Three days later, dirty dishes were piled in the sink, dirty laundry lay in clumps around the house, all the beds were unmade. She had folded the carpets over and torn up the floorboards, and she stood in a housedress, pulling her hair out. The stash was gone. Moved.

And then she went into early labor.

Something wasn't right with the baby's head. It was scrunched up inside and the wrong way up. Gracey went through withdrawal in a stark hospital room while days flipped over into nights until she was in delivery, screaming to God. Two doctors and twice as many nurses tried to help. Lakeisha and Mamma stayed by her side while Gracey's eyes darted from the medical screens to the surgical masks, and pain shot down her legs, across her stomach and back. She screamed until she broke a blood vessel in one eye and then she had no spit or voice left for yelling.

The child came out the wrong way, feet first, minus the joyful hooting and hollering and crying. Shut your eyes, the nurse said.

Gracey is silent. Kelly and Cole watch the table. Cole's throat constricts. He dares not look up. The three of them let minutes pass.

Gracey's voice is a thrown rock through ice. The umbilical cord was wrapped twice around my baby's neck, she says. I strangled her. The thing that keeps a baby to its mamma killed my little girl. Son wasn't even there. He ain't seen me through none of it. When I called home, nobody answered. The doctor come in and give me twenty-five millis of Dem for my pain.

That ain't gonna do shit, Gracey told him.

You can't use this hospital to get high, he said. He was writing something on his chart, his pink face real proud, his eyes like two mean BBs in his head.

I'm shootin a hundred dollars' worth of heroin a day, Gracey told him. And you think twenty-five millis of Dem is gonna get me high? You the man did my lapro whatever that thing is, goin way up there and flingin around my used-up, half-dead fallopian tube, and you think that doesn't hurt like a son of a bitch? Then you chargin me fifteen bucks a Tylenol and tellin me that should aid my pain?

Well, the doctor said, flipping his chart page. I don't want you to OD.

Hell, Doc, Gracey said, you talkin to a girl who's popped pills, smoked reefer, shot dope, and taken methadone all in the same day and you don't want me to OD? I'm not braggin, but my system can handle more than your winky-assed system.

The doctor hung Gracey's chart at the end of the bed and gave a tight little smile. That may be so, he said. But I'm not giving you more painkillers. You have a drug problem, and if this baby'd been born alive, you wouldn't have been able to keep her anyway.

If he thought that made me feel better, Gracey said, he was dead wrong. I was so tired. I just closed my eyes and hoped he be gone when I opened 'em again.

Sonny didn't call. He never came by.

On Friday, her mamma drove her home. The house was quiet. Keisha was at Tyrone's. Jackson was nowhere to be seen. Gracey'd suspected since that night with TBird that her son was out finding his own high, stealing again, skipping school, but she was too concerned with her own life to worry about his. Sonny wasn't there. All his clothes were hanging in the closets. Dirty dishes were in the sink. When she looked under the floorboards, there was nothing.

Gracey leans her back against the door to the interrogation room. I couldn't even think where to look, she says. I sat on the couch in the living room all day and all night waitin on him. It was spooky. She stares at one spot on the floor as if watching the memory emerge. That phone didn't never ring, she says. I didn't eat or move or sleep or nothin. My handbag was still on my shoulder and I was wearin the same dress I came home in.

Four o'clock the next day, the phone rang. Some lady said, You Sonny's girl?

I said, Who's this?

She had a fake, falsetto-type voice. He your man? she asked me.

He is that if you livin, I said.

I'm sorry, she said. Sonny had been sold some bad stuff. Filled with salt. Your man is dead.

Then she hung up on me.

2.

THEY'D LEFT THE GROCERY STORE carrying a rotisserie chicken, roasting stick still inside, whistled all the way down the sidewalk and then, turning the corner, ran. JP's finger-size dreads bopped up and down while Frazier followed him. Jumping over the railroad tie bordering the parking lot, they'd passed through thickets and brambles, charred trash bins and pieces of automobiles, a steering wheel half broken, empty cartons of milk, and a hole in the chain-link fence next to Cabbage Town.

Now JP's sitting on the couch with a chicken bone in his mouth, watching *Bugs Bunny*.

Frazier hangs up the phone and stands behind him, biting the side of his thumbnail.

Is she comin over? JP asks.

She's in Buckhead. I don't have time to wait for her. With Feather down, there's gonna be a line if anything gets there tonight. She said she'd meet me there.

That's your jones talkin, man. You shit-house crazy. She can't meet you there.

She'll be all right, says Frazier.

Elmer runs, shotgun in hand, after that wiseass rabbit.

She ever been there before? JP asks.

No.

Don't let her fire up the first time, JP tells him. She got that sad look lately, she'd be hooked on tight. Beautiful girl like that don't need to be ruined by this shit.

Frazier glances down at the chicken, thinks about pulling off a leg. His stomach turns over with the idea of it. I know that, JP, he says.

JP nods. You got it covered. He lifts up two fingers in a peace sign and eats.

You're just as in love with her as I am. Frazier smiles at him.

JP doesn't look back. He laughs. I am that, my man. I am that.

3.

GRACEY SITS CROSS-LEGGED on the floor, a cigarette burned down to the filter smoking in her hand. She tells them about the day the feds came and tore through her house, repossessed it. She and Lakeisha watched from the car. Lakeisha had to use all her strength to fight a grown woman, her mother. Gracey flailed her arms. Let me out, she wailed. I gotta be outta here. Finally, the car door slammed and Gracey Fill ran husbandless through the alleyways of inner-city Atlanta.

She says she went crazy, stalked drugs through the streets. Days, weeks, and months went by in a blur. For almost three years, she lived in rooming houses for two dollars a night, buying doses the size of her fingernail for five dollars, breaking the crack up, rolling it like cigarettes, flame-broiling the lactose, procaine, and speed powder. She learned quickly that car antennas burn your lips. She used two-dollar stems, glass straight shooters, and watched the lazy smoke come through to her.

She could get anything she wanted all over the city, K4s and K2s, oxycutter, morphine on Cleveland Avenue, Pool Creek, Perry Homes, Fair Street Bottom. Always someone to talk to, get high with, whip up ideas about conspiracy theories. Dealers set up on Kennedy Street, and a little white boy named Larry sold sheets of animal painkillers out of the Alamo. She'd water it down and inject it into her skin.

We was all doin that for a while, Gracey tells them, picking out another cigarette and lighting it with a match struck on the wall's baseboard. But you already know that, she says, glancing at Kelly. 'Cause you were the one supportin us. Thank you very much. In Zone Three, near Grant Park, there was a whole group of you po-pos protectin the dealers, tippin them off, providin muscle for money.

Kelly will not look at her.

You want names? she asks.

He sits white-lipped, his eyebrows rimmed pale.

I don't think you do, Gracey tells him. You the one I seen. I'm sure of it now, and I got a lot of sisters and brothers seen you, too. We know what you did and what you doin. I don't give a shit, Mr. John Q. You do what you need to do to get on, but you better drop that high-and-mighty attitude. Truth is, we all the same.

Kelly shifts in his seat. Droplets of sweat stand out along his upper lip. His ears have turned a brilliant red. He does not look at Cole.

Gracey keeps talking. I lived bad, she says. She tells about the smell in rooming houses, smoke and sex and death and blood. People sneaking in, pulling knives, selling their goods for a little pleasure. Outside, old La-Z-Boys sat in dirt lots under oak trees next to Jesus memorabilia and rotted in the rain. Inside, people got their freak on, died in the middle of their dreams, crawled on the floor, paranoid, cutting themselves with dull razors. They sat on bug-infested mattresses, held up by cinder blocks. Rats big as felines made their nests in the floorboards, their inky eyes watching side-long while the roomers sexed one another. No paint on the walls, Sheetrock and nails and caved-in roofs, electric fires, squatters' rights, and the desperate scream of an addict at four A.M.

On Summer Hill and Reed Street, teenagers were dying for the sake of the pipe and the needle. I don't recommend that to nobody's child nowhere, Gracey tells them. Cole sees her hand tremble when she brings the smoke to her mouth.

She explains how she got money: till tapping at convenience marts, stealing girdles from Maidenform downtown, then walking into department stores and stuffing merchandise in them. She went to warehouses that sold things in bulk, and she'd buy fifty-roll toilet-paper boxes and take the inside rolls out, shove video cameras, stereo equipment, jewelry in there. She would get six hundred dollars worth of items for ten bucks. Or she'd tell the manager she was moving and needed boxes. She'd stack two dummy boxes on top and fill the rest with hot products. Afterward, she took it all to Simpson and Ashby and sold it for money for drugs.

Sometimes she rented her body out to filthy men with rotting teeth and gray tongues, skin and bone and track marks and bruises, abscesses and cracked lips.

Only thing I don't want is the AIDS, Gracey would tell the men. You don't got no condom, I don't got no condom, ain't no shit goin down.

There were places you could get free condoms, Gracey says. That health van come around every week and that lady doin needle exchange on Jones, she and hers used to do the walk on Ponce and Boulevard and we'd get us condoms and needles that way. You people don't want to give those programs money. Politicians think they save a buck by not givin us needles and condoms. Our hospitals are gonna fill up with drug cripples. They spendin up the yazoo for people who are sick and don't got insurance. Addicts waitin to die in Grady with the AIDS, wearin nose harnesses and needin IVs, swallowin hundreds of dollars worth of AZT a day. You give 'em clean needles and some condoms, you can clear some of them patients out of your medical centers.

When Cole looks over, Gracey has her eyes fixed on Kelly. He ain't the culprit, she says, nodding at him. He just a puppet of the culprit. Kelly keeps his eyes on the scribble pad, bouncing his pencil by its eraser.

Gracey tells them the thrill of the drug ended early. It was just the motions. A year passed, then two, then she lost track. Time bent and stretched like a Dalí painting, the clock melting into a surreal landscape. Gracey could not get out. She knew she was headed for a granite block, a wood box in soil, but she had no recourse, no other way to survive.

They got them meth clinics every which way, she says. One is set up right near Grady. I'd walk by there a lot. I knew Earl Kay worked there. He real tall and skinny, with a face like a eel. When I was eighteen, he'd picked me up walkin home from Crystal's and tried to rape me. I wanted to go in, only I kept thinkin, How am I gonna get better if I got that memory starin me in the face? Then one day I was on Kennedy shootin up behind the church. I thought I'd caught a vein, but I was shakin so bad from not using for twenty-four hours, the plunger missed and my whole arm went lumpy. That shit traveled to the left side of my heart muscle. I couldn't move. The next day I was in the meth clinic. I decided if I didn't think that rapist could get better, how am I ever gonna? It was early September, weather like a bitch in heat. This woman at the meth clinic say, How can we help you?

I say, I want to get me on some methadone.

What's your addiction? she asked me.

You name it, I told her.

She was white, with brown hair curled up at the end and these tiny glasses no bigger than her eyeballs. Her hands were raw and chapped and she kept dippin her fingers in a plastic thing of Vaseline petroleum jelly, rubbing them over each other. We was in a little office with a clock on the wall and nothin else. No windows. She said, Well, you won't do anything else but methadone while you are on this program. No marijuana, alcohol, pills, cocaine. Nothing. If you do, you will be put off the program.

I told her, Right now I just want to get off heroin, I can deal with the other stuff. Heroin's always been my main thing.

She raised them pale eyebrows and said, Well, you do what

you want. But we will test your urine and if it's not clean, then we will have to put you off the program.

Ain't gonna cost me a nickel on the street to buy me some clean urine, I told her.

She sighed real big, like I was the imposition of her life, and said, Look, if you feel like you can't keep off drugs right now, you're not ready for the program. We'll give you a few more months on the street with the other junkies and the Red Dogs and see how you like that. I mean, isn't that why you are in here?

Gracey tells them she started to cry. I was afraid I wouldn't never stop cryin, she says. I just blubbered on. I need love, I told her. I want to be treated here, Gracey points to her heart. Not here, she points to her bladder. I told the lady, You can't see it right now, 'cause I'm all messed up, but I'm more than dirty urine. I been tossed every which way the wind blow and now I need somebody to uplift me. I want somebody to say I got purpose in life and that my time's not gone. In order to get off this shit, I need not to be scared, always lookin over my shoulder for somebody to hit me. I need someone to let me know I could still be somebody, be loved properly.

When I looked up, that lady had her hands in her lap and she was nodding her head like she done heard it every day. We'll start you out with a maintenance dose, she said it like I hadn't told her nothin. I'd just poured my heart out to her and she showed me the methadone chart with her pencil tip.

Cole watches Gracey's fists open and close in her lap. She looks up at him and shakes her head. That lady hadn't listened to a word I said.

Soon as I got out, there was dealers at the meth clinic door. That night I was back at the roomin house. I went to the meth clinic today, I told Henry Cool. I wanted to try to get off this shit, little by little.

My friend C.C. was in there. She say, Girl, let me tell you a thing or two. I was on meth for six months. Them people think they know what you need 'cause they got a diploma. But they just as bad as the junkies. They gettin high and havin sex in the bathroom. They got guest rooms at home full of the methadone they stole. And at the same time they sendin you to Narcotics Anonymous, which is sayin you gotta be honest in order to get better. The next day them meth clinic workers be robbin you blind. You can't never ask to see your dose 'cause they play mad with you and say you're being difficult, but you can feel it in how they hit you when your dose is off. That ain't gonna get you better. What you gonna do about it? Sure, you could stand up and tell all till you blue in the face, only who gonna listen to you? You a junkie.

Everybody in there, noddin and smokin and sayin, Word. Right on.

4.

THE OLD HOTEL IS BUILT from the remains of an antebellum mansion. All shades are drawn so cops can't look in from the rooftops. Candles burn in cracked saucers on glass tables. The thick wood-and-plaster walls are muraled with fantastic scenes painted by acid heads. Pregnant swirls of red violence burst from a blood-colored palette. Overstuffed couches line the rooms and dim lights frame half-shadowed faces. Fingers grip mirrors and rolled twenties. Boys glance around and duck their heads, slinking through secret doors with businessmen. Gone. Into a widened mouth. Pants around the businessman's pale thighs, his hands in the boy's hair, his thighs shivering. The boys work to aid the money holder in his escape. Their post-carnal depression is relieved by soft green paper money that buys them relief. No longer crawling on their bellies like snakes, they are flying. True birds.

Suspended in space are the smells of tobacco and dope, the sounds of low conversation. Lighters fire up tinfoil and powder. Glass tubes clink against teeth. Young sixteen-year-olds cry with happiness, lay their alabaster bodies down, and let them be entered.

Their imaginations inhabit peaceful galaxies. Their blood goes heavy with the drug. Their libido turns indolent.

Audrey's fire-colored hair falls loosely around her. She's still a little high from those five fat lines of her mother's, but she's coming down, moving like a smoke billow through the room. Faces stare up at her with dilated eyes and sweating brows. They are smoking cigarettes, talking importantly about very little.

Frazier is not there. JP is not there. Finally she sits on a beige leather couch in the first room, to the left of the front hall. The ebony table before her is shaped like a sperm. A black girl, neat and tidy in long braids, sits next to her. Hey, she says, glancing at Audrey with her big, almond-shaped eyes. A tattoo on her arm reads: JULIAN 1969–1997.

I'm supposed to meet Frazier Sky here, Audrey tells her. Have you seen him?

A red-haired boy comes and sits beside the black girl, who is shaking her head in response to Audrey's question. He says hello and sets his works in front of him, a square piece of tinfoil, a spoon, two packets of powder, his tie and needle.

Audrey was sent to Japan once with Howe when he had business there. They'd sat for hours in a teahouse witnessing the ceremony involving porcelain pots, cups, saucers, and steam. The Japanese had an ancient, practiced way of pouring, high and then low. There was an art to it. She transposes the two in her mind while the red-haired boy lays his things on the table. Beside and a little behind her is an open door and people talk in the hallway, leaning against doorjambs. Their voices burn a low-flame fire. The listeners are a simple blue glow.

She leans over the girl and speaks to the redhead. Do you know Frazier Sky?

Uh-huh. He checks the hallway behind her, then turns his eyes to hers as if noticing her for the first time. He looks her up and down and smiles slowly at what he sees. You ever done brown before? he asks her.

She shakes her head.

He glances down at the table. How come?

My boyfriend won't let me.

You with Frazier Sky and he won't let you shoot brown? What a fucking hypocrite.

Audrey fiddles with her hands on her lap. The boy has straight teeth, blue eyes, and a strong jawline. He's wearing a white T-shirt and under the sleeves his muscles contour perfectly. Frazier may never come. The thought leaks despair through her and there isn't enough cocaine left in her system to jam it back into place, deep within. She tilts her head at the boy. I'm not with him now, she says.

He watches her, nodding slowly.

The black girl has her head back against the sofa, watching this interchange. She touches Audrey's hair. Her smile is drowsy; it starts on the left side of her mouth and travels in an unrushed wave to the right side. Her fingers feel sensual on Audrey's neck, a breath of touch. Don't you think she's pretty, honey?

The boy nods.

We been waitin on someone like you, she says. She sits up and puts a bag of cocaine in front of them on the table. You want to hang out with us tonight? We could dip in while he's setting up. I'm Sistine, by the way. This is Otis.

Audrey smiles and says her name.

They do three lines each, then set out nine more. They are talking like old friends by the time the mirror is licked clean. Sistine goes to Spelman College, Otis is a junior at Emory; his father is a top scientist at the CDC and hers works for corporate sales at Coca-Cola. They think corporations are the cancer that is eating America. The disease of the gentry, they call it. Audrey tells them about the party, her parents. They nod, compassionately rolling their eyes. Authority sucks.

By the time Sistine gets up to go to the bathroom, Audrey's hands are sweating and she can't keep her nose from running, pulls a finger beneath it every few seconds. Her teeth grit together and her gums and cheeks are numb. She wants to tell this couple everything she knows, which is a lot. She believes she has learned the whole of the world in her seventeen years.

Otis leans back and looks at her. He points to the square plastic bag of grainy brown powder. This is the best you're gonna get, he says. It's not anything like cocaine. It's gonna make you calm, gonna be real cool with everything once you're on this. We copped from Feather couple of days ago. He just got in a Rocket stash, never let us down. All of them, he nods in the direction of the hallway, are waitin on Feather, but we know where he is, so we don't have to wait in line. He trusts us.

Audrey nods, pulls her hair in back of her, and looks at the bag. How do you know Frazier? she asks.

The boy shrugs and gestures vaguely. Around, he says.

If there was a phone, I could call him, Audrey tells him.

He looks at her for what seems like a long time. Phones aren't allowed in here, he finally says. Anyway, what are you all in love with Frazier Sky for? He doesn't love anyone but himself.

Her dander rises and stays a violet-blue color within her. You must not know him very well, she says.

He shrugs. I know when I see a heartbroken girl beside me who needs somebody to pay her some attention. I got a good eye and a nose that smells trouble ten miles away, and you're in for some painful times if you stay with Frazier Sky.

Sistine comes back and sits down next to Otis. The front door opens and they both lean over the side of the couch to see who it is. Rain drips from the top of the jamb.

Deneeka stands at the threshold. She's wearing a fur coat found on a passed-out drunk lying in front of the Krispy Kreme on Ponce. It's got bald patches on the sleeves and the hem is unraveled, but in it she is a queen, twirling around, bringing cake for her subjects. Behind her the door opens to breezy rain, a night swollen with humidity. Jenkins Labor, squatter's rights on the place, small-time dealer, and addict in training, comes in after her. He bangs his chest four times and two vials vomit out his mouth. He fists them while the crowd circles. We got five-o-in-the-hole, he says. Comin down the street. Y'all better get away from that bomb. Quit your smokes for a minute, hold your high. Daisy, get the light in the bathroom. There's a candle in the front window needs to be blown out.

In the dark, someone calls out, Where's Feather?

Deneeka's voice is high, shrill, promising. Here I am, she calls. You don't need him any more. Eyes adjust and shapes emerge out of darkness. She swirls in her coat, pats the young boys' heads, and swishes her thighs at them.

The place goes quiet for seven long minutes while the cops pass by.

Then Jenkins yells out, All ye, all ye, home come free.

Someone switches the lights on.

Hi, baby, Deneeka says to the good-looking ones. You doin anything after this?

Some laugh, good-naturedly flirting back; they are the ones nursing chippies, in no real hurry for their Saturday-night fun. But others stand rigid, eager, having held out too long for the drugs.

She sits on the bottom step of the long stairway that used to lead to the guests' rooms and begins to pull out her goods while the crowd gathers.

Jenkins is telling everyone about the sweep that morning. They took RJ's caps, his cocaine, all that, he says.

Others can be heard initiating novices. You think cocaine is good, you should try ice, crack, heroin.

In the side room, Sistine and Otis are hovered about Audrey. She is scared, eyeing the needle. I didn't even want to get my ears pierced, she tells them. She stalls, thinking maybe Frazier will come through the door, her familiarity, her savior.

You don't have to put it in a vein, says Otis. But it's better if you do. If you're gonna sniff it, you're gonna wish you skin-popped it. If you skin-pop, you're gonna wish you shot up.

5.

KELLY HAS HIS HEAD back and his eyes closed. On his arms and forehead, fat blue lines protrude in swollen rivers. He hasn't said a word since Gracey revealed the knowledge of what he has done. It is as if he were no longer in the room. Gracey sits on the floor below the window. Her dress rides just above her knees and she makes circles on her kneecaps with her pointer finger. When she starts to speak, Cole lets his mind's eye see the pictures she paints with her words.

I felt bad goin to Mamma's, she says, but I didn't have nowhere else to go. I couldn't keep track of time. Gracey waves a hand over her head in a sweeping motion. It just flew by. But I knew it had been a long time since I tried the meth clinic. I was so wore out and hungry, spent all my money on bags of girl and boy. I couldn't get a trick right 'cause I was shriveled like a prune inside and some white stuff was comin out me that smelled bad. That shit made me nervous. I needed a good meal and a warm bath before I saw Mamma. I went anyhow.

She remembers for Cole how the lawn on Jett Street was crabgrassed over. The roof was peeling and a railing dangled from the porch. Gray paint splintered under her feet when she walked on it. One hinge was rusted through on the front door. She stepped inside. The house was still. A smell like unwashed skin assaulted her.

Mamma, she called out.

Her mother's thin voice called back, Who's there?

Mrs. Moore was in her bedroom with Kleenexes on her lap. Her dilated eyes were swimming in shit-colored gook and her skin had turned an ashen color. A jelly jar next to her bed was filled to its brim with urine. Her mamma's belly had swelled to pregnant-looking hardness. Gracey held her mamma's hand, burning hot in the middle of April in Atlanta. I'm not feeling too well, her mamma said, but May Clark has been takin good care of me, and Lakeisha comes by at four most days.

Gracey's heart sank. She argued furiously with her mother about going to the hospital. Finally, she wrapped her in a blanket and carried her out. May Clark stood on the side lawn with her concern, explaining about the meals and the weekly washings. Lakeisha's been so good, she said while she followed them down the hill, toward the bus stop. She didn't know where to find you. May's voice, tinged with accusation, trailed off.

In the city bus, her eighty-pound mamma sat rigidly, drowning in the red afghan from her mother's mother.

A two-hour wait in Grady before the nurse came out and called her name.

After the initial check-in with the doctor, Gracey was told to stay in the waiting room. She had no money, was strung out on drugs, and going into a jones.

Gracey describes how the woman entered, wearing a skirt and leather boots, her hair cut short in an Afro. She was holding the door for two young kids, coaxing them, laughing at the little dawdling one with her finger in her nose. Their mother is Mrs. Heather Smith, she told the receptionist. A nurse came around and took the kids by their shoulders, then disappeared through the swinging doors while the woman stood waving at their backs.

She was almost out the exit when Gracey called to her. Everyone in the place watched Merridew Lewis walk forward, take Gracey's face in her hands, kiss her wasted cheeks, and say in a soft voice, Gracey Fill, Gracey. Tracing the contours of her jaw with one delicate finger, she looked in her eyes, then she sat her down so they could talk.

Gracey was in a Salvation Army Dumpster outfit, no bra, tangled hair, shaking limbs. Merridew wore fabric-softened clothes, her skin was honey-scented. She was making a name for herself in the field of recovery, counseling crack mothers and fund-raising to get a home for their children.

Without sugarcoating, Gracey explained to Merridew, honest as she could, how she'd been living, vomit and blood, fight scars and stomach pains, joneses and fixes, always the dream of a high. Merridew listened and nodded, watching her closely.

I went to Mamma's 'cause I don't want to do it anymore, Gracey told her. I want to stop. I don't know how to pull the lever so the ride slows. And now this, she said, pointing to the doors leading to the sick. Mamma's pancreas and liver are full up with cancer. They knew as soon as they saw her.

Merridew's gaze did not follow Gracey's finger to the door. You want to get clean? Her eyes glinted with the flame of low-intensity hope and her voice was strong. How you gonna do it? she asked.

Gracey's soft answer, I don't know. I don't have a clue. She spoke in wearied nostalgia of the first time she kicked. The peaceful quiet of her days with Merridew. How clean I got, said Gracey. And stayed that way for one long while.

Merridew didn't answer.

Sonny died, Gracey said.

A breath of relief escaped Merridew's mouth.

When the doctor came out, he thought they were sisters and called them both over.

They stood leaning against the nurses' station while he flipped through the chart. Most likely it started in her ovaries, he said. And spread from there.

They nodded in unison.

Three months left to live. If that.

Her mother would not stay put in the hospital. The doctor insisted on admittance and then gave up, succumbing to a hopeless case of near death.

6.

MARTA'S GOT A HALF–EMPTY train and Frazier ducks into it. On the other end, white boys, wanna-be gangsters, stare at themselves in the plate-glass windows, their reflections warped and ghostly in the blackness. Frazier fingers the scarf he stole for Audrey in his pocket and leans against the pole, thinking how much forty will get him and who will be dealing now that their connect's down. He remembers Feather's blue face and the woman-man bending on one knee next to him.

Five minutes into the trip, while they are under a tunnel, the train's lights flicker and go out. The white gangsters whoop and holler. Frazier's hand goes instinctively to his breast pocket, holding his wallet. The car slugs to a sudden stop. All goes quiet. His eyes adjust to the light. He notices the ropes and tubing of MARTA's inner belly out the window. Someone brushes against his back, and he turns to see the shadowy figure of a thin-haired man with fat cheeks slinking into a near corner, soliciting him. Frazier almost says something to ward him off, then doesn't. Another man seated in the front watches him, eager and needy. The man in back breathes heavily.

Over near the side window, the whitesters recover from the silence and start to make farting noises, talking in loud tones about chicks and ass, man. Tits and ass, says another. I'm a butt guy, says the first. They laugh, skullcaps and waists down to their knees.

What time is it? Frazier nods to the man in the front seat.

The passenger leans forward, puts his hand behind his ear to show he hasn't heard. His whole face gets into the act, ardent, overzealous.

Frazier wonders if he's deaf. He moves closer and asks again.

The guy stands, shows him the face of his glow-in-the-dark Timex. It's ten-fifteen. He sidles up, not a half foot from Frazier. Nice night, huh? he asks.

Frazier stares at the aisle in concentrated disinterest.

The man slides his fingers over his belly and Frazier understands the wheezing man huddled in the corner is stroking himself inside his own trousers. They are accomplices and competitors.

How did you pick me? the man with the watch asks.

I didn't pick you, Frazier says. I asked you what time it was. He walks toward the end of the train, where the kids are. The teenagers' din quiets for a second. He sits. The boys ignore him, continue their talk. For twenty minutes, he endures adolescent braggery, then slumps farther down in his seat, his hood over his eyes, and falls into a half slumber. Finally the lights sputter on and in one asthmatic gasp, the car lurches forward and gains speed. At the next stop, he switches trains. He gets off near Morehouse College, pulls the hood of his sweatshirt over his head, and starts walking toward the hotel.

Audrey is watching Otis dump heroin into a spoon, put a few drops of water and vitamin C on it, cook it up with a lighter until it boils. He drops the cotton ball in the liquid, presses the tip of the needle into the cotton, and draws it into the syringe.

Always kick the needle with your pointer finger, he tells Audrey, those little bumps can travel to your heart and kill you.

The two teach her how to do it, a verbal trial run before the real thing. Release the tourniquet as soon as you've jacked. And if you're gonna do it again, use a new pick every time so you don't get infected. You don't want a dirty hit, either. These guys are using cigarette filters and shit. You got to use this. Otis points to his bag of cotton.

What is it? Audrey's pupils are big. She is excited. This is a new high, like cocaine the first time. But better, they keep telling her. I swear.

Dental cotton, Sistine says. It's already rolled into a ball and nothing will get in your mix. You can use toilet paper if you don't have any dental cotton.

Splitting through Audrey's mind is a flash of layered memory: her father, dead on his office floor, his face still and sad. He used to take her to underground Atlanta, where she was allowed a birch beer and two cookies. His hand tossing her hair, he'd tease his fingers beneath her chin and call her Sunshine. He was nothing like her slippery stepfather, coming at night, riding his loneliness into her room. Her real father stood in pajamas and slippers, holding hot chocolate with marshmallows he made for the two of them, taking calls from patients at home about toothaches. I know how bad that can hurt! he'd say into the receiver, winking at her, his eyes crinkling at the corners from years of laughing before her mother came and offered her youthful, beautiful self, then followed it with pouty dissatisfaction.

When they'd found him that day, Audrey had turned to Rebecca slowly. While her mother flung herself around the sterile room, crying, Audrey had looked in her tear-stained, horrified face and said, logically, calmly, You did this to him.

Audrey, twelve years old, stood hoping he had died happily, knowing he hadn't.

In the hazy upset of this party, she thinks perhaps using this kind of cotton could bring her to him.

Don't inject anything hot, Otis tells her around the needle in his mouth. The tight squeeze of the tourniquet on her upper arm is a pleasant bruise. You'll cook your vein, he says.

Sometime we'll do a speedball with you, Sistine tells her. She watches the rubber being tied. It's like a double-loop roller coaster, she says. It's like going up on an elevator and then someone cuts the cable. Very scary. Very fun. She throws the Evian bottle into her leather knapsack on the floor. It's summertime now, she says. Every junkie on the street's lookin for water wherever they can get it.

Otis holds the full needle and smiles at Audrey. I'm gonna give you your wings, baby. You gonna do some heroin now.

In the dim light, Audrey watches her crimson blood being replaced by this new juice in her veins.

Frazier wipes rain from his jacket while Deneeka's coat swings before him. It smells of stale beer and looks maggoty and old. She is selling drugs by the pound. Coeds and prep schoolers run to it like kids at a piñata.

Hey, good lookin, Deneeka says to Frazier while she folds a fist of money. You took you a shower and didn't even invite me?

He shakes his damp head. Two fine-looking legs are coming out of the room next to the hallway. The calves are thinly muscled and cream-colored. He can't see the girl's face. She is lying sideways on a couch, her torso hidden behind the wall of the next room.

In a minute, he'll go find Audrey. First he'll buy in case the goods run out. Reaching into his pocket for his billfold, he counts out four tens. He watches a guy in a black raincoat across from him try to sneak away with two free packets. Jenkins sees him, throws him down in one swift motion, and puts a foot on the boy's forehead. No way, kid. Do we look stupid to you?

When the boy tries to stand, Jenkins pushes his forehead farther down. He hands out bags while the kid lies pinned to the floor, turning red, his eyes bulging with fear. You stay where you are,

Jenkins says to him. I'll take care of you later. Jenkins nods to Fred Matsue, a Japanese guy Frazier's known since grade school. Matsue, what you got? What you want?

Matsue has two twenties and a Ben Franklin and waves them around, his spectacles hooded with light.

The legs are still there, draped in a lovely way. Frazier wants to touch them.

They have not moved.

She cries when she first tries it. Audrey Sullivan. Her head back in slack pleasure. Unfortunate are those somewhere else, far below her. Lovely bursts of words come to her from far off, the sounds low and beautiful. Sistine takes the belt from her upper arm. Her arm is motionless, perfect. She's got it, says the boy. When she throws up, she loves him for the plastic bag he puts beneath her mouth, for ripping a slice of his T-shirt and wiping her nose with it. He kisses her neck, her throat. The black girl puts her hand on her thigh. Audrey's eyes are closing, she enters a tunnel, one long dream of unreality, flying her backward into a space of safety, no recoil, no evil. Pure. Nodding to the deep eroticism of forgetting, her neurotransmitters sugar over. Memory is calmed and eaten by the mouth of new redemption. All her life becomes one fluid moment of pleasure. Shame flees with its siblings: embarrassment, judgment, and fear. A white mass of honey-colored bliss stands in the doorway of Audrey's body and glows steadfast, brilliant warmth throughout her.

She is whole.

7.

GRACEY HAS BURNED the end of her thumb with a match and sucks it like a small girl.

You want some ice for that finger? Cole asks her.

Oh Jesus, cowboy, I've had so much worse than this. This pain feels *good*. She shakes her hand back and forth and smiles at him. Her eyes turn glassy.

Kelly rips a Styrofoam coffee cup into small pieces while she talks memory into the room once again. The Ford Mustang convertible carried her and her mother and Merridew through Atlanta. Mrs. Moore said she was hot, wanted the top down. Her hair blew in the passing wind. The car had faded seats, but it was still clean and stylish. I've had to live a little less high, Merridew said while they rode. She checked in her rearview to make sure Mamma was okay. The recovery business isn't as profitable as selling book covers. But I'm good at it, she told Gracey, smiling, the white scarf blowing around her face. I'm really good at what I do.

Mamma didn't look up when they helped her out of the backseat. She walked away from them toward her front door, trailing the red afghan across the weeds. I ain't never goin back to that hospital again, she told them while she walked across her overgrown lawn. So don't you make me.

It was the gruffest Gracey had ever heard her mamma's voice.

That night Merridew and Gracey lay in the twin bed in Gracey's room, where she'd once endured the rhythmic, sick pounding of her now dead father. Gracey listed her mother's sweetest qualities, the goodness of her soul, the drawer in the kitchen she used to sleep in while her mother cooked and told stories about her own childhood. She was again under the oak tree with summer-reading books from the library. Her mamma was always persistent about the worthiness in every human being. I can't save her, Gracey cried into Merridew's arms while she held her. It's the saddest thing I can think of.

Kissing her forehead many times, Merridew told her, But you can save yourself. That would be the best gift.

They slept. When they woke, Gracey tried to get through a jonesing day. They swung by Merridew's house for pills to aid withdrawal so the pull wasn't as bad. When they arrived back at Jett Street, Gracey slept for fifteen hours while Merridew cooked and cleaned, stood on the porch with May Clark and told her the whole of it. They planned a schedule. Merridew set out a fee scale so the woman would get paid.

When Gracey woke, it was to Merridew's hand on her forehead, rubbing her hair. I want to be clean, Gracey said. I really do. And I want to love you again like we used to. Always did.

Merridew smoothed the blankets. She had spent the day planning Gracey's freedom from this house so she could be saved. She had become again an angel flying on recovery's wings to help her. I'm loaning you five hundred dollars, she told Gracey. To help pay for your mamma. I set it all up with May Clark. If you want to kick now, you got to go now. To recovery. You can't wait for your mamma to die. I know you want to, but you can't stay here, especially in this house where it all began. How much do you want to get clean?

Wide-eyed and earnest, Gracey sat up in bed and looked at her.

I'd rather die than not kick, she told her. I know now I don't have time. I don't got much life left to figure out what's wrong with me, where the glitch in my motor is at. I feel real deep in my gut that something's not right, but there ain't nothin I can do about it alone 'cause I can't figure out where it all begins at. If I could just find that place it starts from, then I'd be okay. I think I could live like I'm supposed to.

Tears ran down Merridew's face. Nodding at Gracey's words, she said softly, You can't have me, either, Gracey. I'm not yours to have. I love you. I'll always love you. But I found my soulmate in a beautiful woman. I hope someday y'all will meet. I'm not helping you 'cause I want to get with you. I'm doing it because I know you're worth it, Gracey. My life's work started when I met you. You're its personification. I knew I had a gift. Now if I can turn around and influence your recovery, then God didn't do bad putting me on this earth. The road back is hard, but it's not long, once you get started. You're going to be all right, Gracey. I can feel it.

Cole watches as Gracey stretches her arms up and looks to the ceiling. The drip of unending rain can be heard out the window. She brings her arms down, wraps them around herself, and says, We hugged like old friends, me and Merridew. Her health went right into me. I could feel how clean she was and I got an idea maybe someday I could be like that, too. It was the first time I'd felt joy in a long, long time. Maybe since I was a itty-bitty girl. Maybe forever. And it was that moment I knew it. Merridew or no Merridew, Mamma dead or alive. I just wanted to be clean. I wanted Gracey back.

8.

FRAZIER MOVES TO the front of the line with his forty dollars. Deneeka eyes his money. Where's that smart-ass African you always with? she asks.

He has to work. I want forty.

Well, how you want it?

Frazier looks down at the stash. He sees the picture of a rocket on it. Feather's vestige from that morning reprises itself in his mind again. The stink. He folds his money in his fist. Is this the same shit that ate Feather? he asks.

Deneeka's cigarette flies out of her hand. She barely watches it land. Glancing around nervously, her words are almost inaudible. Feather just did too much, baby.

Frazier toes her cigarette out on the floor. He holds his money and looks around. The kid in the raincoat is still on the ground. Matsue has disappeared. There is a line in back of him.

How do I know that? he asks. Seemed to me Feather knew pretty well how much to do.

Deneeka shrugs him off. You want to decide? Go somewheres else and don't scare off my customers. Pushing Frazier away, she gives six tight smiles in quick succession all around. He stands at the doorway of the first room, watching her sell. People buy their guiltless high and move through the line. He tries to think what he can say without getting himself killed. Maybe he should go find Audrey and hightail it out of there. There could be walking skeletons all around if the stash is really bad.

He turns his head an inch to the right and sees the girl whose legs he was looking at. Her body is flung lengthwise across the lap of a red-haired boy and a black girl. Her mouth is open, and her eyelids are closed. She's not moving. It is Audrey.

He shoves his billfold back in his pocket and turns into the room. Bending down, he goes to pick her up from the boy's lap. He is leaning over her, kissing her mouth. The girl has her hand up Audrey's dress. Before them, their works wait. These two haven't jacked off yet. They are getting it on with Audrey first.

Mr. Sky, says Otis Libech when he lifts his hand from Audrey's hips, you stealin our fun?

Audrey is limp in Frazier's arms, a heavy, malleable weight. Her limbs are obedient to gravity.

This here's my girlfriend, Libech. What in hell did you give her? When he pulls her over his shoulder, her head bangs against his back. Panic seizes him. He begins to sweat.

We copped from Feather a couple of days ago.

Are you crazy? You gave her that shit?

What the fuck, man, she's your girlfriend. You done ten times as much as this before. And you're always copping from Feather, I seen JP there.

Anxiety grips its massive hands around Frazier. That could be poison, he says, nodding his head to the table. Feather's dead.

He doesn't listen to their response. Passing Deneeka and the others with Audrey slung over him, Frazier sees the onlookers' eyes swell, their breath momentarily kicked out of them. Questions come at him that he doesn't answer.

He takes Audrey to the bathroom across the hall. A stained yellow bulb emits fierce light. There's a porn magazine across the floor, spotted and wet. The linoleum is cracked and grimy. He puts her in the curtainless, plugless tub, and leans over it awkwardly. Aud, hey. He feels her faint pulse with his fingertips. Come on, sweetheart, he says, slapping her face. When he tries the faucet, it doesn't work. Son of a bitch. Words fall out of his mouth without his say-so, curses, prayers, her name. Angry with his tears for how they blur his vision, he is in slow motion, his hands cooperating at half speed, slipping on the metal fixtures. Aud, wake up, baby. Hey. Please. The shower is a trickle above them. He turns the faucet until his fingers hurt. Sliced, rust-filled water gushes out as if grumpy to have been awakened. Audrey's head bangs on the basin before he can catch it. Then they are both under the copper water. He thinks he hears her say something and puts his ear under her mouth. What? Aud, please, don't do this. I love you. C'mon.

The toilet beside them is filled with feces. He wants her to throw up. Get sick, he tells her over and over. Get that shit out of your body.

She seems to smile, her head still lolling. Someone is banging on the door. He needs to get her out of there, to a hospital, to someone who knows what to do. Except for dealers and Jenkins, no phones are allowed in the hotel. They'd never let him call an ambulance to this address. There must be a house somewhere nearby. Hang on, he says. He carries her like a bride to the door and reaches for the knob.

9.

THE ELECTRICITY HAS gone out. In other rooms in the building, generators hum. This room doesn't have one. Around them are the remnants of coffees drunk and food eaten. The smell of stale smoke rests in the air. All of Gracey's filters are piled in the corner. She sits holding a match like a girl at a concert, her face a glowing mystery, her eyes two flickering gems. The vision she presents is otherworldly.

Kelly is skeletal in the darkness.

When she continues, her voice is stronger and proud, telling them about her twenty-eight days at the Fulton County Alcohol and Drug Treatment Center on Boulevard. Sixty beds. Gracey soiled the sheets and nurses came in and out, caring for the disease within her. Detoxing was bad. She put up with diarrhea, nausea, stomach cramps, body aches, hot and cold flashes, sweating, clammy skin, terrible dreams, shakes, fever, drooling agony, and no energy. For a week, she existed on cocktails of antidepressants, vitamins, and guanidine.

They say you can't die from withdrawal, Gracey tells them. You can. Sure. You livin for the drugs. You think that's all in your mind? It's in your body, too. But I came out of it. And I started in on the program. You can't leave once you're admitted. There ain't no weekend passes or nothin. You can call home, and I'd do it every single day, talk to May, talk to Mamma. I think Mamma understood I was finally gettin better. She'd say to me, I love you, Gracey. You're my angel. You're my good girl, so smart. Mamma always thought the world of you, she'd say. It made me cry when she talked that way. And it made me want to try harder at Fulton.

I didn't never have a real friend till I came there. I found people just like me. Women sittin on the day-room couch with their elbows on their knees talkin about what a piss-poor ride it's been. Also some about the good times. How we got double-crossed by the feeling.

The schedule kept me sane, wakin up to spiritual meetings, breakfast, group, lunch, group again, twelve-step, dinner, community meetings, and then sleepin it all off. The next day same thing all over again. I got me a routine, friends, a hot meal, a bed, and a new spirituality. Energy started to come into my life. Sure, sometimes I battled that nasty feelin my life ain't worth shit, but I wasn't doin it alone.

Cole watches her count them off on her fingers: Jasmine, Tamara, Olivia, Yolanda, Marsha. Friends who could help her not get sucked back into the vacuum of drug use.

I got NA meetings, she says. They teach you how to lift yourself up. Easy Does It, One Day at a Time. Sometimes I'd call Merridew while I was in there. I love you, I'd tell her, thankin her till I was cryin.

She'd be laughin. I'm so glad for you, girl, she'd say.

I got outpatient now and I'm jonesin for my meetings. I already missed 'em today 'cause of y'all askin me to save your honky ass. Those meetings make me see clear. They make me want to go to the Bluff and sing my thankful praises, turn the whole world on to it. Only I know ain't nobody listenin till they ready. It's near impossible to go backward. Smokin that first rock. Mainlinin that first time. That's just your primal step toward the dungeon of hell. So many demons wantin to pull you down and sink you under. You can't even do it once. They got you in their iron claws from the get-go.

The lights come on. Kelly looks straight at the bulb as if daring it to go out again.

Gracey blinks at it. Better with it off, she says.

Cole nods.

She smiles. When I got out, I went to Merridew's first. We had a lasagna dinner with candles and pie. I met her girl, Angie, who beats the socks off anyone I could have wanted to hate. We celebrated, toasted with bubblin grape juice, and said a prayer with our heads bowed, all three of us holdin hands. Then I went to Mamma's. It was nine o'clock at night. I took the bus over there and come into the house. I didn't say Mamma's name 'cause there was somethin in the air, a silent cryin like she used to do when Daddy hit her. Her ghost was grievin.

Mamma was sittin up in bed, those stone-river eyes starin at nothin, like they'd seen too much and got fixed that way. I felt her hand with mine and then took it back quick. I never touched nothin like that before. I went back and touched it again. I got used to the feeling. I made myself hold her hand and I prayed to God she was safe where she was. Then I closed those eyes so they didn't have to see nothin no more. I sat with her. I love you, Mamma, I told her. I'm healed. Maybe it took you dyin to do it. I laid down next to her and told her about the girls at Fulton and what I learned about me and about her, about blame and shame and makin choices that'll deliver you up instead of down. Finally, I stopped talkin. The phone was sittin on the table next to me. There was a lot of people I needed to call, but I wanted to be in the house with Mamma a little longer. Around midnight, I went back to my girl room and slept there with nothin around but memory that could only hurt me if I let it. I got up at dawn so I could walk to May Clark's and tell her. The sun was comin up a real pretty pink. I was clean for the first time in years. Even though I got to deal with my mamma dyin, I felt good. It was a new day and I wasn't hooked on drugs.

Gracey stands up and puts her hands on her hips. She looks down at Kelly. Ain't you guys have a way with timin? That unmarked Ford sittin right in front of Jett Street, idlin, wantin to sniff up my asshole about Sonny Fill, the only person who could make me go back to that shit-hole life I come from. But what was I gonna do? Run?

She goes to the window and looks out. I told you all I know, she says. It's more than you need to make your big-boy decisions. Now you got to set me free. Let me bury my mamma and get on with my recovery. She puts her face in a crack between the window boards. Closing her eyes and smelling the breeze, she tells them, Lettin me go is about the best thing you ever gonna do.

10.

AN ATLANTA MAP is plastered across Tyler Sky's passenger seat. Night distends around him. Rain streams down his front window. His doors are locked. Behind him is the rain-slicked city and Rebecca's party, her scared face. He is lost. He catches terrified glimpses of an unexplored forest of poverty. He slows to try to see the elusive numbers on the houses. He'd found the street name written on his shaded paper, but there were no numbers on the buildings and finally the street had taken on some other name. On one corner, three girls stand hip to hip in thigh-high boots, their bodies gathered in at their waists, their mouths looming carnal promises. Hey, baby, hey! They kick at his taillight and laugh cruelly, ghastly in their sensuality.

Fear follows him through this maze of neighborhoods filled with salmon-colored houses, no streetlamps. Honks sound in back of him. When he slows, a pedestrian bends toward his window with a solicitous face. Some drugs, you want to buy some drugs?

She moves.
Aud? Frazier looks down at her. Baby, come on.

She says his name and he kneels on the space of grass between the sidewalk and the curb beside the house next door, hollow with darkness. Her voice is slow, weary. I don't feel well. You never came. She chokes back tears.

He flips her over so she can vomit. I'm sorry I was late, he tells her. The train stopped.

She does not get sick. She collapses against herself. One puff of air escapes her throat. She is limp again, limbs dangling. He puts his arms around her waist. Rain mixes with his tears. Aud, he tells her flaccid form, we're meant to be together. Please, hey.

She does not answer, is gone again.

He is half-dragging her. There must be a house somewhere around here. He hears himself call for help to a figure in a Lakers jacket stepping on three tires to see over the top of a Dumpster. When the person stops to look at him, her face is a gruesome compilation of burned skin. Oh, help, he tells her. Can you help me? I need a phone. The mouth opens up to laugh and shows large horse's teeth, rain licked and yellow. Insane.

His legs go weak beneath him. He tells his girlfriend he loves her. Wake up, he tells her. We're kicking. We're finished. You're too good for this. He stumbles once on the cracked sidewalk. Rain slides down his face, into his eyes, his hair is long with it. There are no cars save the empty ones across the street in the lot of a torn-down Kmart. I'm getting you to a doctor, a hospital, he tells her.

As soon as he sees a lit house, he will just stop and knock. Someone will answer. He carries her another full block until he comes to the park at the corner. Water bleeds from the sky, merciless, indefatigable. Up ahead a gang of four guys is walking toward him, wearing baseball hats turned backward, hoods, dark glasses, and gold chains, four deep around their necks. They stare at Audrey while they walk. They don't give Frazier a second glance. What is he? Nothing, just some skinny little white kid in the wrong neighborhood late at night, crying. And he's got an ivory glory in his arms. One guy starts to smile while he walks. Frazier stands frozen, holding her like a sacrifice.

Headlights blare down at him. The passing car screeches to a halt, U-turns in the road, and veers up onto the sidewalk next to Frazier. The gang starts to run toward him as the driver of the car opens the passenger door. His father is leaning over the seat. Get in, he says.

Frazier ducks inside, managing to pull Audrey awkwardly across his legs just as the first guy in the gang reaches the car. Out of breath, the guy pounds on the hood. Hey! he says. Frazier slams the door. He locks it while his father peels out. Which way? his dad asks.

Audrey's head lolls over the seat's side, her chin faces the ceiling, her mouth is open and her eyes are half closed. Frazier sobs and manages words of direction from somewhere in the logic part of his brain. End of park, take a right, go until you hit the next light, take a left, Grady Memorial is on the left, six or so more streets.

Frazier puts his face beside hers and lifts her weighted head. Leaning over her, he breathes into her mouth, sobbing. Wake up, Frazier tells her. CPR, Dad, what in hell is it? His father's eyes are steady on the road. He shakes his head and takes quick glances at his son and Audrey. I don't know, he says.

Frazier blows in her mouth, a futile act.

The Lexus takes turns at seventy-five miles per hour. Silence between boy and father. Guilt enters the car, a shared disease. Defrost blasts over the dash. His father's left hand grips the wheel, the knuckles are white, marblelike, capable. The right hand reaches out and holds Audrey's shoulder. In this moment of curdling terror, Frazier feels a slice of relief. His father is here. His car can handle the road. He is a good driver. Aud, please, hey. He slaps her cheeks, sees she is pale. Lifeless.

No. Dad.

His father lifts his hand. Frazier grasps the fingers.

Rain presses against the windows.

I want to marry her. I never want to let her go.

Tyler Sky believed before that his heart had broken. He was

wrong. It begins to break now, a terrible torment, the ripping sound of lives taken and delivered at will when no one is looking. An irreversible moment throws him back in time. He remembers his son playing alone with figurines when he was a small boy, putting the military men where he wanted, making them fight, kill, in the grassy lawn outside their house on West Paces Ferry. Tyler would stand by the back window watching Frazier. One day he realized that adults were trying to do that in the very lives of their children. An army of people waiting in line for something from you.

He brings the car to the side of the road and he reaches over to hold his son, rocking him back and forth, Audrey between them. The car goes silent except for wiping blades, the constant of an engine, and Frazier's weeping.

Audrey's hair hangs from her head, a gorgeous lake of auburn. Her lips are an iced cobalt and her heart, too tired, stops to rest. Life slips slowly through her pores, reaches ground, and takes off. The heavens on the night of her death belch a terrified thunder. Great veins of lightning break the sky in angry hieroglyphs. Olympus weeps.

11.

GRACEY IS DONE TALKING. She sits smoking while Cole and Kelly gather up the last of the trash and pile it in the wastebasket. Her shoulders are bent and she seems to stare off into space at a world only she sees.

Kelly stands at the threshold and motions for Cole to follow him.

They go out in the hallway, closing the door behind them. Leaning against the wall to talk, Kelly does not look straight at Cole, he watches the baseboard. We don't got shit, he says. You really think she believes The Rocket's dead?

I don't think she's lying, Cole tells him. About anything.

Kelly stares at the floor. His face reddens. Silently they both attest to Gracey's knowledge of him. Kelly wipes his hand across his mouth and swallows. Thing is, he says, I can't believe she doesn't know about The Rocket if she's been out on the streets.

Maybe she knows about him, but she doesn't know he's Sonny, Cole says. Why don't you just ask her?

Kelly shakes his head. Sarge said not to let her know we knew about The Rocket. If she's in with him and we let her go, she'll run back and tell him. If we ask her, we'll have to keep her in isolation.

We don't have grounds for that, he glances up at Cole, but we could make grounds.

Cole watches his partner's jaw tighten and release. You want to hold her? Kelly asks him.

Cole doesn't answer.

Kelly stands up straight and lifts his chin at Cole. Look, Feather Hay is dead and The Rocket is his connection. They need to find him, and if they do, this woman's gonna have to testify. If she knows that, she might run, and she's the best witness. If we keep her here, we make sure she testifies.

Cole watches his partner's darting eyes and flexing jaw. He understands Kelly is pretending he doesn't care about what Gracey knows, but really he doesn't want to keep her here any more than Cole does. Cole's being tested. He studies the linoleum's squid marks and lines that shoot this way and that across the hallway's floor. Kelly will lose his career if Gracey testifies and tells what she knows. Cole could expose his partner, but then Gracey couldn't get on with her new life. Gracey's voice enters him, *Sonny Fill, the only person who could make me go back to that shit-hole life I come from.* He doesn't want to keep her here. He wants to help her. The integrity of his heart wins. He knows Kelly is counting on this. That'll kill her, Cole finally says. There are other people who can be found to testify. We've got to let her go. He pauses. She needs a chance.

Are you a cop or a psych worker? asks Kelly, sarcastic now that he knows he is off the hook. You gonna save one woman or the world?

Cole considers hair-raising bravery, ripping off his badge and throwing it at Kelly, saying aloud what he knows about his partner.

Instead, he looks him in the eye. I think we can do both, he says.

Back in the questioning room, Gracey shivers. Night has come and the early morning hours are approaching. She is empty without her history. She has splayed her life in this room and now there is only air, memory stretched over long hours. She has learned in recovery what it means to talk about it, get the story out, demystify and face shame.

They walk in. This time, the sweet one comes first. He stands at the door, as if the room was her home, and he needed an invitation. The traitor strides right through and opens his little mouth to these words: You're free to go. She starts to take off the coat. It's still raining, he tells her. Keep the coat. As if in defense to some invisible fourth person, he says, We don't need it.

Gathering the coat about her, Gracey stands. They part in order for her to exit, their arms falling awkwardly at their sides, their eyes shifting from her to the floor and back again. She walks out the door. Behind her, the air is thick with her story, and each officer is left lonely. Gracey has made the world a frightening place, a vacuum of evil that only the strong and brave can survive.

The uniformed woman gives Gracey her discharge papers and tells her she can fill them out in a cold tile-and-metal room to the left of dispatch. The lady at the desk does not look at her when she slides them over. Gracey keeps having to scribble to get the pen to work and she goes back to get another one.

While the woman passes it to her, she glances around the command post. This is the last time she'll be in a place like this. Mamma dead, Merridew in love with Angie. But she's clean. She's got meetings and new sisters she knows through the program who care about her story. They say, Girl, don't we know it, tell us more. What you got on your mind? She can brew herself a pot of coffee and call one of them to come help her with the funeral arrangements. She needs to get a job and find Lakeisha and Jackson so she can let out all the apology piled up in her.

The parking lot is empty of people. Cole stands in the cool, misted air near the entranceway waiting to talk to Gracey. He wants to speak with her outside the questioning room. Ask if maybe he can be her friend. He is standing in the building's shadow when the black BMW drives in. It pulls across the front of the entrance-way and the woman in the passenger seat does not wait for it to stop all the way before she opens the door. She is wearing a pale dress and heels and no coat.

It is his mother.

Before he can go to her, she is through the front door. Her hus-band opens the driver's-side door and stands holding the steering wheel, watching her. One foot is still in the car and his other foot is on the pavement. He has white hair and his trench-coat collar is turned up. He touches his collar once, then gets back in his car, puts it in gear, and drives to a parking space.

Cole follows her. She is leaning against the green cement wall across from the sergeant's office. Her hair is falling out of its gold holder at the back of her neck. Her mouth is the color of blood. There are three officers around her. One moves his hand to her arm to try to calm her. She pulls away. There is a wild look about the way she flings her arms around. The sergeant comes out of his office with two officers from the Red Dog squad.

Ma'am, says the sergeant. He walks toward her. He gestures to the bench. Why don't you have a seat?

Cole watches her eyes go from one officer to another in an unbalanced look of lunacy. She does not take a seat. She looks the sergeant in the eye and in a low voice she says, You have the wrong girl. They watch each other. Around them, the fidgeting officers turn clumsy as schoolboys. Overhead lights illuminate their boots and weapons. He can see clearly the wet makeup around her eyes and the perspiration beaded on her forehead. The door beside Cole opens and her husband stands at the threshold, folding his umbrella and eyeing his wife.

Cole backs into the radio-dispatch room. Sandy is hunched over the desk, riffling through papers. Her hair roots are dark and the ends are yellow. She's painted her fingernails purple. She looks up at him and snaps her gum. Yeah? she says. The ballpoint pen behind her ear falls to the desk blotter. She puts it in her mouth.

His voice is hoarse. That woman out there, he says. What happened?

Sandy takes the pen from her mouth. Her kid OD'd. Her husband's friends with the mayor. If city hall wasn't choppin at our business before, they're gonna start today.

Cole walks out the door. He watches his mother turn and notice him. Her pale countenance is splotched with red. His face burns, and his legs turn to liquid while she looks at him. Pulling her arm from the sergeant's grip, she begins to walk forward on wobbly heels. The officers stop talking.

It seems to take her a long time to get down the hallway, and when she does, she stands before him. He sees everything: her gold-speckled green eyes, the long painted lashes, the faint freckles across her nose, her trembling lips. The room swirls mirage-like around him. She smells as she used to.

All is quiet in the command post while she searches his eyes. Bringing her arm up, she puts a palm on his cheek. Her breath is quick and shallow. His own shaking hand rises, and he touches her fingers.

He does not speak before her weight is on him. Her torso leans against his, and she brings her arms up to his chest. He feels her tears when she puts her chin on his shoulder and her face to his neck. He wraps his arms around her waist and holds her. Their bodies heave together when she sobs. The sergeant watches. Her husband steps around and faces Cole. He puts a hand on the back of his wife's neck. Cole feels her shrug it off. Her knees give out and he tries to hold her up; he finds they are slumped against the back wall. Taking a breath in, he lifts her from him, puts one arm around her back and the other across her stomach, and begins to walk her forward.

The men part for them. Cole and his mother do not look back.

Seated in a metal folding chair in the coffee-and-smoke room with the vending machine and a wire-paned window behind her, his mother bends over her elegant thighs and cries. She cannot catch her breath. She moans. She says her daughter's name. Cole kneels on the linoleum beside her. He watches her hands, the length of her fingers, those knuckles, how slender her wrists are. He sees the soft golden hair on the back of her neck. She rocks back and forth under fluorescent lights. Cole does not speak. He understands that words cannot absolve her pain.

Cole has never met his half sister. He does not know she is seventeen and beautiful, that she has long auburn hair and a boyfriend, that on the night of her death she wore a black dress. The first time he will see her will be when he stands beside his mother in a morgue. His sister will be pulled out in prone position, face to the ceiling. His mother will not speak. She will collapse sideways against him. Holding her up, he will look at the girl before him, and he will not turn away. For years afterward, Cole will see her sleeping face in his dreams.

When his mother looks up, he wants to apologize for the seat she is sitting on. He wishes it were more. But words have left him. She takes his hands in hers and brings his fingertips to her mouth. Tears make black trail marks down her cheeks. She asks him if it is true. He watches her. Then he turns and looks back at the sergeant, who nods his head once. She stares at Cole, and he tells her he is sorry. Her head shakes back and forth and her forehead creases. In his hands, her fingers go cold. They feel fragile. The bones in them might break in two, should he let go.

Behind her, droplets of water stroke the windowpane. The rain starts again. For five minutes it beats a torrential downpour while his mother, in the worst grief she has ever known, holds him.

In the hallway, he hears footsteps and he turns to see Gracey go by. She looks in briefly and keeps walking.

He turns to his mother's husband, raises a hand for him to come closer. Taking the man's elbow, he pulls him toward them. The man tugs at his trousers and begins to kneel before his wife. Cole slips out of his mother's grasp and lets her head rest on her husband's shoulder.

He stands. Excuse me, he tells the room.

He moves through the building and hurries to the front

entrance. The rain has stopped. A well-lit parking lot and she is one lone figure, making a long shadow across the blacktop. The coat they let her have turns into wings in the breeze. The bus stop is a few feet away.

He comes up beside her and speaks softly. Thank you, he says.

She stops and turns to him. Touching his jaw gently she says, You're a good man.

They watch each other.

If you want me to, I'll drive you home, he tells her.

She nods for a long time without moving.

Just as he is about to speak again, she says, The girls at Fulton told me he still out there as The Rocket but I'm not goin to give you their names. I don't want none of them implicated. He's at the Alamo. Stewart Avenue. Number three-fourteen. You take it yourself, Justice. It ain't for your partner in there to get none of the prize. Go with the Red Dogs and the GBI and the whole force. Do it tonight. He'll be clearin out soon.

The bus comes and halts its massive, screeching brakes. Gracey touches his hand briefly. I gotta go, she tells him. I have a mamma to bury. She smiles. A life to live.

She heads toward the bus in a jog, not looking back, her head bowed against an onslaught of soft rain.

He watches her mount the steps and move through the late-night vehicle. Her life of sorrow is deep within her, a briar mark, trailing her body. She steadies herself against the bus's inside metal railing, blows him a kiss, and is gone.

The imprint of her photo's negative lives in him, branding his heart. He watches those taillights until they are red dots in the distance, holding knowledge in the silent night.

Dawn

———

Epilogue

JP PICKS UP his newspapers at two A.M. for the Sunday run, twelve stacks wrapped in rain plastic and tied with burlap rope. He piles them on his new bicycle like he's seen the Mexicans do. One named Ruben helps him, a shy boy, quiet, doesn't smoke cigarettes or dope with the rest. His gleaming ebony hair covers one eye. His teeth are white and straight. He lives with his mamma on Boulevard.

Thanks, JP tells him.

Ruben nods, stands back from the bike, looking it up and down. He pats the left side a little and moves back again. You think you can balance it? he asks. His English is thick with Spanish. JP nods. It's a gamble. He grins. But I think I can handle it. Thanks again.

When he hops on, the bike wobbles and the other boys jeer at him and laugh. Hey, JP, what you tryin to do, turn Chicano, man?

JP manages to get one hand off his handlebar and flip them off. It's better than walkin, he calls back.

The rain has slowed to a drizzle. He likes these Sunday mornings, the quiet in the streets like an inert muscle, people sleeping soundly in their homes, the glow of one light somewhere far off. He has three blocks to go before he reaches Little Five Points.

Once he starts to deliver, he falls twice, then gets the knack of reaching back for the newspapers and throwing them on the porches. Dogs muster up their energy to yelp at him. Hey, mutt, he says. Lawns with their mowed grass hem paths to front doors.

He watches himself reflected in black windows. Dawn is arriving and the blackest, coldest part of the night enters him.

JP is fraught with experience. It weighs him down when he is alone. The lives of a hundred men have been lived in his eighteen years. He has loved a mother and lost her and fathered girls when he was just thirteen and loved another boy his age at fifteen and lost him to the needle and then fell exhausted into the body of a girl who turned to whoring. He watched helplessly while her strength was wasted on the pipe and finally on men devoted to her habit. Her exposed self-hatred blinded him. He'd left her and withstood his own withdrawals from the pipe. Now he's doing heroin. He has been slipping back. He knows that now. The H is his magnet toward destruction.

He thinks of Feather. Again and again throughout the day, he's considered this. He didn't tell Frazier, but he believes it is an omen. He is sure God gives out signs. Like this bike. He hasn't ridden a bike in years and now suddenly these wheels are wings. This is so fine, he tells the sleeping world. He has a vision of himself on a bicycle, racing with his head down, scenery flying by. They say endorphins are the legal man's high. It's not a lazy high, like shooting it in your foot, smoking it up a hollow piece of glass. He tries to remember the name of the bike race he's heard of in France.

He believes in divine intervention because it has been practiced on him. Not just once he's been shot at and the pistol carrier misfired. He's come close to buying a bad stash and then an invisible hand laid out his fate in another way. The girl he was with died of AIDS, and HIV still hasn't claimed him. He knows because he gave blood for money last week and they tested. The Lord loves me, he says to the ebony sky.

After Little Five Points, he gets on Ponce de Leon and sees that transvestite, Deneeka, with her hay-colored hair. She's wearing an old fur coat, and limping. His habit almost calls out to her, he got paid this evening, but he catches himself and watches her go.

As if someone whispered in her ear, she looks up at him and raises her chin. How far can that bike go? she calls.

He half-smiles. It could take you cross-country for the right price.

All I need is South Rampart Street, she says.

He thinks while he pedals down Ponce, Where's South Rampart Street? Somewhere south of here. New Orleans maybe.

Fuck South Rampart Street, he says to himself. This bike's gonna take me to heaven. All the way to freedom. A check in his pocket, money, a job. He'll tell Frazier he's kicking and maybe try to get him to do it, too. If they got enough money together, they might move to California or somewhere. If Audrey goes with them, they could fly all the way to Paris. The Tour de France, that's what it's called. He could buy him a better bicycle. Save the world his trouble.

One of Deneeka's heels breaks while she is walking past that smart-ass African, to the Majestic Diner, where late-night lights greet her.

She sits huddled over her coffee with four creams and two sugars watching Sissy eat toast and fried egg with her pinkie finger out.

Teenagers, two boys and two girls, their faces smirched with the pink stain of a passing pimple, sit laughing at the center table. Deneeka watches their moist, red mouths and their clear eyes. They eat stacks of pancakes. Their pale, slender fingers grip utensils. The girls are dressed in bubblegum-colored dresses, and their hair is tied back with ribbons. The boys have loosened the bow ties of their rented tuxes, exposing necks red from new razors.

Deneeka smokes. The end of her filter carries a rust-colored stain. She sits uncomfortably on her own bulged member and ashes the cigarette in a plate of old hash browns at the table next to theirs. A dollar tip is pinned to the Formica by a saltshaker. Left-over rain sneaks down her wrists and neck, into her eyes. She blinks. Her mascara has run over her face in black smudges.

The boys' pink cummerbunds are wrinkled and the girls' corsages are going brown. One girl looks at the clock. This is the first time I've been out past midnight since New Year's, she says.

I heard Feather's dead, says Sissy. Sissy Crew, man turned woman, wears robin's-egg blue and her heart on her sleeve.

Deneeka plays cool, raises her eyebrows. Who'd you hear that from?

KC got put in lockup, Sissy says. She was there when they came to get him. She went crazy. You know how in love with him she was.

Feather's a junkie, says Deneeka. You can't be in love with a junkie. When she brings her cigarette to her lips, she tries to keep her hand from trembling.

An hour later, Deneeka will be seen walking away, exercising her thumb on the I-85 bridge while behind her, future deaths lie down like dominoes, ghosts of what's to come, leaking their entrails into the night. Junkies' veins will shrivel, their starving hearts ceasing in cold blood. College boys' torsos will convulse on Oriental rugs, their faces slowly turning blue. The dabblers, businessmen with chippies fucking blond cokeheads, will become rigor-mortised in the middle of their pleasure.

And Deneeka, not her real name, will chance escape. Only one person knows her destination, a black boy on a bicycle, running free. Telling all.

Acknowledgments

Thank you to Janna Cordeira and the women whose lives she shared, Paige Adair and Hopey, Maryanne Downey, Mona "Love" Bennett, the Atlanta Needle Exchange Program and the Atlanta Harm Reduction Center, Cynthia Connor and Synergy, the Narcotics Squad of the Atlanta Police Department, the Atlanta Center University Library staff, Fulton County Drug and Rehabilitation Center, Amanda Ippolito, Laura Sperazi, Joanne O'Sullivan, Andrew Gates, a belated thank you to my jefe Kevin Brennan, Jan Frazier and her writing groups, William Gay, Patty Krasner, Evie Lovett and Jeff Shumlin, Marshall Brewer and John Calvi, Tara Fleming, Stacey Pope and the WOTN including Seb and Asher, Peter Towle Jr., Leigh Feldman and everyone at D,V & F, Scribner especially Rachel Sussman and Gillian Blake, and in gratitude to Karen Schulsted Duffield and my guardian angels, Marc, Margaret, and Uncle Tee Duffield, Wolfe O'Meara, and Johnny The Whopper Little. In memory of John Watson.